Dark Equinox and Other Tales
of Lovecraftian Horror

DARK EQUINOX

and Other Tales of Lovecraftian Horror

Ann K. Schwader

Hippocampus Press

New York

Acknowledgments: see p. 259.

Published by Hippocampus Press
P.O. Box 641, New York, NY 10156.
http://www.hippocampuspress.com

Cover production by Barbara Briggs Silbert.
Hippocampus Press logo designed by Anastasia Damianakos.

First Edition
1 3 5 7 9 8 6 4 2

ISBN 978-1-61498-129-9

CONTENTS

Dark Equinox and Other Tales
of Lovecraftian Horror

DARK EQUINOX

THERE WAS A CRACK in the gallery's front window. In one of the small top panes, but still obvious, just as last fall's leaves on the porch were. Or the doorknob's accumulated grime, though the sign inside that door read OPEN.

Not for much longer, I'm guessing.

Jen frowned. Despite its website optimism, this place was on its last financial legs after the holidays—with any remotely valuable photographs long gone.

The door's anemic bell did nothing to boost her optimism as she entered. Beyond a desk cluttered with large-format books and brochures, there were only two narrow display rooms divided by a staircase. Their carpets, though good once, bore worn ghosts of patterns, and the walls held more faded rectangles than images for sale.

What she could see of those images didn't leave much hope. Still, Leonie Gerard was listed among the gallery's artists—and she was local to the Denver area.

Or had been.

Shifting her messenger bag across her back, Jen started her search. The first room held photographs of the modern West: no photomontages, nothing remotely experimental. She recognized few of the artists, though a spatter of tiny red stickers showed most were already sold.

The second room, though smaller, seemed more promising. One Uelsmann. A couple of Bonaths. One remarkably contorted Michel Pilon, and—

Not possible.

She stepped closer to the print. Against a carefully composed mosaic of landscapes—ruins, mostly—three oval objects descended in

9

series. They were almost, but not quite, eggs. No visible light source defined them, yet the closest bore faint scrawls of shadow.

Or perhaps harbored them within its shell. Waiting, and growing stronger, and testing for cracks—

She blinked. How had *that* thought come up?

Before her imagination could distract her any further, she checked the print's bottom border. Last year's date, in pencil . . . 3 / 7 . . . and a signature. Her signature.

Footsteps sounded on the stairs behind her, followed by a soft clank of bracelets as someone turned up the overhead light.

"You know Leonie's work?"

An elderly woman in Southwestern clothing stood in the doorway. She wore more silver than Jen had ever seen on one person before, and her long velvet skirts looked vintage. The gallery's owner, she guessed, hoping for one final sale this afternoon.

Jen nodded. "I did my thesis on her, two years ago."

Even at the time, she'd been dissatisfied with it—as had her thesis committee. To their minds, Leonie Gerard's photomontages were less a subject for contemporary art history than for science fiction, or possibly horror. Though Gerard limited herself to black and white, her juxtapositions of image-fragments from exotic locations had grown increasingly bizarre.

Jen suspected her thesis had only been approved out of loyalty to the local arts community. CU Boulder, got to love it.

Silver rang at her elbow. "And you followed her career . . . afterwards?"

"All the way."

In the silence that followed, Jen finally checked the print's information tag. *Vernal Ascension*. The date, again. Archival silver print. No red dot. And no mention of a price, not even NFS.

"So you'll know what this one is, then." The older woman's voice quavered. "Her last."

Three of seven, but only three had ever been printed. Jen hesitated.

"I've read about it, and seen a reproduction in an article. But I've never actually—"

"It feels different, doesn't it?"

When Jen nodded mutely, the other woman took the print down and turned it over, revealing the handwritten label. It gave her the same chill Van Gogh's *Wheat Field with Crows* did, though the image itself was oddly tranquil.

But was it for sale?

Before she could ask, the gallery owner replaced the image and stepped back, motioning for her to do likewise. Weak afternoon light from the front window picked out details: the shattered top of an obelisk, vine-smothered carved steps, the snarl of a jaguar god.

"I don't think she ever made anything else quite like it."

Jen nodded again. While researching her thesis, she'd seen reproductions of most of Leonie Gerard's work—and experienced a few in person at museums. None of those skillfully assembled images worked the way this one did.

She couldn't say why, either. Something in the angles, perhaps, or the sites themselves. Where had the artist traveled? Though she recognized sacred sites in Belize and Turkey, and one T-shaped doorway from Chaco Canyon, most of the locations eluded her. She wondered how many were on the State Department's no-go list.

"I never got the chance to talk to her about it, either." The older woman's skirts swished as she walked back to the print. "Her brother brought this one in."

Now or never.

"Just for display?"

The gallery owner produced a tiny silver pen and a pack of business cards from her pocket. She jotted a number on one before extending it to Jen.

"Are you, um, sure about this?"

"For the right collector, yes." A shadow smile crossed the older woman's face. "And don't tell me you don't own anything else of Leonie's. It doesn't matter. You take her work, and her life, seriously."

Present tense. As if she already knew Jen's struggle for a Ph.D. Her failed applications, her need for more original work to get the attention of the right people, at the right schools.

Jen swallowed hard. "Thank you."

To her surprise, the gallery owner lifted *Vernal Ascension* down at once and headed for the front desk. Clearing herself work space, she began swathing it in bubble wrap.

"Don't you want to wait until your show's over?"

The shadow smile returned. "It's perfectly fine."

Minutes later, her card had been charged and Jen held the dreamed-of image. The gallery owner thanked her, but made no move to leave her desk.

"Is there anything else?"

Jen's fingers tightened on the bubble wrap. "You mentioned a brother." She hesitated. "Does he live around here? Would he be willing to talk with me about her work?"

The wrongness of the question hit her immediately. Mumbling an apology, she turned to leave.

"Just a moment, please."

Behind her, Jen heard a desk drawer open, then a rustling of papers.

"Sebastian Gerard," the other woman said, still digging. "I met him once. Interesting man, used to teach world mythology—Joseph Campbell stuff—at some community college. Now he owns rental cabins up in Estes Park, but it's the slow season. I suspect he'd have time."

She exhaled satisfaction as she shut the drawer again. "Here's his card."

Jen took it and thanked her, then hurried out of the gallery with her purchase. No sense taking chances. This wasn't a bad part of town, but there weren't a lot of good parts this late in the day.

She was barely off the porch when she heard a noise behind her.

Glancing back, she saw that the gallery's door sign now read CLOSED. Only the building's upstairs windows were illuminated. When even these began falling dark, she tightened her grip on her prize and walked faster.

*   *   *

"I'm glad you called, Ms. Maxwell."

Sebastian Gerard's voice was older than she'd expected—and better informed. Jen frowned. How the hell did he know her name?

Insight hit a couple of seconds later. "I'm assuming the gallery told you—"

"—who bought Leonie's last piece? Yes. I'm afraid I asked them to."

Sunk deep in the folds of her beanbag chair, Jen still felt a chill. This was getting into stalker territory—aside from *him* waiting for *her* to call, of course. And it had taken her days to work up the courage to do that.

"I guess I can't blame you," she finally said. "It must hold a lot of memories."

"That's . . . putting it mildly."

Whatever was skewing his end of this conversation, it didn't sound like grief. Or even resentment.

More like anxiety?

Start over. "I'm so sorry for your loss, Mr. Gerard. Your sister's imagination was incredible. In those later images, it was as if she was assembling a whole new world."

"She was."

The chill she'd been blaming on her landlord's control of the thermostat deepened.

"I didn't realize she'd discussed her work with anyone. When I was researching my thesis, I didn't find many letters or notes. She didn't do a lot of interviews, either."

"No, she didn't." Gerard seemed to be gathering his own courage now. "Ms. Maxwell, I'd appreciate the chance to buy back *Vernal Ascension*. Every cent you paid—and some extra for your trouble." He hesitated. "I never should have put it up for sale."

Jen's frown deepened. Hanging above her futon couch in pride of place—assuming pride even applied to this place—Leonie's last image pulsed with life.

The background ruins looked sharper than they had in the gallery, as if some jungle mist had started to lift. Their juxtaposed locations no longer felt jarring, but exuded an organic sense of rightness. The egg-objects were descending toward an earth womb prepared for them. Or perhaps there was only one object, plus two earlier reflections of the journey—

"Ms. Maxwell?"

Gerard's voice sputtered from a fold in the beanbag. Extracting her dropped phone, Jen started to apologize.

"You were looking at it just then, weren't you?"

Go with the weirdness. "Yes."

"I had the same experience with numbers one and two of that image, and I didn't know why at the time. Now I've at least got suspicions." Another silence. "Which is why I'd really like to buy back number three."

Jen glanced up again at *Vernal Ascension.*

The jaguar god's tongue lolled faintly red.

"I can't do that," she said quickly. "I'm working on my Ph.D. application. I'm not sure what that gallery told you, but—"

"—you need to start publishing. Which means original research."

He sounded tired. "Ms. Maxwell, I understand your fascination with my sister's work. And I'm deeply grateful for all the time and energy you've spent bringing it to the attention of academia. But this just can't—"

He took a ragged breath. "—it can't really be researched. And if you saw Leonie's studio, I think you'd understand why."

Jen froze. *Her studio?*

Almost a year ago, Leonie Gerard's career—and her life—had ended in a darkroom fire, which might or might not have been accidental. None of the references she'd found could tell her any more, and the rumors she'd chased in the arts community couldn't be confirmed.

All she knew for sure was that Leonie's studio had been in the Colorado mountains.

"Are you saying you could arrange it?"

"My sister lived up here in Estes when she wasn't traveling. I lent her one of my cabins, and we built her studio together." Gerard hesitated. "There's not much left of that. But the cabin's just as she left it."

Not *in* Estes Park, she knew, but somewhere outside it. At the end of an unpaved road knee-deep in snow. Or mud.

Owned by a guy she'd never met.

Way too far from help if he turned out to be dangerous.

Mentally sighing, Jen reached for a notepad. She'd need driving directions.

As it turned out, she had been wrong about the road. What twisted and plunged its way down to the Triple G Cabins office was more of a goat track, and almost a match for her aging Subaru.

Killing the engine at last, Jen drew a deep breath and rested her head on the steering wheel. What was she looking for here? In the handful of days since she'd spoken with Sebastian Gerard, she'd been unable to figure that out, despite her certainty that Leonie's studio—or its remains—held answers.

At least she and Gerard agreed on that much.

Moments later, the man himself tapped on her window. She lowered it halfway.

"You can't drive in to the studio. We'll have to walk from here."

Leonie's brother looked even older than he'd sounded, with a short gray ponytail and a lean, weary face. He barely waited for her to lock the car before heading toward a nearby stand of pines.

There was no real path through, but she'd worn boots and there wasn't all that much snow. Just discouraged grimy patches after a dry winter, with long-range forecasts not much better, and wildfire season looking worse. She'd always imagined it being beautiful up here, but this was—

"I don't suppose you brought your print with you?"

"Uh, no." Her mind flittered back over their phone conversation. "Were you expecting me to?"

The weariness in Gerard's face deepened. "No, just hoping."

They walked on in silence through the trees. A lot of them looked unhealthy, with brittle needles and trunks clotted with resin. Not hard to imagine a fire up here, even without darkroom chemicals or amateur wiring.

Not hard to imagine it not being an accident at all.

Even so, Jen wasn't prepared for the view beyond the pines. Sticking up through the snow like a charred skeleton, the remains of Leonie Gerard's studio looked as if the tragedy had happened last week—not almost a year ago. Tattered blackout curtains flapped from window frames. Glass shards glinted on the ground. Even the ruined door still hung in place, barely.

Breathe. "Did you ever find out what happened?"

"She died."

No point in asking what volunteer fire brigade had tried and failed, what EMT had done likewise. What official conclusions came weeks later. The details of that March night were surely burned into Gerard's mind, but nothing she could say right now would bring them to the surface.

Apologizing, Jen moved closer to the doorway. "May I?"

Gerard nodded. The afternoon air felt suddenly colder, and very silent.

Pale sunlight through breaks in the roof revealed scorched trays, a shattered light table, sodden boxes of files and supplies. A wire drying line had survived, but held only curled strips of black in twisted clips. A much larger tangle of metal and half-burned paper blocked the path to the door.

She squinted. The metal looked like picture frames.

A sharp, improbable drama played through her mind: Leonie, distraught, piling up her work in the first convenient place. Igniting it. Realizing too late she'd blocked her exit—unless she'd never intended to leave in the first place. And all this inside her studio, destroying negatives and contact prints as well.

What had she wanted to burn so badly?

When she turned to ask Gerard, he was already standing beside her.

"She'd been preparing for a group show down in Taos, working nonstop. She was still recovering from her last trip . . . Sierra Leone, good God . . . but *Vernal Ascension* wouldn't wait. She said she needed to put the images together right away, while she could still see what they were trying to show her."

Jen started to ask the obvious question, but he went on.

"Meanwhile, the Taos gallery was getting antsy. Leonie printed the first three and shipped them off, but they kept calling. The night of March nineteenth, she locked herself in her studio to finish the other four—"

Jen held her breath, waiting.

"—at least, that's what she told me she planned to do."

Turning away from the ruins, Gerard began walking fast, heading even further into the trees. She scrambled to catch up.

"Ms. Maxwell, how much do you know about my sister's work methods?"

"She did digital photography for a long time, but switched back to film for the last couple of years—when she started doing photomontage exclusively."

Scraps of interviews she'd read came back to her. "She wanted the 'greater reality' of print over pixels. The tactile experience of fitting images into new wholes. Each image leads to the next, but it's like a jigsaw puzzle: you've got to have all the pieces to know where they fit."

Gerard swore under his breath.

"Each image leads to the next. You don't know how often I heard that from her, without understanding what it meant. Or even trying. She was chasing all over the world to get her precious images—South America, Africa, Mexico, places nobody sane goes these days—and all I did was argue with her."

His voice cracked. "I never asked the right questions."

When the stone-built chimney and plank walls of another building came into view minutes later, Jen knew without asking that this had been Leonie's cabin.

And that her brother, too late, had found his answers here.

Fishing a plastic-tagged key from his jacket pocket, he headed for the porch. "We had an agreement about this place. I own it, but I wasn't supposed to go inside—not even when she was traveling—unless there was an emergency."

He unlocked the front door and pushed it open for her.

"Depends on your definition."

The main room looked more like a crime investigation than an artist's living space, with cork boards mounted on the walls and propped against furniture. Black-and-white photos of various sizes had been pinned to the boards. Most were accompanied by handwritten notes, and each was linked to others with yarn. Red yarn.

As she moved closer, Jen recognized familiar images. A doorway from Chaco Canyon connected to a clump of megaliths swirled in Cornish fog. Which led on to the jaguar god—from Belize, its note explained—which connected to part of a Hindu temple, which led to the shattered obelisk.

By the time she'd traced a strand to the three egg-objects descending through their anonymous sky, sweat trickled inside her collar.

"Where did she take this one?"

"No idea." Gerard moved closer to the cork boards. "All I know is that she wasn't setting up shots in her studio. They could be anything." His brow furrowed. "Or *mean* anything. The shadows in the largest one don't help, because—"

"—they change."

Gerard stared at her. Jen swallowed hard. "Or at least the ones in mine do."

Without commenting, Gerard retraced the red yarn to its starting point.

"This is where it started," he said, indicating the Chaco doorway. "Her last series. The one that made her career." His voice dropped. "And ended it."

Jen nodded for him to go on.

"She had this ratty little travel trailer. Loved to stay at the campground down there. She said the night sky was phenomenal, so dark and clear she could just fall into it. Then one night she stayed up watching until dawn—"

He took a long breath. Jen held hers.

"—and she never stopped working after that. Traveling, shooting rolls and rolls of film, then back to her darkroom. No more digital. All old school. Fitting images together on her light table, doing enough prints to keep some gallery happy, then packing again and taking off."

He frowned.

"Sometimes she left me an itinerary, sometimes she didn't. Never when she was going somewhere risky—which was most of the time as the series went on. I never could figure out what she was after. Or why she couldn't stop."

Until she did. Jen shivered. While writing her thesis, she'd seen most of Leonie Gerard's last series, and it hung together in a way she couldn't explain. The diverse images created weirdly believable landscapes—not dreamscapes, as one reviewer had insisted, but real places a person might walk through.

Never willingly, though. Something about those landscapes—the angles, the light, the juxtapositions of objects—turned them alien.

As if an entirely different aesthetic was at work.

"*Vernal Ascension* was the worst. The traveling, I mean. She'd started off back at Chaco, and I hoped it would calm her down, but it did just the opposite. Something about that clear dark sky . . . She even set up a camera for long exposures, though she never used those images. Just blew them up—eight by ten, sometimes larger—and hung them around her darkroom."

He frowned. "She said they showed her how the pieces went together."

Moving away from the Chaco doorway shot, Gerard returned to the egg-objects—with their enigmatic sky much darker than Jen remembered from her print. And were those faint background flecks of white *stars?*

She was about to point them out when he directed her attention elsewhere.

A little above the descending eggs, a last small image had been pinned. No yarn linked it to any of the others, no note accompanied it, and it wasn't a ruin or a sacred site. Instead, an amazingly ugly little statuette stared back at her.

"I do know where this one came from," he said. "Sierra Leone. Somewhere in the south. The people there call them *nomoli,* but no one seems sure of much more than that. A few tribes even claim they were left behind by spiritual beings."

His expression hardened. "Whatever they are, Leonie took some awful risks to photograph them."

Jen looked closer. The statuette was carved from something like soapstone, which didn't allow for fine detail. Its exaggerated features

and dwarfish body were partly obscured by a reptile (crocodile?) the
little figure was grappling with. Or holding.

Or becoming?

She rubbed her eyes and checked again. Not two figures. Definitely one in the process of transforming, and the reptilian aspect was
stronger, but vaguer: neither a crocodile nor anything else she recognized. Its scales flowed up the figure's arms to the shoulders, and—

Gerard pulled her away from the photograph, dragging her to the
middle of the room before releasing his grip.

"It did that to me, too." He sounded more nervous than apologetic. "For a couple of hours, because I was alone and I'd had a few
drinks. I was trying to figure out where Leonie fitted it into the picture."

"She didn't." *Why was she so certain?* "I've been over and over my
print, and there's nothing like this in it."

Without asking for permission, she took out her phone and started
photographing the whole sequence, taking close-ups of the notes. It was
time to quit freaking out. Sebastian Gerard had some seriously weird ideas about his sister's work, but she couldn't let them mess with her head,
not more than they already had. She'd come up here to gather material
for a couple of articles, at least. Maybe even a book. Real Ph.D. stuff.

By the time she finished, she'd nearly convinced herself.

Gerard sat silently in an armchair, watching her—or maybe watching nothing, staring into memory space. He had a big Ziploc bag on
his lap. She didn't remember him leaving to get anything, but she
hadn't exactly been good company these past few minutes.

"One more item for your research."

The bag held something flat and scorched. Jen took it gingerly.

"Leonie kept travel journals, always. Mostly work notes, but sometimes details about a location she'd visited, or a place she'd stayed. After the fire, I went looking for them. I don't know what I hoped to
find. Maybe some explanation for all this—"

His voice faltered.

"—but it turned out she'd burned them, or tried to. The whole
pile. In her darkroom, along with everything else. I only managed to
recover part of her last one."

Jen slipped the ruined object out. It looked like a book cover plus a very few pages, much the worse for smoke and water. If there'd been any entries on those pages, they weren't—

Wait a minute.

On the final page, partially protected by the cover, was a list of five names. They'd all been written in ink, then crossed through in pencil.

"Make any sense to you?"

Jen read them through. One or two looked familiar from her thesis work.

"Other photographers, maybe. At least a couple of them are—but I'm not sure how Leonie would have known them. They're foreign."

Something else gnawed her memory. "And I think at least one of them is dead."

Tipping everything back into the bag, she zipped it with unsteady fingers and tried to hand it back to Gerard.

"Keep it. Maybe you'll figure out something I haven't been able to."

With a last glance at the boards with their red yarn and cryptic notes, he headed for the door. "And call me when you're ready to sell your print, OK?"

Jen hurried past him onto the porch.

Then away from Leonie's cabin, willing herself not to run.

Researching the names on that list hadn't been the hard part. There were only five, after all, and she'd had plenty of experience. Internet, academic databases, people who knew people: questions in, information out. Repeat. Compile.

And wish that compiled information made a little more real world sense.

Or at least that it ruined less sleep.

Jen rubbed stinging eyes and reached for her coffee, carefully swiveling away from her laptop before taking a sip. She'd had some close calls lately—*gee, I wonder why*—and she couldn't afford to replace the thing. Not after clocking in late at work for the third time last week.

One more time, from the top.

Only three of the names on Leonie's list had been photographers. The other two were muralists whose fragmented styles resembled photomontage. All the photographers had used film rather than digital media. The muralists had worked directly on their walls. And all had traveled extensively to snap or sketch their images on-site.

The same images. On the same sites, minus the mysterious eggs.

It hadn't been quite that obvious: the sites had been visited at different times of year, captured with wildly varied approaches. One of the muralists had Picasso envy, and a couple of the photographers loved their filters. Fortunately, most of them had done more interviews than Leonie had—though not all were in English. She'd been able to piece together the rest from personal sites and gallery images. From what she could tell, they'd even visited each place in the same order Leonie had.

Glancing over the top of her mug at *Vernal Ascension,* she felt her stomach clench. Oh, yes, it was all one world.

And not her world.

Less so every day, though she tried to ignore the not-quite-green of formerly monochrome leaves. The mutating contours of those Cornish megaliths. The jaguar god's tongue reaching to the ground, starting to split into writhing, coiling—

Jen swiveled back to her desk and set the coffee mug down. Hard. *Way too much caffeine, girl.* Still, there was no arguing with that haunted landscape. The names of its ghosts now mocked from her laptop screen, annotated with the details of five disturbing deaths spaced one year apart: none of them natural, most of them violent.

All on the same date: tomorrow's date. Almost today's.

She wondered how Leonie (number six?) had found out about the others, though she suspected she wouldn't like the answer. Maybe those stars above Chaco Canyon had held more than a blueprint for the shared world she'd been creating. Maybe she'd seen herself there— the latest link in a chain it was too late to break.

Jen sighed. In the days and weeks since acquiring Leonie's last image, she'd almost gotten used to thoughts like that. Random acts of neurological chaos, she suspected, brought on by living with art she had no hope of understanding. There weren't going to be articles from this one, after all.

Some impulse made her stand and head back over to *Vernal Ascension.* Her rumpled futon couch—where she'd been collapsing most nights for the past week or so—creaked as she stepped onto it.

Descending through their deepening patch of twilight, the three egg-objects hadn't appeared in any of the others' images, yet they'd been the centerpiece of Leonie's. She'd given up trying to figure out why. Or where they'd come from. Nose to nose with the largest one, now, she watched shadows crawl across its surface like a storm seen from space.

Something new curled beneath that surface. Spectral, fetal, it clutched itself with curiously mottled limbs.

No, not mottled. Scaled—

Stumbling backwards off the futon, she landed hard and felt one ankle twist under her. *Sierra Leone*. The words throbbed in her mind as she dragged herself back to her desk chair. *Nomoli*. Leonie's last trip, her last shoot, her last big risk.

You've got to have all the pieces to know where they fit.

Each image leads to the next.

It cost breathless minutes to find the number on her phone, but Sebastian Gerard picked up right away. Or she thought he had. The connection hissed and popped and faded at random, garbling his words no matter how loudly he spoke them.

"... hatching. It's what eggs do, right? World eggs ... half the origin myths on the planet ... ours just raw material for the next ..."

This wasn't helping. Raking a hand through her hair, she tried again.

"Are your prints doing this, too? The crawling shadows? The—"

"—*Hundun* ... Primordial chaos, in some translations ... buried in the stars ... worn-out worlds breaking apart, worlds remade from the shards ... not ours any more ..."

There was something familiar about the connection noise.

"Are you driving?" Jen sucked in breath as her ankle throbbed. "Where are you?"

After a long moment, their connection seemed to clear.

"Just got into town. Left Estes as soon as I realized ... what I should have from the beginning. When I might have stopped her, if I'd been listening ... Are you in your apartment, Ms. Maxwell? Is it still—"

Even from her desk chair, she could see the image. Couldn't stop seeing it. That solid knot of dark, just under the surface—

"Yes."

"Get out. Tear it up if you can, but get out."

She stood up cautiously, good foot first, testing the ankle. White pain stabbed through.

"Can't."

Gerard swore indistinctly. "I'm nearly there. Stay away from—"

"Are your prints doing this, too?"

"Not since I burned them."

Someone else's horn blared, followed by a screech of tires. He hung up abruptly. Still clutching her phone, Jen felt a cold wave of disbelief as she stared at *Vernal Ascension*. That spectral knot was still there, curled at the heart of the largest egg, but it hadn't changed since she'd fallen. There were no new changes at all. No cracks in that other world which was not her world.

Insomnia, she told herself firmly. Plus caffeine, plus academic desperation, plus this damned ankle she'd probably broken in a fit of stupidity. Maybe Gerard could drive her to a clinic when he got here.

Swiveling away from that strange patched landscape at last, she turned to her desk and the window beyond it. The street below was poorly lit, weeknight quiet, too iffy for pedestrians at this hour. There were only a few parked cars. Part of a moon.

Her world after all.

Gerard's old pickup showed up minutes later, nearly clipping a traffic sign on the last corner. It slid into a parking space across from her building, sputtering to a stop as the driver's door flew open and a coatless Gerard scrambled out. He stared up at her window. Then, without pausing to lock his vehicle, he started across the street at a run.

The massive van came out of nowhere, one headlight out and not even trying to stop. Somewhere beneath her screaming, Jen felt rather than heard the impact as Gerard's body flew. An answering crack of midnight sounded behind her, but it was only when the fire flowed up her arms—the gnaw of flesh transforming to reptilian scales—that her trance broke and she turned to face Leonie's final creation.

And beheld its occupant ascending at last, the world of its remaking streaming through.

A darkness more brilliant than light.

THE SWEETNESS OF YOUR HEART

S O NOW YOU ARE DYING, my love. At the end of your long proud
drive lined with cypress, beyond the double-planked doors of your
ancestral home (no home to me, though I dwelled therein), you lie pallid and speechless at last. The physicians come and go like so many
ravens in their tight black coats, disturbing your household day and
night with their harsh voices and nostrums and fees, though there is
nothing to be done. Nothing at all.

Nothing but to wait, and to watch. And I do.

I dare not fail in my task, for there are many who rely upon me
now. Many who are bound too strongly by age and habit and . . .
change to stir far beyond their accustomed haunts. It is strange to be
so free now—I who was never free—and I revel even in this duty beneath our lady moon. Beneath your wide sheer-curtained window,
where the shrubberies have not been cut back for years, I wait with
infinite patience and observe all that I can.

Observation, you might remember (but your mind does not remember anything, not now), is among my most notable virtues. Observation and silence. It was while I silently observed you from my
exile's corner at a crowded ball that you fell in love with me at first
sight. Or so you claimed. Surely there was little else to fall in love with but
my virtues, for my mirror had been a poor friend since my earliest youth.

Too thin, it whispered in its harpy tones. Too thin, too pale, too
graceless. Nothing my dressmaker devised could please it—or my father, either; for he saw his investment in my future dwindling year by
year. Season by season. Three seasons and a girl is done, a failure forever. And it was in my third London season that you plucked me from
that dismal garden of dashed hopes, waltzes, and wicked tongues,

25

whirling me away to church as quickly as propriety (and settlements) allowed. You could not rest, you said, until we were one eternally. Until I was truly and wholly yours.

And all this, I believed, from the sweetness of your heart.

There is a tolling now disturbing the chill air. A solemnity of iron and sentiment nine tailors long. Your passing bell, my love, ringing out from the squat gray chapel where your ancestors have been married and buried for centuries. And beside that stone toad of a building, well fenced in by more solemn iron, the churchyard dominated by a single outsize crypt of leprous marble.

Your crypt, my love. Soon. Soon you shall join that society of the smug and justified dead, another brick in its proper niche in the family wall. You showed it to me once, soon after we were married. A shallow cold bone-slot . . . but how proud you were of it; and of the niche immediately beneath, where I should be placed one day.

There were other niches below yours as well, and more than one of them sealed. When I stooped to read their engraving, though, you took me by the arm and hurried me out of that place. "Never speak of them," you said. "I could not bear it."

But driving away that dying afternoon, I stared back out of the window and thought of them. Called to them out of my heart, wishing them happy where they were as I was now happy beside you—until you caught me leaning out too far, and pulled me back in. Such flattering anger! The sweetness of your heart could not bear that I might be injured by falling from your carriage.

Or perhaps you too had seen—from the corner of your eye, as I did—certain shadows in the day's last light, flitting among the constellation of lesser stones. *Never speak of them, either,* said your fixed expression.

Your habitual expression, as I learned soon enough at the end of that cypress drive, within the endless cold rooms and rambling wings of your ancestral monument. Monument to some infinitely more important past, when your family name was a conjuring-word for counties around and each November's hunt rode out in a glory of surging hounds and horns and expense. Now only the monument itself remained, sustained on diminished lands and investments you never spoke of—not even to my father, or his solicitor.

Or to me, of course, your most recent investment.

I was truly and wholly yours along with my passions and my virtues and all I possessed, but only the latter held much continuing luster for you. The rest was a troublesome packet of inadequacies demanding constant management. Discipline, even, though you never struck me. You only shrank my world around me, like distant sun drying up a puddle.

Another physician, now. And a surgeon, hurrying fast into the house. The silhouettes at your bedside flock thick as a murder of crows.

There were crows outside my sitting-room window every morning until the last. Or perhaps they were ravens, though I never dared to ask you. You had, you said, no patience with ignorant women. My shrunken world made ignorance too easy, and so I resumed silence instead. For some months you accepted that (welcomed it even, I think), but then my silence became a barrier to be pecked away at, if only because it was mine. It was all I had left.

And when that was gone too; when I had no peace from what passed for your conversation ... at meals, in the endless evenings, even in your bed on rare occasions ... I knew nothing but hollowness and a longing for death. Remembering the churchyard shadows of that long-ago afternoon, I felt a bleak kinship. Surely they would take me now if I went to them.

The moon hung like a suicide blade in the night beyond my window. Slipping outside in my nightdress, I ran up that long drive like a penitent, welcoming each stone beneath my bleeding feet. Mortality's black angel haunted my soul now, harrying it on toward the tall spiked gates that had tempted me with their shadows.

They should, of course, have been locked now, so long after sunset.

I had not thought of that.

Ignorant, your brandy-whetted voice rasped in the ear of my memory. *Too ignorant even to die.* And perhaps you were right, my love. The thick chain—thick as a young child's wrist—which should have bound those gates coiled snakelike on the ground inside, its lock broken open. Pushing through with my last scraps of strength, I heard only the silence of oiled hinges where I remembered no such blessing.

And still further inside, beyond that great crypt crouched like a pallid sphinx, beyond all but the meanest clumpings of headstones, I came upon my shadows at last.

Or rather, they came upon me.

Even now . . . even to myself . . . I can hardly describe such horrid magnificence of limb and feature. Bestirring themselves suddenly from their strange feast, they seemed at first like a pride of she-hyenas sprung out of hell, with eyes of kindled amber and dripping crimson jaws. Such jaws they were, too!—for the long bones of a human leg were nothing to them, and the soundest-woven graveclothes merest tissue.

Then a wind licked through that churchyard and brought me the scent of them, and I knew I should die where I stood. It was an exhalation of the conquering worm and the death-gorged earth, every rank impurity of the flesh and the unshriven spirit, all mingled within a miasma of ancient brimstone.

"So," breathed the most twisted of these apparitions, impaling me with her incarnadine gaze.

But now there are sudden stirrings of light in the frugal dankness of your rooms. Exclamations of something that passes for grief. A great cry for candles and lamps and messengers goes up, and I fade further into these shrubberies that have served me so well. The violent apoplexy that struck you down on the morning after my escape has won through at last. The Demoiselle D'eath lays her chill kiss upon your brow, marking you as truly and wholly hers.

Or perhaps not wholly. Only truly, for the pageant I have watched through this long night for—this night, and two before it—now stirs to life, a massive and hideously costly creature.

In its masque of crape and bombazine and jet, in its mummery of mutes and prayers and priests, it will ravage your lands like a fire. Ancestral pride, as manifested by obscure relatives and hangers-on, must squander what it cannot lay claim to. A burnished ebony hearse and four matched blacks, with nodding raven plumes to their headstalls— nothing less will suffice for your final conveyance. Dripping guineas in place of honest tears, this dark pantomime shall wind its way to the burying-ground of St. Toad's.

And there, behind the verdigris doors and poxed marble of your ancestral mausoleum, after the last hireling mourners have departed . . . while your distant relations are pillaging the choicest vintages from your cellar . . . there we shall be reunited at last, my love. All of us.

Eternally, just as you wished.

Si'lat, my shadows call themselves, in the esoteric Eastern tongue of ghûls: sister connoisseurs of the new-dug grave, female adepts of the truest possible consumption. But they bore other names once. Names you could not bear to hear spoken, names you saw engraved and forgotten under niches sealed against prying eyes. However you willed yourself to believe in their deaths—by drowning or laudanum or lethal melancholy—they were merely used up, and not dead forever. Only inconveniently missing, when you so wished and needed to marry again.

But, of course, you managed anyway. Over and over, with all the proper certifications of your widower's weeds in hand. Some thrice-damned, thrice-perjured solicitor, no doubt. And some soundly black-mailed surgeon as well, to sign where the solicitor could not.

There are no surgeons waiting in this final twilight, my love. No solicitors. Only we who were utterly devoured by you, in full view of the world and without recourse. Hollow and aching in our esuriance, we await what is by right of nature—red-fanged Nature, who rends to rebirth—ours alone.

And to me alone (for I have been promised) shall go the most highly esteemed tidbit of all. The delicacy I craved always, yet waited a lonely lifetime to savor.

The sweetness of your heart.

WHEN THE STARS RUN AWAY

THE NIGHT SKY TEARS beneath her touch. Slowly at first—then faster—the worn spot her fingers found becomes a rip, a narrow gap in the spatter of stars. Megan doesn't need to watch. Her father had told her all about it: why the universe is getting bigger and emptier, how the stars are running away.

At the other end of the sunny library, her teacher is reading *Charlotte's Web* to the rest of the class. Megan used to cry when she read it, but she doesn't any more.

She has real things to cry about.

Black cold seeps through, numbing her fingertips as the rip grows longer and wider. She pinches down tight, trying to stop what she's doing, but she can't feel the sky any more and the tear opens like a wound.

Don't look down. Keep your glasses on.

Prying her fingers from one side of the rip, she reaches up to her face. Her fingertips are ice. They dig into her hair, find one bow of her glasses, and start tugging.

"Megan!"

Her hand falls away from her face, leaving her glasses cockeyed. The book thumps onto the library carpet.

Her teacher is staring at her from across the room.

Everybody is staring.

Megan's eyes sting with tears as she pushes her glasses straight. Her hands are shaking. *What were they trying to do?* Wadding them to fists, she crams them into her lap and sits staring down, not looking at anyone at all. The book sprawls on the floor, its torn page in plain sight.

At least she has her glasses on.

The murmur of *Charlotte's Web* begins again, though she can still feel her classmates sneaking looks. After a long time, her teacher stops reading. Twenty-four pairs of feet thud out of the library.

"Not you, Megan."

Her teacher thrusts the open book back into Megan's lap. She is frowning a complicated frown.

"Why did you do this? You know we have to be careful with library books. They don't belong to us."

Megan's eyes tear up again, smearing her glasses. Big and glossy and filled with facts about space, this book is one of her favorites.

And now it's ruined. Her fingers ruined it.

"Please answer me, Megan."

She knows her teacher is being nice to her because of her mom. Because of what happened with her mom after Christmas, when she had to go talk to the counselor and use up all his tissues.

Her teacher doesn't want to hear about her fingers doing something, even though Megan thinks she knows why.

"Because it's true," she finally says.

Her teacher's frown gets even more complicated. "What's true?"

"The universe *is* ripping. All of it. Everything's coming apart."

Her teacher's frown wavers to sadness.

"I know, sweetheart. It sure feels that way, doesn't it?"

Her father reads over the note from school once again before he looks up at her. His face is thin and tired—always tired—but he doesn't look mad. Just confused.

"Your teacher sounds worried about you."

"I know." Megan presses her fingertips together to feel the lingering cold. "But I told her the truth!"

She starts explaining what she said and why she said it—though not what happened with the book, exactly. She still doesn't know why her fingers did that. Or why they almost took her glasses off at the worst possible time.

Her father's confusion turns to something else Megan doesn't recognize at all. Then he crumples the note.

"The Big Rip is just a hypothesis, Meggie. You know what that means, right?"

"Not even a theory?"

He nods, but his expression doesn't change. Reaching for the book on the dining room table, he opens it to page twenty-seven. The tear in the night sky looks even worse now.

"Some people think so."

He runs one fingertip down the tear, but his gaze is somewhere else. Megan follows it to the shiny new frame on the buffet. It holds most of a photo of her with Mom and Dad, taken last summer in the mountains.

Dad tore the bigger picture apart after Christmas. Megan remembers the careful, terrible sound of Mom's third being peeled away, though she doesn't think he saw her watching. It was way after her bedtime, and the wind was howling in the foothills the way it did most nights nowadays. A few days later, the reframed picture was back in place.

With a little piece of Megan missing.

"Ripping is real," she finally says. "Like redshifting is real."

Dad told her about redshifting last summer, during that same vacation when he took that picture. He and Megan were out on the porch of their rented cabin one night, talking about the stars while Mom was inside on her laptop.

Her father loves telling stories about the stars. He teaches astronomy at CU Boulder, when he's not analyzing data from the South Pole Telescope.

Last summer, neither of them knew Mom was going to redshift.

"Redshifting is a lot more certain," her father says, frowning down at the book. "And what's that got to do with what you did?"

She hesitates. After Mom disappeared over her personal event horizon, she'd noticed other things doing it: a jacket she left at school overnight, the neighbor's Sheltie when a gate latch broke, the classroom hamster whose cage just wasn't there one morning. None of these things ever returned. When she asked why, nobody had a good answer.

Even bits of her favorite constellations started winking out. Maybe only a star in Orion's belt Dad said he couldn't see anyhow, but it was still happening.

Then, a couple of months ago, Dad had told her about the Big Rip and how too much dark energy—*phantom* dark energy—might make the stars run away until everything tore apart. Even for him, it was a weird bedtime story. He'd gotten home late from a night class, after Megan was already supposed to be asleep, and just sat in her room telling it to her.

Everything made sense after that. If the big things in this universe had started to rip, it shouldn't surprise her when dogs and hamsters and jackets disappeared—or when she and Dad came home from the library one afternoon to find Mom's closet empty and her car gone.

She hurt just as much, but at least she wasn't confused any more.

Until she stared too long into the dark one night without her glasses.

"My fingers did it," she finally mumbles. "I was thinking about how the stars were running away from us, and it just started happening." She swallows what feels like a rock in her throat. "I'm sorry."

Her father shuts the book and gets up, coming around the table to put his hands on her shoulders.

"I know you are, Meggie. You're a smart girl, but sometimes you like stories too much. When I told you about the stars running away, I didn't mean that they were doing it . . . like that."

Just for a moment, his grip tightens.

"Tell you what. After dinner tonight, if it's clear, we can go take a look for ourselves. OK?"

They haven't done much stargazing together since last summer, but she makes herself nod.

"Seventy-three percent of the whole universe?"

Megan stares up in sick disbelief. It's May, the back yard lilacs have been blooming all week, but her fleece pullover is suddenly not enough. She wiggles her glasses more firmly on her nose.

Meanwhile, beside her, her father rattles on.

"Hard to believe, isn't it? Everything we can see with our eyes—out in space or on Earth—is only maybe four percent of what's actually there. Then there's dark matter. That's another twenty-three percent . . ."

His voice trails off as he notices her confusion.

"Don't feel bad, Meggie. I don't have a clue about it myself. I don't think anybody does—it's just a fudge factor to make equations work right." He snorts, and Megan giggles. "Besides, the South Pole Telescope isn't trying to find dark matter."

She stops giggling. "Just dark energy?"

"I told you you were smart!"

Even the pride in his voice isn't helping. He's just told her that what's tearing the universe apart is most of what the universe *is*—except she knows that's not true, either. This universe, her universe, has nothing to do with why the stars are running away.

But she knows what does.

Curling her fingers around the binoculars, Megan grips hard until she stops shivering. When her father starts telling stories about Ursa Major, the Big Bear who was her very first constellation, she tries hard to pay attention. Surely the Big Bear is full of good stars. Stars that stay put and don't redshift, don't vanish over event horizons where she can never see them again.

Not like Mom.

"Do you remember the secret in the bear's tail?" her father asks.

It's an Indian secret hardly anybody knows. "The horse and rider?"

"Mizar and Alcor, right." He points up toward the Big Bear's tail—the Dipper's handle—and traces it to the second star from the end. "Why do you think I told you to bring your binoculars?"

Mizar and its faint companion Alcor, the horse and the rider, were a vision test. Only a keen-eyed warrior could see the fainter star, which means she definitely needs binoculars.

Without her glasses on.

Bad idea. Megan puts them carefully in the pocket of her pullover anyhow. Then she raises her binoculars, settling both eyepieces into place.

As she adjusts the focus, blobs of swirling liquid shadow leak into the edges of her vision. They have no shapes she can identify, no purpose she understands. They are, however, alive. And intelligent: she knows this as certainly as she knows rips don't just happen.

Rips aren't empty, either.

Second star from the end. Breathe.

The first time she actually saw them, it was the middle of the night about two weeks ago. She'd just gotten a drink of water and was having trouble falling asleep again. Lying there with her thoughts and without her glasses, she'd almost screamed when one seeped out of the corner of—

"Have you found the rider yet?"

Her binoculars jerk sharply. When she settles them back on Mizar, there is nothing else in her field of view. Only a twinkle of light, out there in space which might be tearing open right now . . . *Alcor. Breathe.*

She's just found that faint bright speck when her father's phone chimes. It's the ring that means work, and he apologizes before fishing into in his jacket pocket and stepping away.

"Are you sure?" he asks, moments later. "Have you confirmed this with anybody?"

Her father's voice doesn't sound like he's talking to work. It's sharp and hard and anxious, the way it sounds when Mom's lawyer calls.

"Well, what did Atacama say?"

If he has more questions, she can't hear them over the wind already whipping through the lilacs. Stray shreds of cloud are moving, too, making it harder to find Alcor again. Megan keeps trying—it's something to hang onto out here in the dark.

Then another swirling blob leaks into one lens.

She yelps as the binoculars slip from her hands, bruising her chest as the strap catches them. Her father doesn't notice. He's already heading for the house, phone still pressed to one ear.

"Sorry, Meggie," he tells her over his shoulder. "I've got to go back in tonight." He lowers the phone. "Some problem with the data coming up from the South Pole."

Which means Mrs. Schmidt and her snoring again. The retired teacher who watches her after school is nice enough, but when she has to come back at night, she has trouble staying awake. Megan can hear her all the way upstairs, no matter what's on TV.

Mrs. Schmidt lives clear across town, too. She won't be happy to get a call this late.

Reluctant to go inside, Megan raises her binoculars for one last try. Alcor flickers into view almost immediately as she holds her breath.

Then, like a blown-out match, it vanishes.

*　*　*

Hours later, a branch thumping her window wakes her from a dream she can't remember—except that she knows not remembering is a really good thing. The wind sounds like winter, when she forgets to pull the back door all the way shut and the cold wails through.

She can't even hear Mrs. Schmidt downstairs. For once, this bothers her.

When she pulls the covers away from her face, her clock radio shows it's after midnight. Is her father home yet? Grabbing her glasses off the nightstand, she heads for the stairs as quietly as possible, glancing away when shadows drip from the corners of her room. Or bead up along the hallway, swirling in patterns that almost make sense.

She tries even harder not to wonder why there are so many tonight.

On the second step down, she finally hears Mrs. Schmidt, as loud as ever over some shopping program. Megan sits listening for a long time, but her father doesn't come home and the wind doesn't let up.

Like dark energy.

Dark wind through a crack in the door—or a rip in the universe.

When she stops running, she's back in her own room and groping for her reading flashlight under the bed. Switching it on low, she slides the beam along her shelves until it rests on a shiny black spine taller than the rest. She pulls the space book out and holds it close.

It may be damaged—so damaged the school didn't want it back—but now it's hers forever. Her father taped the ripped page, so that's probably safe.

But the wind isn't.

Blowing through from where?

Cross-legged on the floor, Megan opens the book across her knees and starts reading. She knows a lot about space for her age—but she needs to know more, and right now. She wants galaxies pinwheeling through the void. She needs to see them making clusters, the way her father told her once that they did. Clusters of islands in the deepest, blackest ocean, all drifting apart faster and faster.

The pages are turning faster, too. Propping her flashlight on one thigh, she skims photos and drawings and blocks of words, finding less than she'd hoped for.

It's only a kids' book, after all. She wants the truth she heard in the wind tonight—the reason Alcor flickered out before her eyes. She wants to know what comes after the redshift—

Then her breath catches. Hard. She's come to *that* page, the one her father mended, but there's something wrong with the tape. It's lifting away from the paper already, up from the bottom in a tiny curl. Underneath that curl is black cold so intense it numbs her finger, which is probably just as well. As she watches, another glob of swirling shadow seeps out from that black.

And onto her fingertip.

Then slowly, greasily, through it.

This hurts worse than any shot she's ever had, but there's no wound. No bleeding. Nothing but an awful piercing iciness as her flashlight hits the floor, jittering its light around the room. Megan slams the book shut and throws it into her closet, then drags her desk chair in front of the closet door.

Abandoning the flashlight, she climbs back into bed and pulls the covers up—all the way over her head, though she never takes her glasses off. The darkness has hurt her enough with them on.

Outside her window, the wind is still tearing at the night. Downstairs (though nothing in this world could make her go check), Mrs. Schmidt is still snoring along with ads for miracle cleaners and fake diamond rings.

She will lie awake listening until her father comes home.

The kitchen next morning stinks of burnt toast and strong coffee. Her father sits hunched over his laptop at one end of the table. The rest of the tabletop is covered with printouts, and wads of yellow paper from the pad by his elbow litter the floor.

He hasn't made her breakfast.

Megan fixes a peanut butter sandwich and a big glass of orange juice, then clears some space at the other end of the table. The printouts look like mostly math from the South Pole Telescope, though a few have Spanish words. Maybe from Atacama—which she remembers is in Chile.

Her father barely looks up from his screen as she moves the papers. He is wearing his same clothes from last night, and he hasn't shaved. His eyes are dark smudges behind his glasses. Every few seconds he pokes a key on the laptop, then makes a noise under his breath.

She takes a big sip of juice for courage. "Dad?"

At first, the wind is the only answer. It still sounds the way it did all night, the kind of wind that blows garbage cans over and tears leaves off trees.

And rips space apart.

As she grabs for a napkin and struggles to stop breathing peanut butter, her father finally notices. Hurrying to her, he thumps her back gently and holds her until the coughing fit stops—but only until.

Then he's back to his laptop, poking that key and making more noises.

Megan's chair scrapes loudly across the kitchen floor. *"Dad."* No answer. "Dad, what's wrong?"

When he does look up, she wishes she'd kept quiet.

"Meggie, do you remember what I said yesterday? About the stars and the Big Rip and how it wasn't all happening . . . like that?"

She sits back down and nods.

"Well, now I'm not sure." His eyes flick to the screen again. "Nobody is. Not at the Pole, not in Chile. They've seen galaxy clusters—do you remember those?—moving farther and farther apart, too fast for our math. Something's changed."

He gropes for his coffee and takes a gulp.

"Dark energy is our best guess—if that even counts as a guess. We needed something to fix our equations, but we never bothered to find out what that something actually was."

More coffee. "Or where it came from."

In one corner of the kitchen ceiling, a hand-sized blob of liquid shadow forces its way through. Smaller drops follow like rain through a bad roof. The big one's surface is swirling with colors that make Megan's stomach hurt, and she's glad when it disappears. It's the largest one she's seen so far this morning.

Rips don't just happen. And they don't get bigger on their own.

Before she can say anything, her father closes his laptop and stands up. Then he starts stacking printouts into neat piles, though he doesn't seem to be sorting them.

"So the stars *are* running away, maybe? Redshifting?"

Her father's hands freeze on a pile. "I don't know."

Not "no." Not "That's silly, finish your juice." Megan does finish her juice, though, and puts her dishes in the dishwasher afterwards. Those are the rules. Suddenly, she likes rules.

Outside, despite the wind, the sky is hazy and gray. Even the foothills have almost vanished. She and her father are halfway to the garage when he starts digging in his pockets.

"What's the matter?" she asks.

"I forgot about the check for that book." He pulls out his house keys. "I meant to write one last night, but I didn't get back until—"

"It's OK. I'll tell the librarian I'll bring it tomorrow."

She starts walking again, leaning into the wind with her backpack. Her father hangs back for a moment. Then he catches up and slips his fingers through hers, the way he did when she was little.

"You're right, Meggie. It won't really matter at all."

She can feel his hand trembling.

When she gets home from school, the driveway is empty. Mrs. Schmidt is never late, and something whispers inside Megan as she stares at that space.

Redshift.

She tries to push the word back out of her mind, but she can't. School today was too strange, beginning with her teacher being gone for no reason the sub knew of. Several of her classmates—all bus riders—were absent, too.

Everybody else kept sneaking glances around the classroom. Megan isn't sure why liquid shadows like leaking through corners, but the big ones usually do. This afternoon a basketball-sized one squeezed in between two ceiling tiles. At least three other kids saw it, but nobody said a word.

None of the shadows tried going through anybody until recess.

Then a little second-grader started screaming and fell off the jungle gym, just like that. He had a long twisty one like part of a squid stuck through his middle. When he hit the ground it was gone, and there wasn't any blood.

Not on his stomach anyhow.

Megan's free hand clutches at her own stomach as she unlocks the front door. By the time she gets it closed again against the wind, her phone is chiming in her jacket pocket.

"Meggie?"

Her father's voice is as far away and hollow as a dream she's having. Or one she's already had. When she tells him about Mrs. Schmidt, he sounds worried but not surprised.

"I'll be home as soon as I can, but you'll have to look after yourself until then. Can you do that?"

She can barely hear him now, but she says yes and I love you. The words drown in buzzing silence. Dropping her phone into her backpack, she hurries upstairs without stopping in the kitchen for Oreos or even hanging up her jacket. Swirling droplets are leaking in everywhere now, and one or two sting through her cheek before she reaches her room.

After her mom redshifted, Megan spent almost all her free time here for weeks. The worn furniture and overstuffed bookshelves felt like safety. Like thick comforting walls against the world, but that world is only four percent of something even her father can't explain, and the wind in the trees sounds like the sky tearing open.

Maybe the stars finally are running away.

The sky outside is the color of thunder, though the shadows splatting through are not rain. Megan watches for a while, hoping for a break in the clouds, but the drops multiply until sidewalks and driveways are paved with shredded green leaves. Green dying. Yanking the curtains shut, she heads for the only other answers she knows.

The space book is lying on some laundry in her closet. *A Child's Guide to the Cosmos* gleams across its cover in bright gold letters—or it did last night. Now the title shines faint as Alcor, winking out as she settles the book across her knees.

And takes off her glasses.

Her fingers find the page on their own, though they're already burning with cold. The strip of tape her father applied yesterday now runs across starless void. The curl at the bottom quivers invitation.

Somewhere beyond her bedroom door, on the staircase of a house half shattered by wind and shadows, her father's footsteps are climbing fast. Megan does not hear. Her thumb and forefinger close on the loose tape and begin to pull. Droplets and drops and gouts of sentient darkness pour through, on a gust of sound no earthborn ear has experienced before today.

The sound of a reality ripping.

"Meggie!"

Her father's arms wrap her with desperate love, but they are not enough. Like all the rest of their fragile visible universe, they are only four percent of what is.

And nothing of what will be.

WINGS OF MEMORY

TIPPING THE LAST BLACK OIL SUNFLOWER into her largest feeder, Edie frowned. Good thing her winter seed and suet would be here soon. She'd waited too late to order, hoping Jase would be gone—that she'd have spare cash to spend on her birds instead of her great-nephew.

He was still here, though. Eating like a horse, maybe still unemployed.

Her only sister's child had meant well by sending him, but this wasn't working out. Whatever trouble he'd found in the city, Jase was probably finding it out here now. Or up the road in Parkerville—

A chickadee's call rang from another feeder nearby. She smiled: her Walt had loved the sassy little birds. Glancing over, she wondered what memory it carried.

Moments later, her eyes filled with tears.

They had set up this area—a complete little habitat—two years before Walt's stroke. The two of them walked hand in hand around this old farmhouse she'd inherited, planning to make it the perfect retirement home. Even then, the property had been a haven for birds, but feeding stations and two heated birdbaths had done wonders.

Walt had even planted chokecherry bushes for food and cover. These would take a few seasons to mature, he said, but they had plenty of time.

Edie dug in her jacket pocket for a tissue. Memories were bittersweet, but she was grateful to the birds for bringing them. Ever since Walt's death last winter, she'd gotten one or two each afternoon while checking the feeders.

Since the beginning of autumn, they'd become more frequent.

Maybe the ravens made a difference.

Edie smiled at her own foolishness: ravens were common enough

43

out here in the country. They just fascinated her, or maybe their myths did. Messengers from the Otherworld, totems of wisdom and memory—

Her breath caught. Perched in a nearby crabapple, the largest raven she'd seen this season settled its polished black wings and stared at her. Into her.

Almost against her will, she stared back.

Then the bird cocked his head, and she understood.

Gravel crunched on the drive a few minutes later. Chilled and stiff, Edie shook herself and turned away from the tree. It was empty now.

But a black feather lay on the grass.

Picking it up with trembling fingers, she hurried to see if her order had arrived.

By the time she reached the front porch, two large cartons were waiting. So was the familiar brown truck with its usual driver.

She was about to call out a greeting when she noticed Jase by the side of the truck. The driver's window was down, and raised voices drifted toward her.

Why was her great-nephew home early?

Before she could reach them, the truck headed back down the drive. Edie's stomach knotted. Their driver almost always helped her put away her orders—or, at the very least, he asked after her health like a decent neighbor. What had Jase done to drive him away?

Something in his face told her not to ask. The boy had a temper, worse than she'd known about before he came. He took after his father, though she'd never had the questionable pleasure of meeting the man. He'd been out of the picture before Jase was ten.

"So," she finally said, "how was work?"

His grunt told her everything she needed to know. Wherever he'd taken off to this morning, it wasn't to the mega-mart outside town—where he had supposedly been employed since this summer.

He scowled past her at the cartons. "Think you bought enough?"

"I hope so. It may have to last all winter."

Jase ambled up to the porch for a good long look. At twenty-three, he was still more adolescent than not, given to sulks that lasted days. Recently he'd started slamming doors.

Edie's sister had suspected his dad of being a batterer.

"So how much did it cost?"

Her own expression hardened as she faced him. "Enough."

She wasn't sure if she meant enough money or enough of his questions. Either way, the boy had just crossed a line. Maybe she had, too.

Jase stared back, then shrugged.

"Since you're home early," she said, "could you help me put things away? There's a wheelbarrow in the—"

"No problem. I can take care of it."

Edie's jaw threatened to drop. Jase's mother had sent him here to help around the place, but he was good at not seeing what needed to be done. Still better at not being around to see it. Even when she reminded him—which she did less and less—chores went undone for days. The more muscle required, the longer they waited.

Now he was offering to do more than she'd asked.

"Thanks," she finally said, forcing back her smile. "I can get an early start on dinner. How about apple crisp for dessert?"

Jase gave another patented shrug, then went for the wheelbarrow. Edie watched long enough be sure he meant it before hurrying inside. The cold settled in early this time of year, and darkness wasn't far behind. Darkness and winter.

Fingering the raven feather in her pocket, she felt her chest tighten.

Halfway through dinner—wasn't that always the way?—the phone rang. Jase barely looked up. Sighing, Edie pushed aside the remains of her pork chop and headed for the hallway. Walt had never liked a phone in the dining room.

"Miz Campbell?"

She frowned as she recognized their UPS driver, then reached for the little chair beside the phone table. *Never stand when you can sit,* her doctor kept telling her.

"I hate to bother you so late," he continued, "but I'm planning tomorrow's route. What time did you want me to come pick up that seed?"

Suddenly, she was glad she was sitting. "I'm not sure I understand."

Or I hope I don't.

The driver sighed. "Since that order I delivered was a mistake, you'll need a tag to return it. I can bring one tomorrow. You've got to send everything back pronto if you want a refund."

"Why would I?"

"Miz Campbell, all I know is what your great-nephew told me. He said you hadn't ordered anything lately. He didn't even want me to unload it. When I told him I couldn't do that, he got—"

"I saw." She groped for the right words. "I'm afraid there *has* been a mistake, but Jase made it. I received what I was expecting, and I'm terribly sorry he bothered you."

Silence on the line. Edie felt iron grip her chest again.

"Thanks for clearing that up." The driver's voice sounded strained. "Miz Campbell, is everything all right at your place?"

"Of course."

She hung up quickly, then sat in the dark wondering why she'd lied. Jase's own lie had cost her a lot of embarrassment just now, but she wasn't feeling embarrassed. More like threatened. Maybe even frightened, if she let herself think about it.

So don't.

Taking a deep breath, Edie returned to the dining room. Jase had helped himself to apple crisp—with a double scoop of vanilla bean ice cream.

She'd checked the carton before dinner. Two scoops was all of it.

"I just had a very interesting talk with our UPS driver. He was under the mistaken impression that I wanted to return my seed order."

Jase kept eating.

"You were rude to the man, and you lied to him."

A shrug. No eye contact.

"Would you like to explain yourself, Jase?"

Her shoveled down the last bite before looking up at her. "OK, but you won't like it."

"I already don't like it."

Jase sighed and wiped his mouth. "It's simple: you can't afford that stuff. I wanted to save you the embarrassment, so I just told the guy it was a mistake. Tried to make him take it back, but he started giving me attitude."

Edie's nails dug into her palms.

"Since when are my finances any of your business?"

She knew the answer, of course. Her money had been his business ever since Jase arrived, claiming he'd already applied at the mega-mart. Maybe he had and been turned down. Maybe he'd never bothered. Either way, he wasn't paying room and board as his mother had promised.

She wasn't about to ask her only sister's child for that money—assuming she had it, which Edie doubted. Walt's pension and Social Security could get her through. She had told herself that all summer, even as cash started disappearing from her purse, then from the pickle jar hidden in the pantry.

Two weeks ago, she'd had to dip into her savings to place that seed order.

"Doesn't matter." Scooting his chair back on the hardwood floor, Jase dropped his napkin in the middle of his plate and stood up. "Fact is, that stuff needs to go back. You won't be able to use it anyhow."

Her breath caught. "Why?"

"Because it's locked in the shed. The only place it's going is onto that truck, so you may as well call and tell the guy you made a mistake."

Hurrying into the hallway, Edie grabbed her jacket and a flashlight before heading outside. There was no lock on that garden shed. There never had been—

Staring at the brand-new padlock shoved through hasps Walt had never removed, she started shaking.

Jase wasn't in the dining room when she got back. For a fleeting moment, she thought he'd gone—run away like the coward he was—but sounds from the upstairs shower dashed her hopes.

She was halfway through the dishes when he appeared in the kitchen doorway.

"I want that lock off my shed. Now."

Jase just shook his head.

"We're going to need the money this winter. Mom told me about Uncle Walt's pension, and it's not that great, not with inflation. Not even with Social Security."

Sick anger knotted her stomach.

"Let me get this straight. My personal finances are a topic of conversation between you and your mother?"

Jase didn't even have the grace to look embarrassed.

"She mentioned a few things. How long Uncle Walt worked for that company, how old he was when he died. I went online and figured out the rest."

When she'd agreed to let him live here, Edie had imagined she was doing his mother a favor—a temporary one. Tonight it didn't look that way. Jase was taking a proprietary interest, and she doubted he'd come up with that on his own. He wasn't that bright.

His mother was, though, and life hadn't been good to her since Jase's dad walked out.

"I'm going to pretend I didn't hear that," she said. "If *we*"—she emphasized the word—"are short of money right now, it's because one of *us* isn't contributing. I've always fed the birds. They aren't the problem."

Jase stared at her, then shrugged.

"Things change. Don't wait up, OK?"

"Where are you going?"

"Halloween party in town. Like I told you this morning."

He probably hadn't. Still, her confusion let him escape, the heavy front door slamming behind him. Edie stared down into the sink as the last of her anger drained away.

Replaced by fear.

Things change. For all his sullenness and pilfering, Jase had never pulled anything like this before. Never locked up her property or told her what she couldn't afford. Never treated her like an incompetent old woman.

Calling his mother now would do no good. If she wanted him out, she'd have to do it herself—and get her locks changed. That would cost money and couldn't be done until morning. Her UPS neighbor might have bolt cutters for the padlock. She wasn't strong enough to use them herself, though, and even asking the favor would mean explaining her situation.

Like an incompetent old woman.

Suddenly the greasy, cooling soapsuds were more than she could bear. Wiping her hands on a dishtowel, she headed toward the back door with its view of her feeding stations.

The security lights Walt had set up last year revealed nothing but shadows and emptiness. No birds feeding after dark, of course . . . and maybe soon, no birds at all. No memories. No messages from a time when days had seemed worth keeping track of.

How had she forgotten that tonight was Halloween? Easy enough, out here with no neighbor kids to remind her—and Jase wouldn't remind her of anything unless it suited his purposes.

Her chest tightened again. Fishing the raven feather from her pocket, Edie held it and tried to relax. *Avoid stress,* her doctor kept telling her—but how? Little by little, she was losing control of her life and her money. That was where it always started, where Jase had started tonight.

It ended with a bed in a cut-rate nursing home. With a grave.

Edie abruptly felt every year of her age. Turning away from the door, she headed back to her dishes.

Outside, under the security lights, a narrow blade of shadow detached itself and flew.

Maybe it was Halloween, but it hadn't been much of a party. With the losers he hung with, it never was, but he'd expected more than cheap beer. Pills, maybe. Pot at least. Squinting through his truck's cracked windshield, Jase swore at the world in general as he headed out of town.

Good thing he'd convinced Edie to give him his own house key this summer. After the fit she'd pitched about that birdseed, there was no way she'd let him back in tonight—not that he couldn't get in anyhow. The back door lock was a joke, and security lights didn't matter without an alarm.

He was half tempted just to force that lock. He could say he'd forgotten his key. It might remind Edie how alone she was—how much she needed him around.

A swoop of motion in his rearview mirror tightened his hands on the wheel.

Cops? Sweat broke on his forehead. He didn't need another DUI. With one eye on the mirror, he concentrated on the blurred lane markings. Not easy. He'd driven wasted before, though, and he wasn't seeing flashing lights.

Just another swoop. Then another, closer to his taillights.

Wings. Lots and lots of wings.

Jase sucked in his breath. Maybe there had been drugs tonight after all, and somebody had slipped him something. Something that messed with his head, made him see impossible things—like a flock of birds out in the middle of the night. Little ones, mostly, the kind Edie wasted her money on.

Not all little, though. With the next swoop, he saw it clearly: sleek and black and substantial, leading the flock.

No way. Cops or no cops, Jase's foot got heavier as he tried to lose his pursuers. This was getting too Hitchcock—especially on Halloween night. Better to get home fast and chill out.

After a minute or so, his rearview mirror showed clear.

His driver's side window was another story.

The night beyond the filthy glass was filled with wings, pale and dark and everything in between. Edie might have recognized them. He sure as hell didn't. All he knew was that the birds were pacing him, speeding or slowing or swerving as he did. Bead eyes stared in, shining with malice.

The principal's letter on their dining room table. His mother sitting there reading it, waiting up even though she'd worked a double shift again. Her eyes as red as the ink she'd used to circle that letter's last paragraph.

Expelled.

Him in the doorway not feeling too focused, hoping she couldn't smell the dope on him. Knowing she could. Her lips starting to move, lips forming the words he hated—words no chemical fog could silence.

"You're just like him." Big angry tears. "You always let me down, just like him . . ."

Cursing, Jase swerved hard into the flock. Wings scattered. A few small bodies thumped against his truck and dropped, crushed under the wheels. Blood streaked his windshield as its crack lengthened.

A girl's face, pretty and pale and miserable. Maybe just disgusted. Maybe more than one girl, one bad moment he hadn't seen coming. "Can't keep waiting for you to get your act together," she/they are saying. "I want a life. A real family. I want something more."

"Don't you all," he muttered as his foot came down harder. He was really speeding now, almost out of control, but the damn birds wouldn't leave him alone.

Smeared blood and feathers made it hard to see out. Still, he could sense the flock surrounding him, its huge black leader swooping above and nearly into the path of his truck. Memories pecked inside his skull: decisions, choices, pain.

His mother again. Skinny and worn in her ratty bathrobe, she sits in her recliner in their apartment, smoking and staring down the hallway into his room. Watching him pack.

He has the mega-mart application in his back pocket, though he knows already that it's hopeless. Drug test required. He didn't know that when he told his mother he had the job already. He'd heard anybody who could fog a mirror got hired there.

"This better work out," she calls to him. "Your great-aunt Edie is all the family we've got. Our last chance."

Jase groaned. Squinting through the mess on his windshield, he saw a narrow side road and turned onto it fast, teeth jarring as his truck's tired suspension met dirt. No telling where it led—to another rundown farm like Edie's, probably—but it beat staying on the highway with his pursuers.

He felt the flock sweep past him as he turned, and the pecking inside his head stopped. Slowing a little, he concentrated on staying in the twisting ruts and wished his high beams worked better than they did.

As he wound through stands of gaunt, leafless trees, he felt something thump into the truck bed. Moments later, a draft hit the back of his neck. Jase glanced up into the rearview mirror—and froze.

His sliding rear window had cracked open.

Poking through it was a long black beak.

The long black hole of the front doorway gaping, letting in a cold wind. His father standing there looking down at him like a bug. Somewhere upstairs, his mother crying again.

A stink of beer and cigarettes as his father's mouth opens.

God, no.

"Quit staring," he says, already reaching for his suitcases. For the end of their family. "You'll do the same, first chance you get—because you're just another loser, aren't you? You're just like me . . ."

Jase screamed, shoving his foot down hard on the gas. His truck bounced out of the ruts he'd been following and slewed sideways, still traveling fast . . . too fast. Another clump of trees loomed in his headlights.

Twisting the wheel with everything he had, he shrieked once more. Then he was hurtling forward, into his spiderwebbed windshield and an explosion of blood and feathers.

Black wings.

Edie leaned into the old tree and closed her eyes, waiting for the iron fist in her chest to unclench. It took a while. Reluctant to risk her sedan off pavement, she'd parked at the top of the dirt track and walked down slowly.

She knew this farm well, or had once. Until last winter, it had belonged to a neighbor as kind as her UPS driver, and considerably closer. Now it belonged to no one. No one had come this spring to do repairs, or to grade the path down through the dying orchard—

You've got to open your eyes again some time.

The raven perched atop the shattered tree opposite cocked his head at her.

Then down.

Edie hugged herself, shivering despite the heavy jacket she'd grabbed on her way out. This, she reminded herself, was what she had come here to find. Why the same raven had pecked at her window just before dawn, shattering an uneasy sleep filled with dreams she preferred not to remember.

Is this another?

Her guide's beak jerked down again, sharply. This time her eyes followed it.

Weak November sunlight glanced off the hood of Jase's pickup, accordioned into one of the biggest apple trees on the property. The impact had sprung the driver's door open. Or perhaps he had failed to lock it, just as he'd failed to wear his seat belt—

Sudden flap of an impressive wingspan. One staccato scream.

All right, all right.

Stepping closer, Edie risked one look inside the truck. A stench of beer and blood and worse greeted her. On the passenger seat amid shards of glass lay another black feather, larger than yesterday's find.

Her gaze skittered across what occupied the other seat. Clamping a hand over her nose and mouth, she backed away quickly, frosted grass crunching underfoot.

When her heel crunched on something louder, she nearly stumbled—then glanced down, puzzled. A half-dozen keys on a cheap ring, its plastic fob now broken, glinted at her.

How had Jase's keys wound up here?

The ground showed no other tracks or footprints. Still, his keys might have fallen from a pocket during the crash, attracting the attention of an animal. Or a bird fond of shiny objects.

Edie picked up the keys with a tissue. The smallest—a padlock key?—looked brand new.

Slipping them into her own pocket, she exhaled sharply and turned away. A pair of magpies had already alighted in the shattered tree. Soon there would be others, and she had no wish to see why. No wish to feel more than emptiness and vague relief.

Or gratitude.

Her chest clenched again as she looked up at her guide. He still perched there, eyes bright with memory—and something more, something she preferred not to believe. Not on this clear, cold morning, with the sun on her face and her breath coming more easily than it had in weeks.

Edie headed for the trail without a backward glance. Perhaps she should phone the police, but someone else would find Jase eventually. She had bird baths to scrub, feeders to fill, suet blocks to replace.

As for her raven, she would see him again soon.

Winter was coming.

HER BELOVED SON

SHE ALONE CAN HEAR HIM crying in the vastness of the attic tonight. Crying for her. His voice is primal ocean breaking on a shore no sun ever illuminated, no human foot touched. It is beast and earth and that howling which fills the spaces between the stars. It is Outside made flesh.

And it is a lonely child's hunger.

Her rocking chair creaks as she leans forward to warm her hands at the dying fire. Almost immediately, the other one snarls at her to be silent.

Lavinia's throat tightens. Across the room from her, aided by a single lantern, the other one sits preparing for the Hallowmass-rite. Heaps of tattered, much-mended books—*her* books, once—surround his chair. The largest volume of all occupies his lap, and she need not strain her weak eyes to know its title. Nor the passages he is certainly reviewing, in Dee's cumbersome English translation.

Once, not so very long ago, she listened to him recite those passages by heart. Kept his grandfather from beating him when he was slow to learn, or mispronounced some crucial word. Speaking came hard for him, with his throat . . . and other things . . . the way they were inside.

Her lips draw into a narrow wound. *So much of his father in him.*

Yet not enough.

For all the hill noises and the thunder on nights such as this, all the bane-fires leaping between the ring stones on Sentinel Hill, his father has never answered. Not truly. The good Doctor Dee offers no remedy for that, however often the other one furrows his dark brow and squints at the page.

She lied when she told the Bishop woman that she did not know what he wanted. What he was, is, trying to do.

That knowledge has finally called the whippoorwills to this ruined house. They began flocking well before sunset, filling every tree on Whateley land before spreading their shadows across the rutted lawn. Soon their cries will grow loud enough to distract the other one from his preparations. He will be angry. And there is no other convenient target for that anger—none he can hurt, anyhow.

It begins with his bark of a laugh.

"You hear them, Mother?" He cocks his head toward the filthy windowpanes. "They're waiting for you, old woman. For that rat's-nest scrap you call a soul. Nothing else left anybody would want, but they'll take *that*."

He smacks thick lips. "Tonight."

Lavinia blinks owlishly. It has been a long time since she knew fear. And only once, despite Mamie Bishop's flea-witted concern.

How the wind had screamed that May-Eve night!

Even then, she had hardly been a girl, though maiden enough for her errand on Sentinel Hill. The purpose for which she was born. Her father had known from the first and offered the necessary teaching, but he dared not offer *her* to the Outside. Some fates must be freely chosen.

And she had been rewarded beyond her expectations—nearly beyond survival.

Never strong, she had taken months to recover unaided from the delivery. And the feedings. Many times, she had wakened to a whippoorwill echoing her faltering heart, but always her father watched over her. Then he himself died, leaving only the other one to watch if he would.

Pressing one hand to her belly, she sets her teeth against deep tearing pain. "Yes, tonight."

Behind the rough beard he has affected since his tenth year, the other one's expression darkens. How can this merely human thing know the moment of her death?

As he rises from his chair with a curse, an immense weariness washes through her. She has been dying by inches ever since that May-Eve, for the Outside does not care for its vessels. She has walked with the whippoorwills these thirteen years, pallid and twisted beneath the shadows of their wings. Her own power can sustain her only so long before it must be surrendered. Or lost.

It shall not be lost.

She tastes copper and salt as his expected blow falls. Spitting into the last embers, she murmurs the opening of a ritual the other one never learned, in a tongue she neglected to teach him.

Within her mind, primal ocean answers. Wave after wave eroding the shores of mortality, making way for void incarnate and Those who wake within it. Walk within it between stars and worlds, on this night when the veil is thinnest—when even the smallest offering of fire and blood may suffice.

The other one hears only the whippoorwills. Turning away with a grunt of revulsion, he snatches up his book again and heads for the door.

"Won't be back till dawn, I expect." A cold smile twists in his beard. "Don't be waitin' up, Mother."

Long after his departure, she continues to stare into the darkening fireplace. Only when the last spark dies does she reach down for the weirdly carved oaken staff her father once carried: the "old stick" the other one has no use for. Strong beyond his years and arrogant past understanding, he has threatened more than once to feed it to the cook-fire.

Now, as she struggles to her feet with its aid, she is grateful for his blindness. There is old power in oak. Older power still in the glyphs twining over it, obscured though they are by use and time. These were the first of her learning, long ago at her father's feet, for not all knowledge can be carried in books. And no book could support her so well now as she climbs the steep and crooked stairs leading to the attic.

Outside, the whippoorwills in their thousands begin to shriek.

Each time she pauses for breath, she tastes fresh blood and spits again. Something long damaged inside is giving way. She must hurry if she hopes to reach the iron-bound door now rattling in its frame, always secured against her by the other one.

But tonight, it waits unlocked.

From inside.

Caught up in the madness of the whippoorwills, swept forward by dark star-winds filling her mind, she reaches for the latch. It falls away beneath her fingertips.

As her father's staff clatters to the floor, Lavinia is reunited . . . entirely and forever . . . with her beloved son.

CUSTOM ORDER

THE MAN WITH THE PERFECT silver-blond hair and tennis tan tosses Caitlin's folder onto his desk. "Looks fine to me. When can you start, Ms. Reilly?"

Caitlin freezes. She is not even remotely qualified, to say nothing of her visa situation. Alexander Blaine can obviously afford the best. From the glass and timber walls of this room jutting out over a deep ravine, to the rustic leather furniture and quarter-sawn oak executive desk he has filled it with, nothing suggests he would settle for anything less.

Even his home—though it does not feel like home to her—is a custom design. Situated well outside town on several acres of pristine mountain land, it has far too much space and too many windows for its few inhabitants. Caitlin suspects that each window and every inch of space is exactly what Blaine wanted.

So why has he just hired a mere *au pair* in place of the nanny he requested?

Admittedly, the toddler crawling on a nearby Navaho rug doesn't seem to need special care. Alex Blaine, Jr., is a fine strong boy, the image of his father. The agency mentioned some congenital problem, but she can't see a thing wrong with him.

Nor can she afford to refuse the only job she's been offered this month. Her savings are nearly gone, and the motel she's been living in wants next week's rent tomorrow.

"Tomorrow," she hears herself saying.

Alexander Blaine, Sr., smiles. "Excellent."

The fourth person in the room, an emaciated blonde, struggles to sit up straight in her chair. Heavy silver bracelets on both wrists jangle as she finally subsides into the cushions.

Her lips tremble. "But Alexander, shouldn't we check her references first?"

Blaine Sr.'s expression tightens.

"I'm sure the agency has already verified those. That, after all, is why one goes through an agency."

Caitlin winces. If anyone here has the right to ask questions, Alex's mother does. Yet this is Teresa Blaine's first—possibly last—contribution, brushed aside like a child's complaint.

Her husband's attention returns to Caitlin at once.

"My wife has been feeling . . . overwhelmed since the birth. It was a difficult pregnancy. I'm hoping that getting her some help with Alex will ease the situation."

His tone holds all the warmth of the spring rain spattering the windows. Blaine Sr. is an entrepreneur, a risk-taker impatient with problems. Whether this one is his wife or his baby son, she's not sure—and if it's his wife, Caitlin is no expert on postpartum depression.

Depression might not even be the whole story. Mrs. Blaine is a young woman, only a few years older than Caitlin, but pain has etched itself around her eyes and mouth. Her complexion is pallid in the dim natural light, and her whole posture hints at something broken inside.

Sensing impatience from Blaine Sr., Caitlin shifts her glance to the toddler on the floor. Bright blue eyes fix on hers.

"The agency didn't tell me how old your son is." She watches Alex struggle to push himself upright. "Nine months, maybe?"

Blaine Sr. grins like any proud papa. "Seven."

"He's doing . . . well for his age, then."

Unless his father is lying for reasons she can't imagine, Alex cannot be only seven months old. His size and muscular coordination are too advanced. Even now, the toddler is on his feet—barely—and wobbling toward his father.

He tumbles moments later with a diaper-padded thump. Caitlin hurries to pick him up and wipe his tears, but there are no tears. His little face twists with fury, and his eyes hold only sullen frustration. With remarkable strength for seven months, he pushes her hands away.

Mrs. Blaine giggles faintly.

"Little Mister I Want It Now. Just exactly like his daddy . . ."

"That's enough, Teresa."

When the thin woman giggles again, Blaine Sr. fishes a bottle of pills from a drawer and tosses them at her. As she fumbles with the cap and dry-swallows two, Alex stares up at his mother. His tiny lip curls. Crawling off to the farthest corner of the Navaho rug, he plumps himself down with a sniff.

Caitlin can't help but stare.

"Amazing what kids will pick up, isn't it?" Blaine Sr. is pushing his chair back now, tapping her papers into their folder. "Look, I've got a meeting in town. Are we through here?"

She nods because he expects her to.

He pulls a set of keys from his pocket and hands them to her. "You can use the Jeep to go get your things. Consider it yours to drive while you're with us."

His wife looks as if she's going to object again, but doesn't. The pills must be fast-acting. Caitlin closes her hand around the Cherokee's keys—very posh, very new—and slips them into her blazer pocket with Gran's rosary. As her fingertips brush the worn jet beads, she feels better and ashamed all at once.

"Thank you," she says—but her employer is already gone, off to deal with his next problem.

Teresa Blaine shrugs and sighs in her chair.

"I'm afraid I'll have to leave Alex with you for a couple of hours," says Caitlin reluctantly. Alex and his mother have both retreated into their own worlds—hers pill-induced, his a fascination with his own toes. For the moment, he looks like any typical nine-month-old.

At seven months.

"Mrs. Blaine?" she says, louder. Alex's mother finally blinks and hauls herself upright in the big leather chair, bracelets jangling.

"You'll have to find Inez downstairs. She's our housekeeper. She can watch him till you come back . . . she'd like that—"

Pink-shadowed eyelids quiver down over glazed eyes. Caitlin waits a moment, then reaches cautiously for Alex. The toddler gurgles and holds his hands up.

She lifts his warm weight onto her hip, ashamed of her earlier misgivings. The weather and the house—this big, new, cold place with too many windows and balconies overlooking nothing but rocks—are playing tricks on her mind. Alex is an ordinary baby, albeit one with very strange parents.

Here in America, many rich people are strange.

Mountain morning sunlight floods the nursery, glinting off the tray of medications next to Alex's changing table. It's a big institutional tray. Caitlin has never taken care of a child who needed as many medicines and supplements as Alex does.

Right now, post-breakfast and nappy changing, his schedule specifies drops from bottle #2. She frowns at the typewritten list. Two weeks in this house now, and no one has told her what any of these carefully numbered medications are—or exactly what they're for. Blaine Sr. calls them "proprietary formulas." He seems to think this is all she needs to know.

They could be bloody rat poison, and she'd be none the wiser.

Suppressing a sigh, Caitlin fills the bottle's dropper with the specified amount of #2 and pokes it in Alex's mouth. Whatever it is must taste good. He swallows immediately, gurgles at her, and reaches out for the dropper.

As she snatches it away from him, something fast and dark scuttles across the changing table. Caitlin yelps and swats it onto the floor with her free hand. It hits the tiles with an audible click and goes on scuttling, stopped only by her foot grinding down.

A cockroach? She peers at the mess she's just made. Cockroaches, she's been told, don't live in most of Colorado—certainly not in a house this well-maintained. Besides, it's a bigger than cockroach-sized spot.

Slightly sick, Caitlin turns away to recap medicine #2.

And sees another large, dark, scuttling thing crossing Alex's changing table. And another. And yet another, even larger than its compatriots.

Sweet Mother of God.

Stifling a rising scream, Caitlin sets down the dropper and starts brushing, swatting, stomping. Filthy things, whatever they are—oily black and grotesque, with long quivering feelers and spiky legs. What if they crawl on Alex? She quits grinding the last one underfoot and turns back to the table, where she left the baby lying placidly.

Alex is still on his back, on a nice soft folded towel. Still placid.

With a particularly ugly specimen crawling across his cheek, headed for his right ear.

Muttering words she's glad Alex can't repeat, Caitlin grabs some tissues and snatches the bug off his face. This one crunches audibly as she stomps the wad of pink paper. No sooner has she finished, though, when she spots wriggling feelers protruding from the corner of the baby's mouth. His mouth! Shuddering, she grabs more tissues and extracts the bug—which she is now afraid that Alex had been trying to eat. Babies do eat the most disgusting things sometimes.

And she's pretty certain Blaine Sr. wouldn't approve of his son ingesting insects, disgusting or otherwise.

Gritting her teeth for the worst, Caitlin wraps her fingers in yet more tissue and gently tries to open Alex's mouth. He twists his face away. She tries again, this time with her free hand cupping his small blond head. His lips tighten against her wrapped fingers.

Then, abruptly, he gurgles and burps at her.

Caitlin shrieks.

A whole stream—sweet Mary, a *river*—of glistening black horrors spews from his mouth, cascading down his tiny chin and covering his chest. This lot seems to be all spiked legs and antennae, with bodies as big and thick as her thumb. Their heads are narrow wedges with vicious sharp snouts, and there's a stench as well. Acrid and chemical, it fills the air so quickly she has no chance to clamp a hand over her nose.

Alex gurgles again. Happily.

Halfway across the room—and whatever is she doing there, with the baby in danger?—Caitlin freezes in shock, then starts stomping. The bugs smell even worse dead than alive, but there's no time for noticing that. No time for calling Inez, either, not that she'd dare for fear of being blamed. Thrown out with nowhere to go, and a work visa she can't risk renewing.

At least she's afraid of something besides the bloody bugs now.

After the last one is a long nasty smear on the nursery floor, she hurries back to the baby. Silent now, he stares up in blue-eyed complacency.

No feelers protrude from his pursed mouth. Nothing scuttles over or around or under the towel he's lying on. Still, Caitlin hesitates before she scoops him up and settles him on her hip.

"Come on," she says, heading for the door. "Let's go find your mama and see what she's got to say about you—"

Doing what? Eating bugs? Some part of her can't believe that, however desperately she wants to.

"You playing bad tricks, trying to spook me."

She has no idea of where to find Teresa Blaine, let alone what good it might do. Mrs. Blaine hasn't visited the nursery more than a few times in this past week. Still, she is Alex's mother. If he makes a habit of live snacks, she's more likely than her husband to have noticed it.

Mrs. Blaine isn't in the sunny breakfast nook downstairs. Inez hurries out of the kitchen to tell her this, smiling as she glimpses Alex.

Her smile fades quickly when Caitlin pursues the question. No, Mrs. Blaine hasn't had breakfast yet. Sometimes she doesn't. Mrs. Blaine has many bad nights.

A shadow crosses the housekeeper's face, too quickly to be sure of. Then Inez is telling her about the spa room where Mrs. Blaine seems to spend a great deal of her time, and has she tried looking there yet?

Until today, Caitlin didn't know the spa existed.

When she gets there, the door is open. Sunlight pours in from a curved window forming most of one wall. Peering inside, she sees a hot tub large enough for a party bubbling away on its raised tile dais, accompanied by a towel rack full of thick white towels and a small forest of potted plants. A massage table waits nearby. There's even a special area for Alex, with a spacious play pen and a toy box.

The hot tub is vacant, however, and Alex is squirming. Hitching him up higher on her hip, Caitlin turns away—and nearly runs into Blaine Sr.

"Can I help you, Miss Reilly?"

"I was looking for your wife, actually."

In answer to his unspoken Why, she continues. "Alex is having . . . a problem with diaper rash. I thought I'd better find out what Mrs. Blaine usually did for it."

Blaine Sr. shrugs.

"She let him cry, most likely. In any event, my wife is not available this morning. She did not sleep well last night."

Is that all? his eyes ask. He turns away before she can reply, though something in the action suggests that he will be watching until she takes Alex upstairs. So Caitlin does, though she does not return immediately to the nursery.

Instead, she turns down the short hallway leading to the master suite. Here, too, one door stands partly open.

From the threshold, she can see very little. The shades in this room are drawn—or perhaps the glass has been turned opaque, since she cannot imagine shades large enough for any of the windows in this house. There is about an acre's worth of tousled bed, with someone curled tight under its covers.

And the faint sound of female crying.

Looking bored and fussy, Alex wriggles on her hip. Caitlin hurries them both back to the nursery, dreading the cleanup ahead. She left so many ugly smears on the tile—with no safe explanation. Settling the baby in his crib, she takes a spray bottle of strong ammonia solution from a high cabinet and hopes for the best.

But she finds no smears when she kneels to start cleaning.

No bugs anywhere.

Mrs. Blaine surprises Caitlin a few days later by inviting her to dinner. Dr. Merelli, "the doctor who helped us have Alex," is back in town for a week or two between conferences (or consultations, or something else Teresa Blaine cannot quite remember). Of course, she'll want to see the baby before everyone sits down. Will Caitlin please make sure Alex is bathed and awake by four?

The doctor arrives in the nursery at a quarter to five, a thin dark woman with cropped hair. She is possibly sixty, though her bones are so fine and her skin so taut that it is impossible to guess. She trails the smell of strong European cigarettes as she heads for Alex's crib.

"Has he been receiving all his medications?" she asks, before even glancing in.

Caitlin shows her the typed schedule's check-off page. "It would help if I knew what they were, though. There are so many possible interactions with non-prescription . . ."

Dr. Merelli stops her with an eyebrow. "You have been giving him something other than these medications?"

"No, but if he gets a fever, or needs something for pain—"

"He should not." The doctor hands her back the schedule. "Give him only what is on this list, and only at the specified times."

She turns away to pick up Alex, but Caitlin is persistent. "What about food interactions? What if he has to go to a hospital? I need to know what these drugs are!"

"They are proprietary."

"To what?"

Alex stares at her past the doctor's shoulder. Something eerily like amusement flickers in his blue eyes, vanishing before the answer comes.

"My clinic."

At dinner that night, Caitlin divides her attention between the baby monitor at her elbow and Merelli's conversation with Blaine Sr., which revolves almost entirely around the clinic. As usual, Mrs. Blaine says very little and eats less. The nervous anticipation she radiated earlier is gone, replaced by drug-induced calm. Supplementing this with Chardonnay is a questionable idea, but neither her husband nor her son's doctor are taking notice of her refills.

They're too occupied with business.

From what Caitlin can piece together between gurgles from the monitor, Blaine Sr. is more than a former client of Merelli's clinic. He is also financially involved in its operation.

She never thought of fertility clinics as profit-makers, but this one must be. Blaine Sr. strikes her as a man who picks his horses carefully, then backs them to the hilt. Whatever services Merelli and her staff offer to desperate couples, they aren't doing it out of medical charity. There is talk of quarterly reports, research and development costs, equipment depreciation. Waiting lists of up to a year.

The hiring of new "research partners" for vital, though unspecified, tasks.

Teresa Blaine watches silently, manicured fingers tight on the stem of her glass. Candlelight makes it hard to read her expression, but once in a while Caitlin sees a flicker of awareness return.

When it does, her glance shifts away from Merelli to her husband. If this is what a grateful new mother looks like—or even a woman in love—Caitlin hopes to Mary that she will never be so blessed.

"So what's new in pharmaceuticals this quarter?"

Blaine Sr.'s question, a bit expansive with wine, breaks into her musings. He isn't addressing her, of course—but this is her opening. The wariness in Merelli's eyes confirms it.

"I've brought you a report." The doctor's tone fairly screams *later.*

Blaine Sr. isn't taking the hint. "I hope it's a good one. You know what the market's been like, and my other offshore ventures haven't—"

"It's all in the report."

Caitlin checks the baby monitor to hide her reaction. In the short time she has lived here, she has never heard anyone speak to her employer like this. Merelli is quietly but unmistakably furious—and, impossibly, she is powerful enough to let him know it.

The tension passes in a heartbeat, but this is as close to off-balance as Caitlin has seen him. Touching Gran's rosary in her pocket for luck, she speaks up.

"About Alex's, um, pharmaceuticals—is there any way I could at least know what they're for? If he had a bad interaction, I'd never forgive myself."

Silence. Her fingers tighten on the worn jet beads.

"Does it have to do with how he was born?"

Caitlin gets an answer this time. Her monitor emits a piercing wail, followed by several more to let her know that this is no ordinary bad dream—or soggy diaper, or gas—Alex is having. Snatching up the device, she shuts it off and heads for the dining-room door.

Teresa Blaine follows unsteadily.

As the two women climb the stairs, Caitlin smiles at her. For the first time, she's acting like Alex's mother. Maybe she'll even be able to help calm him tonight.

At the top, though, Mrs. Blaine shrugs and turns for her own rooms.

"I'm sure he'll be fine." She glances past Caitlin toward the nursery. "He's always been difficult, but there's never anything wrong with him. Healthy as a horse."

As though this burst of speech has exhausted her, she yawns.

"Alexander would rather talk to our guest anyhow. He's always eager for news on his investments."

Caitlin frowns. She's guessed this, but still—"Your husband is a shareholder in her clinic?"

"Major shareholder. Maybe *the* shareholder. He doesn't talk to me about business, or haven't you noticed?"

Booze and pills. Bloody hell.

Murmuring sympathy, Caitlin edges away, listening for anyone else coming upstairs. Alex isn't making it easy. Even through the solid nursery door, she can hear impending tantrum in his cries. It's going to take at least an hour to calm him down.

But the moment she opens the door, everything changes.

Alex lies on his back just as she had placed him hours ago, head turned to watch her. His plump cheeks are streaked with tears, but that's the only wetness evident. Caitlin picks him up to be sure, then considers other possible triggers for the vocal storm. Not hungry, surely. No gas. He's not overdue for any medications.

And she's pretty sure the horror-bugs haven't returned, though she's not about to look.

A surge of frustration grips her. So much for any more hints about the Merelli clinic! Blaine Sr. isn't likely to be caught off-guard again.

"What's your problem, anyhow?" she asks that alert blue gaze.

"Why, I'm bloody dead, Caits. Dead and in Hell, but aside from that—"

Seamus. Caitlin's stomach twists. Her brother's voice is rasping through those baby lips, edged with whiskey and bitterness. The same bitterness she remembers from pub nights at home, her nursing one pint while Seamus chain-smoked and chain-talked, drinking more than she'd ever tell Gran. Drinking and watching the door all the time, waiting for his friends.

His brothers in the Cause, as he called it. His brothers who had gotten him killed.

Or at least helped him get his own idiot self killed, and make sure she could never risk renewing her work visa. Not with paranoia running high here in the States.

"No." The word is a whisper between her teeth as she backs away. "You can't be. *He* can't be . . . Alex, please—"

"Just me here, Caits. Or what's left fit to look at."

Alex's wide eyes stare at her unblinking. Not Seamus's eyes, thank God, but not like any baby's she's ever seen. "Don't know what bollocked up that timer . . . loose wire, maybe . . . but it did for me proper, didn't it? An' the priest wasn't keen on Last Rites for a pile of—"

"Stop it!"

Caitlin's hand dives into her skirt pocket. Clutching the rosary, she edges back to Alex's crib. Maybe the bright silver crucifix will distract the baby. Make him stop doing . . . *what he can't possibly be doing, oh no . . .* and start gurgling or even crying again. Anything but that nightmare spewing from his mouth.

Swinging the crucifix gently at the end of its jet beads, she dangles it over the crib.

Alex doesn't gurgle. Doesn't reach out for the pretty shiny thing. Instead, he shrieks and curls in on himself like a spider in a candle flame, writhing and whimpering. A horrible stink rises from his formerly clean diaper.

But Seamus's voice is gone.

Caitlin fumbles the rosary back into her pocket. Alex is fussy now—no wonder, the mess he's just made of his nappy—but the shrill indignation is all little boy. As she gathers wipes and baby oil, she murmurs a prayer of thanks to Mary. Never mind the task ahead: Alex clearly had an attack of . . . something, just now, despite Dr. Merelli's proprietary medicines. Gas and crankiness, that was all she'd heard.

She repeats this under her breath while she scrubs and powders and generally sanitizes Alex. By the time he's clean and medicated (three drops of #4 at the first suggestion of diarrhea, says the schedule), the litany is wearing thin.

A part of her *knows* what she has just seen. It does not understand, but it knows, just as it knew to reach for Gran's rosary. And it knows what must be done next.

After settling Alex in his crib, Caitlin picks up the skinny local phone book.

The town's sole Catholic church is a cramped little building, its rough-hewn stonework dating to mining camp days. The schedule of services is posted in a verdigris-green box with cobwebs on the inside and a hairline crack in the filthy glass. Its lawn looks ragged, the small prayer garden overgrown.

Caitlin feels a surge of guilt as she parks the Jeep. She has been to Mass here all of twice this summer.

How dare she ask for help now?

Because I have no choice. Her lips tighten as she lifts Alex from his safety seat. *I need a priest old enough to believe me. To remember what might need to be done.*

She tries to recall whether the priest here is a Jesuit. She thinks so. That would be good.

"Come on," she whispers to Alex, settling him on her hip. "Time to get some religion, boyo!"

Alex blinks at her, or perhaps it's the sun in his eyes. She knows very well that her employers have never taken him to any church. They—meaning Blaine Sr.—do not condone time-wasting superstitions. Alex has not been baptized, assigned a godparent, or otherwise spiritually processed.

So why does he clutch at her waist so tightly as she approaches the building?

The question vanishes in relief as the narrow double doors open. Father Thomas—at least she has remembered his name—emerges, one hand adjusting his collar. His smile is sincere but uncertain, as though he recalls last night's phone conversation but isn't sure of the details.

Well, that makes two of us. Caitlin presses Alex more firmly to her hip. *And we all know where the devil is, don't we?*

"Miss Reilly?"

Caitlin wonders abruptly whether this visit is a mistake. Father

Thomas looks nearly as old as his tiny church, and in equally poor repair. Even if he does believe her, what can he possibly do?

Still, if he is a Jesuit, that's something. The Jesuits are scholars as well as believers. Caitlin forces a smile. "Thanks for agreeing to see us this morning, Father."

"It's no trouble." The priest's smile wavers as he glances from Caitlin to Alex. "Anything to help a child—though I wish you had explained his trouble more clearly."

"I'm not sure what it is myself, Father."

Can you go to Hell for lying to a priest? Caitlin suspects so, but she does not *know* what is wrong with Alex. She only is afraid of what might be.

"Well, why don't you bring the boy in, then? It's a fine morning, but looking like a hot one. I've got some fresh iced tea."

It happens even before she clears the threshold.

As her right foot touches the age-darkened wood, Alex seems to explode against her. A horrible stench rises from the plastic pants covering his diaper. Thick greenish mucus streams from his nostrils. Small face twisting scarlet with rage and fear, he digs his fingers into her side and shrieks.

It is that raw, primal cry only the very young or the insane are capable of—a *No!* in the face of the universe. It echoes through this narrow holy place like an intruder, and Caitlin stumbles backwards into the priest.

His hand closes on her shoulder.

"Perhaps the garden," he says, voice strained above the howling. "The lad seems a bit . . ."

Neither of them finish the sentence. Caitlin at least doesn't dare to. Alex's screams abate as she lugs him back to the Jeep for a change, but the little boy doesn't release his grip for at least another minute.

When he does, she finds she is bleeding through her thin cotton shirt.

The ragged prayer garden looks different when she returns. So does Father Thomas. The priest has removed (or at least concealed) the large silver crucifix he'd been wearing earlier, and a statue of the Virgin is missing from its brick grotto at the garden's center.

Alex is calm now, playing in the grass at her feet. Father Thomas watches him quietly for a few minutes, his face unreadable. Caitlin watches the priest.

Now do you understand?

"From the beginning, please." His eyes never shift from the child. "Anything unusual he's done since you began working for his parents."

He hesitates. "Particularly anything which might resemble a . . . sign."

Relief strengthens her. This man is a proper priest, as Gran would say. A believer and a scholar, old enough to recognize what she has been struggling to deny. He is not going to spout child psychology or suggest that she consult Alex's doctor.

At first, the priest listens to her as he has watched Alex: seriously, but without impatience. As she reaches last night's events, though, a change comes over his face.

"That's two." His forehead creases. "And you managed to stop it?"

Carefully, without letting its crucifix flash, she draws Gran's rosary out of a pocket. "With this. At least, I think that's what did it."

He nods, motioning to her to put the rosary away.

"That would be three."

Relief evaporates. She lets the jet beads slip through her hand, but continues to touch them.

"Have you any idea *why* he might be manifesting these things? Anything in his background? Perhaps his parents' earlier lives?"

Caitlin hesitates. The Blaines are private people. And, in Mr. Blaine's case, not particularly forgiving. Still, Father Thomas *is* a priest. And Alex—

"I think Alex might have been an in vitro pregnancy," she finally says. "From a clinic."

The priest's gaze sharpens. "What kind of clinic?"

"A Dr. Merelli runs it. I've met her once. She's prescribed a lot of drugs for Alex—proprietary medicines, she calls them—and I have to give them all on a schedule . . ."

"Merelli?"

There's a harder line to his mouth now. Something less fragile about his jaw. Father Thomas is still old, but no longer elderly.

She hesitates again, then nods.

"I've heard odd things about the Merelli clinic. Scientific impossibilities, astounding arrogance. A truly frightening disregard for natural order. Nothing I was inclined to believe . . ." His gaze shifts down to Alex. "Until now."

She waits for him to explain himself, but he doesn't. After a few minutes, Father Thomas gets up from the stone bench and brushes off his cassock. A hot breeze lifts his sparse gray hair as he turns to her.

"I think I'd like to sit with Alex for a few minutes alone, if you don't mind." His voice is gentle now. Quite ordinary. "If you'd like to go back to your car, I'll come get you when we've finished our chat."

And if he chats with you the way he did with me?

Biting back her apprehensions—and her reluctance to leave her charge with anyone, even a priest—Caitlin retreats to the Jeep and its air conditioning. By swiveling one mirror, she can watch Father Thomas sitting back down, hands on knees as he bends to speak with the toddler. There's a brief flash of silver as he brings out his crucifix, but she can't see whether he leaves it in sight for long.

Or how Alex reacts.

After a few minutes, the priest lifts the toddler onto his own narrow shoulders and carries him back to the parking lot. Caitlin's mouth fills with questions, but Father Thomas says nothing until Alex is buckled into his safety seat.

"Well?"

He shakes his head, motioning to Caitlin to step behind the Jeep. There is a terrible sadness in his eyes.

"What is it, Father?" Her stomach clenches. "Is Alex . . . is he . . ."

"I'm sorry."

Caitlin frowns. Even if he has confirmed her worst suspicions, regret makes no sense. Knowing what's wrong is the start of fighting it.

"I thought so," she murmurs. "Not that his parents would believe me if I told them." Her frown deepens. "How are we going to manage this without them . . . ?"

"I'm not."

She stares at the priest. What she has come here to ask for is dangerous—in ways the modern world cannot imagine—but she hadn't expected him to refuse outright.

Is he afraid of her employers? The Blaines are wealthy, but this town is full of rich people.

"I've performed the rite before," he continues. "More than once, over strenuous objections from some of my colleagues. I have no qualms about it, intellectual or moral. It's just that—"

Father Thomas glances past her to the child in the Jeep.

"In the simplest terms, it's a battle. The priest and his . . . adversary . . . contesting for the soul of the victim, no holds barred."

His voice drops. "But in this case, I found nothing to fight for."

The summer air is suddenly chilly. Caitlin wraps her arms around herself, wincing as one elbow digs into her waist. She has to force herself not to glance back at her charge.

"That's not possible!"

Father Thomas suddenly looks even older. "I do not understand the hows or the whys of it, Miss Reilly. I only have experience in seeking the human soul. I found none in this child, though I cannot tell you why. I cannot even explain how he lives."

A shadow crosses his face.

"It is as if something was left out, from birth."

By the time Caitlin returns home, it is late afternoon. The usual threat of rain blusters outside the windows as she carries Alex carefully inside, into the pine-paneled great room where Inez is vacuuming. When the housekeeper stops to ask if they had fun in town, Caitlin barely knows how to answer.

"We had ice cream." It's the easiest truth. "Alex wanted double choc, of course, and I had a lemon gelato."

She glances toward the inside door. "Is Mrs. Blaine around?"

"In the spa room, I think. Not feeling well." Inez's broad face hardens. "*He* won't be back until late tonight."

Caitlin thanks her and heads for the spa, still lugging Alex. She would prefer to leave him with Inez, but the housekeeper is busy and she doesn't dare leave him alone. At least he's being a good boy. No crying, no fussing.

No dead brother's voice. No hell-bugs.

The door to the spa room stands open again, wafting chemicals and perfume down the hallway. Teresa Blaine sits almost submerged in the tub, head lolling on an inflatable pillow stuck to the tiled rim. Her eyes are closed. A plastic table nearby holds an open bottle of white wine, plus a large glass of the same half full and a couple of pill bottles.

Caitlin waits to be certain she's still breathing.

After shutting the door behind her, she carries Alex to his play pen. Then she adds an armful of toys from the chest nearby: stuffed animals, a ball, a whole box of soft plastic alphabet blocks. Her hands shake as she dumps the bright cubes around the toddler's feet. How can she ever tell his mother—

"Inez?" Teresa Blaine's eyelids flicker. "Inez, is that you?"

Courage. "It's me, Mrs. Blaine."

Caitlin moves forward, making eye contact. "I'm sorry to disturb you," she says, "but I need to ask some . . . important questions."

Her stomach clenches. "I'm afraid there's something very wrong with your little boy."

Mrs. Blaine sits up with a splash, revealing a black tank suit sagging on her body. She reaches for her glass.

"Don't you mean Daddy's little boy?"

Mrs. Blaine doesn't sound intoxicated, though she is working on it. Nor does she sound unusually medicated. The edge in her voice is genuine, her eyes focused.

Caitlin takes a deep breath. "Excuse me?"

"His daddy's little boy. Not mine. Exactly like his daddy, custom ordered. Bought and paid for and then just incubated by yours truly, never mind it damn near killed me."

Her hand tightens on the stem of her glass. "Too bad it didn't. I can't ever have a kid of my own now. The clinic doctors said delivery tore me up too much, they had to operate . . ."

"Clinic?"

The word emerges from Caitlin like a gasp. Mrs. Blaine takes another sip to wash down a few pills, then forces a smile.

"Dr. Merelli's very special institution, of course. So special it can't operate on American soil . . . which I suppose should have warned me, but then there was the pre-nup, wasn't there? *Any necessary medical assistance* to have the child Alexander wanted—that we both wanted—because he had 'fertility issues' and it's not like he's in his twenties. But I was. I was young and stupid and I thought it would all be just fine."

Caitlin nods slowly.

"Well, it wasn't. I think I realized that when we first toured the place. While Alexander was asking about fees and investment opportunities, I kept noticing security everywhere. Locks on all the windows and doors. Cameras in the pretty tiled hallways. Orderlies built like pro wrestlers."

Yet another long sip of wine.

"Funny thing was, I never saw another patient while we were there. Not ever. I heard women's voices once in a while, but it was always a nurse or a lab tech. Merelli was the only woman doctor there—hell, maybe the only doctor. She took most of the samples and ran all the tests. She did the implant."

"You mean Alex is a test tube baby?" Caitlin blushes. Talk about sounding like a poor ignorant superstitious—

"Little Miss Vatican. You *are* Catholic, aren't you?"

Mrs. Blaine looks as though she would laugh if it hurt less. The edge in her voice is gone now, lost to wine and pills and her own mental demons.

"I'm sorry," she finally says. "I'm sure the Church doesn't condone any of that, but it's OK. Alex wasn't an *in vitro* pregnancy. Not an ordinary one, anyhow."

Somewhere behind Caitlin, small bare feet scuff plastic. She glances back to see Alex pulling himself up in his play pen. A part of her wants to grab him and get them both out of here, but she can't. She can't do anything now but keep listening.

"All Alex got from me was one scooped-out egg. No DNA. No nothing. Just an empty shell, like his so-called mother."

Caitlin stares at her.

"You know what that makes him, right?"

Recalling her conversation with Father Thomas, she nods. "But isn't that illegal here?"

"Very. As Alexander was happy to remind me once, when I threatened to leave him."

Mrs. Blaine's words are blurring toward memory. *How much wine has she had? What kind of pills?* Caitlin is uncomfortably aware of the toddler behind her, watching intently. She wonders whether she should call for Inez.

Whether she dares to.

"I'd had . . . a few, I guess. A few more than usual, and don't ask about usual. I wasn't always like that, but after the baby—"

Teresa Blaine shrugs, splashing water. "Anyhow, I was sick and depressed and I wanted out. I knew there was something wrong with the way we'd had Alex, though nobody would tell me what. I knew I shouldn't have had so many drugs and tests, all that bed rest in the clinic for months on end. I knew I shouldn't still be hurting the way I was."

The way I am, say her eyes.

"That was when he told me just exactly what Merelli did. We'd both been parties to it, but he had the lawyers and the contacts and the friends. If I left and went public, I'd be the only one prosecuted. The fines would kill me even if I didn't get sent to prison, which I might . . . and then he'd divorce me. No benefits."

Her voice trails off momentarily into the gurgle of the spa.

"Or I could stay right here and keep my mouth shut. Play like Alex's doting mommy, only I was never much good at doting or even changing crappy diapers. Too sick all the time." Teresa Blaine sighs. "I nearly made the U.S. Ski Team once, did you know that? My body used to work right—my *mind* used to work right—but nothing does now. Not since—"

She glances back at the play pen, then sighs and reaches for her glass.

Despite the steamy atmosphere, Caitlin suppresses a shiver. Mrs. Blaine is far more troubled than she suspected. Worse, there's nothing she can do for her. Nothing but listen—and try to decide how much of this is real.

Postpartum psychosis is a definite possibility.

"What I don't understand," she finally says, "is why. Why would your husband risk it? If you couldn't have your own child . . . together, I mean . . . why not adopt?"

Teresa Blaine giggles. It is not a pleasant sound.

"You mean take a chance on just any baby? That wouldn't have suited Alexander. You see, he'd been married before. He had three kids by his first wife—a real head case, he claims—and they all disappointed him. Who knows how? Maybe they dropped out, or did drugs. Maybe they just didn't get the right jobs.

"Anyhow, they weren't what he wanted. So he divorced her, dumped them out of his will—and met me. God, was I stupid! I thought he wanted us to have a baby together because he loved me. All he saw in me was a damn incubator for his perfect little son and heir."

She starts to giggle again and stops. A familiar, peaceful glaze is creeping into her expression.

"But you didn't want to hear all that, did you?" Mrs. Blaine struggles to sit up, fighting the pills one moment longer. "Of course you didn't."

Wordlessly, Caitlin nods.

"Now what was it you came to tell me about Alex?"

Another plastic squeak sounds behind her. A soft gurgle, and the thump of blocks. Caitlin covers the blood on her shirt with one hand.

"He made a fuss in town today, that's all. I took him into church with me . . . tried to, anyway . . . and he—"

"Church?"

"Yes, Mrs. Blaine."

The pill-glaze is winning. "Just don't ever tell Alexander you took his son to a church. He wouldn't approve."

Caitlin hears her exit line. Heading for Alex's play pen, she lifts the toddler out. To her surprise, he starts whimpering . . . then crying inconsolably, reaching past her toward his mother.

Mrs. Blaine emits a last giggle. "Oh, leave him with me. He'll be safe in there for an hour or two, won't he?"

As Caitlin obeys, the toddler's tears cease. Plopping himself down among his toys, he reaches for a block and tries shoving it in his mouth. His tiny fingernails have pinkish stains.

Caitlin stares at them helplessly. *What are you?*

*   *   *

Still half asleep—dragged from a nap she does not remember starting—she feels a strong hand on her shoulder, shaking her hard. Caitlin moans in protest. The fingers dig in, lifting her off the bed with their desperate energy. A voice accompanies them, though she cannot make out the words.

Only that something is very, very wrong.

"You have to come! You must come now! She locked herself in, in the spa, and Mister Blaine—"

Caitlin shakes off the hand and scrambles to her feet. The bedroom is dim with the beginnings of sunset. How long has she slept? Inez is wearing an apron freshly stained with some sort of sauce, so she guesses dinner is ready.

Inez tells her as much as they both hurry down the hallway, then the stairs, then another corridor. Their feet echo on the hardwood. This house has never felt so oversized and empty, though Caitlin files that thought with all the others she keeps to herself.

"... so I shouted through the door for her to please come out now, I had the salad all ready, but she didn't say anything." Inez's breath is coming in short gasps. "Then I tried the door—"

Caitlin's own breath catches. "I left it unlocked!"

"Well, it's not now."

The housekeeper gasps again as they round the last corner. Alexander Blaine Sr. is already there. The corridor resounds with his fist on the door, his repeated demands that his wife open it *right now*. As he catches sight of the women, his face floods with color.

"Where's my son?"

Caitlin feels sick. "She . . . Mrs. Blaine . . . she told me to leave him with her. Alex seemed to want that, too, so I—"

The impact of his shoulder against the door cuts her off. After three tries, the lock gives way, and something clatters to the floor as they rush in. Bright metal glints up at Caitlin. A key, falling from inside . . . from the lock—

Inez starts screaming.

Caitlin and Blaine Sr. run past her to the hot tub platform, nearly tripping over Alex. The little boy crawls contentedly among the potted plants, poking fingers into the soil and gurgling.

His mother is slumped face down in the bubbling waters. Pale hair floats out around her until her husband grabs a handful to pull her upright.

"Teresa!"

He sounds more angry than frightened. Lifting her out of the tub, he stretches her limp body on the floor but makes no attempt at resuscitation. When Caitlin offers, he waves her back.

"It's too late." He indicates the table with its empty bottle and scattered pills. Shards of crystal crunch underfoot as he moves. "Did she say anything to either of you about this?"

Inez stops screaming and starts crying. Uncertain how to help, Caitlin glances away.

Then she freezes, staring down at Alex.

What are you doing out of your play pen?

Before he can cut himself on his mother's broken glass, she scoops him up and hurries over to the play pen. Various stuffed animals sprawl inside, embroidered eyes offering her no clues. The ball she tossed in is likewise still in one corner.

But a few of the blocks are now outside.

Caitlin's grip tightens on Alex as she stares down at the seven colorful shapes. Soft plastic, rounded corners. Utterly safe. Their line is ragged, but the order is unmistakable.

L. U. C. I . . .

"Miss Reilly, get my son out of here!"

The blocks skitter across the floor as she complies.

Inez is gone the next morning. Her replacement arrives that same day: a thin frightened-looking girl who speaks little English. Caitlin expects to be replaced as well, but Blaine Sr. is otherwise occupied. He spends most of the next two days in his study, sorting out his wife's death.

The chief of police—a personal friend—phones to offer condolences.

A medical opinion of Teresa Blaine's mental state postpartum, signed by Dr. Merelli, arrives by certified mail.

Dr. Merelli herself returns to town soon afterwards. She spends a great deal of time with Blaine Sr., often joining him for meals at the house. Caitlin is not invited to these meals. Nor is she present when Merelli insists on examining Alex "to be certain his development is on track." Alex is now nine months old and looks a full twelve months. If he misses his mother, neither Caitlin nor anyone else has noticed.

A secular memorial is scheduled at the best hotel in town within a week. There is no question of a funeral, let alone a wake, and no viewing of the body. As per Mrs. Blaine's private wishes, she has already been cremated.

When Caitlin goes to Mass on the evening before her memorial, there is another priest in Father Thomas's place. The substitute tells her afterwards that Father Thomas has left his parish duties indefinitely. He is thinking about retiring—or at least relocating to somewhere warmer. Is there some concern he can help her with?

Caitlin quickly shakes her head no. No one but Father Thomas would believe her.

And even his Jesuit scholarship had offered no hope.

Caitlin packs her luggage that night, keeping the keys to her own small car handy. The Jeep's keys and her letter of resignation sit on the dresser like talismans. She tries not to think about her expired visa. She tries not to picture Alex in his crib next door, his small face looking so innocent in sleep.

Above all, she tries to forget her last talk with Teresa Blaine.

There is a post-memorial reception back at the house, though none of Mrs. Blaine's friends stay long. Relics of her skiing days with indelible tans and uncomfortable expressions, they offer condolences to Caitlin—and, less readily, to the new widower—before slipping out for cigarettes or air and never returning.

As soon as she decently can, Caitlin returns to the nursery. Inez's replacement is minding Alex, and the girl strikes her as unlikely to cope with the unusual.

Besides, Blaine Sr. will hardly miss her. There are still plenty of guests: his friends and business associates and the ubiquitous Dr. Merelli. There is also plenty of catered food—along with a remarkably well-stocked bar. Perhaps this *is* a wake.

Secure in being forgotten, Caitlin changes and feeds and medicates Alex, then puts him down for a nap. She is considering one herself when Inez's replacement returns, looking nervous.

"Mr. Blaine wants to see you in his study," she says. "Now."

Before Caitlin can ask why, she hurries away. Alex wakes and whimpers in his crib. Left with no options, Caitlin scoops him up before detouring to her room for the letter and Jeep keys. She has not been in the study since the day she was hired, and can imagine only one reason for this summons.

That reason makes her slip her own keys into a trouser pocket as well. As they clink against the crucifix of Gran's rosary, Alex squirms against her.

Holy Mother, not now!

"Patience," Caitlin tells the unhappy toddler. "Not much longer."

A breeze greets her as she walks into the study. One massive window doubles as a sliding door, and it now stands half-open, giving access to the balcony. Blaine Sr. occupies a chaise lounge near the railing, his back to the ravine below.

He has a glass in one hand, which he does not bother to set aside as she approaches. There is another chair a few feet from his—not a second chaise, but a straight-backed metal item with no cushion.

He gestures toward it, not actually inviting her. Caitlin sits anyhow and holds Alex on her lap, hoping he won't start squirming again. The balcony railing is barely waist high—a strange, arrogant touch in keeping with the rest of the house. She will be glad to be free of this place, no matter how hard job-hunting proves to be.

Blaine Sr. finally sets down his glass on the deck and clears his throat.

"I'm glad you came so promptly. Given recent events"—he glances at his son—"there need to be some changes around here. The sooner we get that established, the better for all of us."

Caitlin nods. "I don't blame you, sir."

She hands him her resignation and the Jeep keys, glad for the lack of drama. She expected, perhaps deserved, much worse. Though she had nothing to do with Teresa Blaine's death, she should never have left Alex alone with her.

L. U. C. I. . . .

Not possible. However Alex was born, whatever vital thing might have been left out, he is still just a baby. Surely a baby is incapable of harboring—

Blaine Sr. hands her letter back.

"This isn't what I meant, Miss Reilly. I don't need you to leave, and certainly Alex doesn't." His eyes fix on the child in her lap. "You'll be staying right here."

Caitlin frowns. This conversation is going all wrong.

"I've already made other plans," she lies. "I can give you two weeks' notice, but—"

"You'll be staying."

Blaine Sr. forces a smile, but its warmth never reaches his eyes. "We've both grown fond of you, Miss Reilly," he continues, still watching his son. "Much too fond to have you leave us."

His glance shifts to her face. "Especially when Alex would so enjoy having a brother."

Initially, her mind simply refuses to process this.

When it finally does—when the shivers set in—Caitlin shakes her head mutely. Then she lifts Alex off her knees and puts him on the deck.

She tells herself it's because she is going to walk out now, but that's only the smallest part of it. The weight of the toddler is suddenly too much, his very nearness a contact poison. He is no longer a child, much less an innocent, but the product of Dr. Merelli's mysterious and unspeakable clinic.

No, not unspeakable. Teresa Blaine spoke quite a lot about it once.

Blaine Sr.'s glance becomes a blue-eyed stare, freezing her in her seat. "Just where do you imagine you're going, Miss Reilly? Job-hopping with an expired work visa?"

She tells herself she is not surprised that he knows.

"If I have to," she says through clenched teeth. "Or maybe I'll just go home."

He shakes his head. "A few years back, that might have been an option. It's a different country now. An expired visa is one thing, but a terrorist brother—even a dead one—is quite another issue. Real IRA, wasn't he?"

Warmth drains from the late afternoon sunlight. Work visas might be easy enough for an employer to check, but the facts of her brother's death are not. Certainly his Cause shouldn't be, when he never even—

"I don't know," she finally manages. "He didn't discuss it with me."

Blaine Sr. shrugs.

"You might even be able to convince them of that. Eventually. After several months in some undisclosed location with no access to counsel, no matter how many lawsuits the ACLU files."

Alex gurgles at her feet, no longer looking up at her. His small body moves restlessly, leaning and then crawling away from her chair.

"Or," his father continues, "you can remain here, safe. You're a healthy young woman with your whole life ahead of you . . ."

So was Teresa, once.

" . . . and a chance to marry money. Talk about American dreams."

When words fail her utterly, he plows on in his deal-maker's voice. With rising panic, she realizes that he himself believes in this deal. He has been planning it for a long time.

Remembering her interview this spring, she shudders. What had he really selected her for? Was Dr. Merelli involved, even then?

Sweet Mary, was Alex?

The strange, chilly smile returns. "I certainly wouldn't want Alex to have a bastard brother! There'll be a pre-nup, of course, but you can still——"

End up a drunken, drugged, dying husk of a woman. Another used-up bit of rubbish to be thrown out.

"No."

Stifled by fear and disgust, Caitlin's voice is hardly more than a whisper.

Still, it carries.

The toddler's gurgling stops. He is staring at her too, now, clutching the toe of his father's dangling boat shoe. His eyes hold a fervid intensity she has seen only once before.

Blaine Sr. doesn't seem to have noticed.

"*No* isn't one of your options. If you choose to leave, you'll never make it to the airport, let alone out of the country. One phone call——"

Caitlin stares back at him, sickened and confused. *This isn't the script we were on five minutes ago.*

Fine beads of sweat are coating Blaine Sr.'s forehead. When he reaches down for his glass, she can hear the ice rattle all the way back up. Liquid dribbles from one side of his mouth as he sips. He is drinking like a man with something to drink about.

Alex drops his father's shoe and begins crawling up his leg, small fingers digging into chino with a too-familiar grip.

Caitlin swallows hard. "No," she says again. "No matter what."

Alex stops on his father's lap, staring at her. His blue gaze is malignant.

Controlling.

"I can have you picked up right here at the house, you know. Right here tonight. You'll be in jail by morning, and on your way to somewhere a lot worse after that."

The last of Blaine Sr.'s drink spills on the deck unnoticed.

"Are you determined to be an idiot, Miss Reilly? Do you really believe I won't turn you in?" His voice rises. "Well, I will. It's a simple choice. You can cooperate and make us all one happy family . . ."

A grunt of pain escapes him as his son resumes his climb, pulling himself up his father's chest hand over hand.

" . . . or you can spend a long time explaining yourself to some extremely unsympathetic authorities."

Above the hard mouth, Blaine Sr.'s eyes are desperate. Red speckles blossom on seersucker as his son continues to climb.

Blaine Sr. grabs for Alex with both hands, then yelps as the toddler sinks teeth into his thumb. Even from where she sits, Caitlin can see the blood and torn flesh: an animal's bite. A rat's bite. Nothing human about it, other than the use of human teeth—

By what?

She stands up so fast that her chair tips, clattering on the deck as she digs in one trouser pocket. Worn jet beads evade her fingers, but the silver crucifix is an easier target. Catching it between thumb and forefinger, she extracts Gran's rosary and wraps it around her right hand, a Hail Mary already on her lips.

Alex has reached his father's throat now.

"Miss Reilly, you really have no choice—"

Crushed by the pressure of the toddler's arms and legs, his larynx barely operates. Twisting his face away from groping fingers, he manages one last appeal. *"Miss Reilly!"*

Releasing his grip on his father, Alex stretches one small bloody hand toward her. Baby lips twist themselves into the shadow of Seamus's most winning smile.

"Ah, Caits, for the love of God . . ."

Biting her lip hard, she thrusts Gran's rosary into that smile.

Alex shrieks and recoils, clawing at his father's face as he tries to climb away from her. Blaine Sr. is shrieking, too. Fastening both hands around the toddler's writhing body, he yanks with all his strength, spitting profanities and blood as he tips back farther . . . farther—

Too far.

Releasing his grip on his tiny assailant, Blaine Sr. grabs for the railing and misses. Toddler and man slide off backwards together, their cries mingling as they fall.

The mountain ravine is a very long way down. Very full of jagged rocks and not much else. When the screaming stops, Caitlin makes herself take a good look over the railing. Green and white striped chaise cushions lie scattered on the rocks. Green and white stripes . . . and red, more red than she could have imagined. Seersucker and khaki and red, red, red, everywhere—

But nothing moving. That's the important thing.

She keeps repeating this all the way off the deck and out of the study, then back to her room just long enough to grab her purse. Teresa Blaine's memorial reception is still going on somewhere below. The house is so sprawling that no one is likely to have heard much, even without the distractions of plentiful food and liquor. Still, there is always a risk—

"Excuse me, Miss Reilly?"

Caitlin freezes halfway down the stairs. Slim and foreign, impeccable in a black sleeveless sheath, Dr. Merelli is staring up at her. At the purse on her shoulder—or perhaps at the jet beads still wrapping one hand, forgotten until this moment. Caitlin's fingers fold around the rosary as she takes a deep breath.

"I'm afraid I'm on my way into town, doctor. We've run out of talcum powder, can you believe the luck, and I—"

A flare of suspicion in the dark eyes cuts her off.

"I wanted to look in on Alex before I left." Merelli's glance sharpens. "You haven't left him alone, have you?"

"Of course not!"

Caitlin makes herself start moving again, circling wide of Merelli at the bottom of the stairs. When the doctor reaches out anyway, she shakes her head and slips past.

"I wouldn't disturb him now, if I were you," she says over her shoulder. "He's resting with his father."

DESERT MYSTERY! GAS & GO!

YOU'RE GOING TO BUY a ticket. You just won't admit it yet. Paying for gas takes five minutes, but you've already been here for fifteen—browsing the magazine rack, picking out a Coke (diet? cherry? decaf?) for the road. The mom with her whining toddlers is long gone. Likewise the road-tripping spring breakers, the two Texan sales geeks, the trio of gals talking nonstop about some spa in Sonora.

It's just us, now. And the Mystery is waiting.

The sign by the cash register makes it easy. Tickets are only a buck, though I'll push it to two-fifty come snowbird season. When I put one down by your Coke and the gas receipt, you shrug . . . then nod. What's to lose? Curiosity happens.

Not often enough, lately. The dreams are getting bad.

I ring up the sale while you go make sure your car's locked. There's nobody else in that car. Or in the parking lot. Nobody headed down from the highway, either, despite those signs strung out between here and Tucson. The keys jangle in my hand as we head over to the Mystery's building.

I like the new paint I gave it this winter. Lime and turquoise: striking without being an eyesore. Black question marks on all four sides, but the stencil looks professional. Don't want folks thinking this is some roadside rip-off, another Black Hills snake ranch. I've got the real thing here.

I've got it.

Must remember that, though your questions aren't helping. Losing focus isn't good right now.

At the threshold, a lizard scuttles across my foot and I flinch. You laugh. It's an uneasy sound: the sleazy sideshow vibe is finally sinking in, and I catch you glancing over your shoulder as I unlock the door.

Still no witnesses. I've already checked.

The air inside could be fresher, but ventilation's a problem and the smell's not bad this early in the year. No windows. One dim light with red bulbs *blood-litten Yoth, gateway to lightless N'Kai and the rites of the Un- speakable* aimed toward the back display.

Waking dreams now? Dear God. Not that I believe any more.

Pretty hard to, once you know what's coming.

I let you see me shut the door carefully, but I don't relock it. Nev- er from inside. Most folks don't notice, that big case is so flashy. Just a museum discard I picked up at an auction, but upholstery velvet and paint do wonders.

That and a little sandpaper on the glass. Can't risk showing too much.

You might try leaving, and then where'd I be?

The answer to that is already seeping through the floorboards, burdening the air with a near-visible taint. There's no smell quite like it—*fetor* would be close, if anyone still had a vocabulary—and your eyes go wide as you start coughing.

What the hell is it? Nothing so mundane as hell . . . but it's time to get things moving. I touch the control in my pocket, and those red bulbs flicker like a Hammer Film effect. Like my dreams. You're al- ready hanging all over that case, staring down.

Depths beyond understanding, where the leavings of a race far older than hu- manity—but no wiser—wax sentient and cunning, vengeful with the slow turning of stars.

Dreaming now? Waking?

Your snort of disgust relieves my mind. We are still in this waking world, you and I. We both know a sand mummified coyote when we see one.

But you bought your ticket for a Mystery.

And I need the dreams to stop.

Turning away from the case's false promise, I jangle my keys again and smile. This marks you out as one of the elect, immune to childish illusions and therefore deserving of truth. Here before you stands your guide to that truth—

Works every time.

I touch my pocket control again, and the red flickering stops. A single spotlight at the back of the room picks out one corner of the planking. The inset door is welded metal, equipped with a hasp and padlock. A very good padlock.

The fetor is even worse here, but you've stopped asking questions. You even edge away as I kneel to open that padlock and throw back the door.

Everyone expects stairs at this point. Maybe a ladder. But the way down into Mystery is a simple ramp, cut from the bedrock though unmarked by tools. There are no lights aside from the heavy flashlight I've just unclipped from my belt.

I'm almost missing your questions now, though their time is over. Better that we descend in silence, past fragments of the cairn that covered this shaft when I found it. Wish to hell I'd left it alone! But the stones with their jagged, incomprehensible glyphs intrigued me, and it was deep winter—too cold for rattlers to be active.

Can't believe I used to worry about *rattlers*.

Of course, the shaft wasn't this wide when I found it. More like a very deep prairie dog burrow, but it didn't look dug: more like melted out, or maybe burned.

Then my flashlight beam caught flashes of eyes looking back.

Clusters of eyes.

I can hear you slowing behind me, dragging your feet. Struggling not to breathe. The smell is *lightless gulfs of lost oceans roiling through time* unmistakable, though we are thousands of miles from serious salt water. Millions of years too late to imagine what spawned in it.

There's a distinctive sound, too. A thick sticky forward momentum like a slug and a freight train combined, but so far away—so deep in the ravaged rock—that it's more vibration than noise.

Not picking that up yet? Better move ahead of me, then.

I insist.

No need to put your hands up like that. I'm not likely to get twitchy at this point. Not the way I got when the dreams first started, all stark white wilderness and dead stone cities glittering with ice. Ice, slime, and ... corpses, I guess. Headless ones, though damned if I know what those heads must have looked like.

I only knew how they came off. And why prairie dogs or rabbits or the odd coyote weren't going to cut it any more.

Size is strength. Time is strength. Time and size and strength against the slaving ones with their star-wings, their ceaseless wars and senseless cities. Tormented into being, reformed endlessly to serve. Mind-lashed, mind-leashed—until the great cold drove Them back and freed us.

Black dust upon the wind. Dust of life within retreating ice. Deep rivers lost to upthrust and fold, sediment and pressure and erosion. Starved centuries of darkness before—

The sound's stopped now.

And you've stopped dead in your tracks, even though that's just what might happen. I can see it in your eyes. You're not going one more step into this Mystery.

But you don't have to. I can feel the darkness gathering itself ahead, cresting like a wave just beyond my flashlight beam. A wave of sentient shadows. Unending hunger. And a multitude of shifting, flickering eyelids, slitting open one by one as I bite down hard on a shriek.

It isn't until much later—after I've dropped the flashlight, nearly dropped the .38, scrambled and slipped and crawled up that damned ramp and groped for the door and locked it down good—that I realize it's not *my* shriek.

I am alone once more in my mind's fragile silence. Tonight holds no dreams. No icebound citadels with strange echoes in their depths. Only coyotes will sing their mysteries to the moon, and the dead stargulfs beyond this ball of dirt and ignorance will go right on being dead.

For a while.

Rehab

THE KNOCK COMES after midnight. Four silent men in dark hooded sweatshirts carry her in, tip her off the stretcher onto the bed, and leave. Dr. Sam stays behind.

Liz stares down at her client. The young model's eyes are open but unfocused, deeply shadowed. Her lips are cracked, her hair matted with dirt. Her pallor redefines heroin chic.

"Did it . . . work?"

"Of course." Dr. Sam's lipless smile curves below his sunglasses. "Her treatment was a complete success."

The doctor rummages in his bag. He pulls out a misshapen bowl the color of old ivory and strips plastic wrap from the top. Then he takes a silver spoon from his pocket.

Liz frowns. "What's that for?"

"The last of the treatment." His black lenses angle toward the girl on the bed. "Sit her up."

A perfect size two again. Liz grips her shoulders as the doctor force-feeds her. It looks like chopped herbs in molasses and smells like nothing on this earth. The girl starts moaning and struggling, her eyes wild.

Liz tightens her grip. Extreme rehab isn't pretty, but she's tried everything else.

Minutes later, Dr. Sam shoves the last spoonful between the girl's bleeding lips. Her gaze is glassy and passive and empty. As the doctor puts his strange bowl away, Liz feels her own hands trembling.

"Now what?"

"Look directly into her eyes and speak her name. Tell her what her job is."

Liz skips commercials and TV walk-ons: the clinic doesn't recommend either after treatment. Photo shoots are fine, though. Runway work is OK. Both make money, which is more than her client has done this past year.

When Liz finishes, the girl nods once. Her eyes are only slightly less empty.

"Sleep now," says Dr. Sam.

Liz takes out her checkbook. Her hands are still quivering, and the number is large and hard to write clearly. Harder than she expected. She realizes she has misspelled the clinic's name, crosses it out, starts over.

L-a-v-e-a-u.

The doctor takes her check and turns to leave, his long coat swinging behind him. As he reaches the door, a last spasm of anxiety brings Liz to her feet.

"Isn't there anything else I can do for her? Pilates? Medication? Special diet?"

Dr. Sam glances back, lenses flaring in the motel lamplight.

"*Never* give her salt."

SCREAM SAVER

THE FRACTAL ON HALPIN'S SCREEN writhed through a dozen color shifts in as many seconds. One flowed into many, many into one—and the gaps between were jagged mouths, gnawing at a void blacker than imagination.

Susan backed away from her colleague's desk. "Where did you download this thing?"

"It's a distributed computing project. Strictly volunteer."

He tapped one corner of the screen, where translucent spikes stabbed in counterpoint to the fractal's movements.

"That's got to be a pig for bandwidth." She frowned, feeling queasy. "The IT Nazis will have a fit."

Halpin's smile was mysterious and deeply irritating.

"*She* already knows about it. Where do you think I got the URL?"

Susan bit back her doubts. Halpin's nose was the brownest around, but his instincts were good. If the new head of Info Tech—some big-ticket foreign hire—hadn't banished this monstrosity yet, she probably had her reasons.

"It's like SETI, but better," Halpin babbled on. "SETI just does space. This does space and time, because they're the same when the angles bend right."

This screensaver was definitely not bending right. "You're not making sense."

Halpin's eyes stayed fixed on the screen. "Time," he muttered, "doesn't exist. Everything that ever was—or will be—is here right now, in some dimension of space. We simply can't see it because our own dimension is too curved."

Were those silver spikes jabbing higher now?

95

"Angles are intersections," he continued. "Points of contact between here-Now and here-Then—any Then. Imagine a time machine where nothing moves. Where you can just step through, back to the beginnings of life on Earth."

His voice dropped even further. "And beyond."

Susan understood now what Halpin's problem was. Pharmaceuticals manufacturing involved unique challenges—like coworkers who sampled.

If she didn't want to lose her own job, she needed to go report him. Bad enough that she'd stayed late—on a Friday night, too—at Halpin's request. He had cited problems with a new tablet coating, but when she got to his desk he'd started in about this instead. Now he wasn't even talking, just gawking as the screen's patterns twisted and pulsed and leaped.

She retraced the cubicle maze on autopilot and adrenaline, heading for the hall as lights throbbed across the ceiling. Random doorways revealed screens all displaying the same fractal, each more twisted than the last.

Where do you think I got the URL? Hard to imagine Halpin working directly with the new head of IT, but it was just possible.

A low, overstressed hum rose around her. Risking a peek at one screen, she saw larger gaps of void between the fractals. Narrow sharp things flashed in those gaps.

Eyes? Teeth?

"Oh God!"

Halpin's desperate wail rose from back in the cubicles, but Susan fought the impulse to turn around. By the time she reached the corridor, she was running.

Think of a time machine where nothing moves. Where you can just step through. Every desk in this building had access to the Intranet, which probably meant access to the fractal program as well.

Access was such a horrible word. It went both ways.

Somewhere behind her came a dry scrabbling, like scales or claws or something worse fighting for traction. Halpin wasn't screaming any more.

Bolting for the nearest elevator, she slammed her hand against the Down button. When the door opened breathless seconds later, she ducked inside and flattened herself against the closest wall, then fumbled with the controls to shut the door again fast.

A squat figure swathed in a long coat occupied one back corner.

"Is there a problem?"

Susan froze at the quiet, vaguely Asian voice. *The new head of IT.* Of all the people she didn't need to look like an idiot in front of—

"I'm not sure. There's a screensaver running on all the terminals, and they aren't sounding good." *Neither am I.* "Halpin said it was a distributed computing project, some volunteer thing, but he wasn't making sense and it just got worse as he went on—"

Her voice trailed off as she realized whose "volunteer thing" the project must be. Still, Halpin *had* been babbling about space and time and angles . . . hadn't he?

As though in answer, the squat figure nodded. "It is the Liao program."

Susan blinked. Was this something she should have gotten a memo about?

"The program was experimental. It generates random angles of opportunity. Halpin was not meant to discuss it, although I suspected that he would."

Sharp dark eyes peered over the top of the coat's collar. "I am sorry you were the one he chose."

Something in her tone made Susan wish she'd taken the stairs.

And what the hell were random angles of opportunity?

"Halpin isn't exactly discreet. He seemed worse than usual tonight, too." *Spit it out.* "Like he'd been taking something—"

"You are so much less expendable than he was."

As the pit of Susan's stomach followed the elevator down, she stared into the eyes opposite her and saw nothing but void. Void in which strange sparks woke. In which something moved.

The head of IT folded down her collar with gloved fingertips.

"Your coworker was correct about one aspect, though. Like SETI, the Liao program assists something: the plight of immigrants. Immigrants desperate for the curved reality of a purer world than their own, which they made foul."

Susan stared at the woman's yellowed ivory features, smooth and perfect as a mask.

"Immigrants?" she croaked. "From where?"

The elevator stopped. As its doors began to open, black eyes flicked away from Susan, toward the angled walls overhead. Toward the inexorable pressure of jaws forcing through at the corners, lean and thirsting shadows shifting from Then to shrieking Now.

The head of IT spread her arms to welcome them.

"It is called Tindalos."

THE WATER LILY ROOM

Mona is the one who finds it, of course. Dusty and unimpressive, the carpet lies rolled in a small room at the back of the house—behind a door that opens to the one unlabeled key on the ring from their rental agent. Not something most people would look at twice.

But Mona knows how the carpet feels.

As she unrolls it, she sees that the floor is good hardwood, scuffed and neglected. The delicate wicker furniture needs repair and paint, but looks sound enough. Two filthy, uncurtained windows once flooded this space with morning sun, and could certainly do so again. This is a woman's room . . . a woman's retreat.

For the first time since coming to this place Jim has single-handedly chosen for their family's summer, she smiles. This room needs her.

Back in its place again, the carpet reveals all the colors of water: green and teal, shadow blue, silver gray. Not nearly as faded as she'd feared, aside from several pale splotches at the center. Straightening for a better view, she squints at them, looking for a pattern.

A loose board squeaks out in the hall.

"Mona?"

She glances up quickly at her husband's voice—then back to the carpet, frowning. Not bleach stains, thank God. Not mere splotches, either. Pale leaves, maybe, or even water lilies. It's an unusual design. Possibly antique?

Before she can examine it more closely, Jim appears in the doorway. Giving the carpet an uninterested glance, he sets down a box labeled KITCHEN and frowns at her.

"Where do you want all this?"

Mona bites her lip. Jim has his problems, but literacy isn't one of them. She'd better get back to work, before he and the kids fill up the hallway with cartons for her.

Jim glances at the carpet again. "Why'd you bother getting that out?"

"Just curious."

Mona flushes. Eighteen years of marriage still haven't taught her to handle Jim's moods—or his lack of them. Jim does nothing on impulse. He doesn't have hunches or inexplicable feelings, and he never gets distracted when there's a job to be done.

"Well, now you know," he says. "It's junk."

As her face flares even redder, his expression softens. "Look, I'm not saying you can't order a new rug if you want one in here. Something cheerful."

"Water lilies are cheerful."

"Lilies?" Jim squints at the splotches. "More like water *stains*—and that color's boring to start with."

He shrugs. "Doesn't matter anyhow. We've got a truck full of stuff to move in, and that rental place closes at five."

Thumps behind him tell her the kids have already gotten this lecture. Mona sighs, turning away from her needy little room. From its carpet, which already looks very much like water lilies to her.

"After we've moved in," she says, "I'm going to make this my project. Maybe respray all that wicker glossy white—"

But Jim is already headed for the front door, yelling at the kids to keep those cartons coming.

By mid-June, the morning light streams in through spotless windows, over freshly painted furniture with new throw pillows and seat cushions. Cut-glass bowls of potpourri mask how long the room was closed up. There's a damp smell, too: Mona hasn't been able to track it down yet, but surely sunlight and fresh air will do the trick.

Sitting cross-legged in the middle of the carpet, Mona feels the sun on her too like an affirmation. All it has taken is a little love, and a little time. OK, a lot of time, but what else has she got to do this summer?

The thought makes her pull her knees up to her chest. Wrapping them with both arms, she hugs her own body so tightly it hurts.

Nobody in this house needs her. And she knows it.

Five days a week—sometimes six—Jim drives in to the city, where some pending deal usually keeps him away until well past dinnertime. The kids do exactly what they would have done at home: sleep till noon, then emerge long enough for a sandwich or a bowl of cereal. After that, she's not likely to see them again for hours. Their rooms are electronic cocoons: laptops, cell phones, DVD players, stereos.

Anything to ease the boredom of this country place Jim assured her they'd love.

If they they'd been four and six rather than fourteen and sixteen, they might have.

Mona shuts her eyes tightly, remembering four and six. Her days had been full then. Skinned knees, lost toys, bathtime, bedtime—but it all went so fast. Now she can feel herself fading into the background, and she is too old to have another baby. The friends who once pleaded with her to get back to her work life no longer even call.

Around her, unseen, the colors of the water lily carpet glow.

Mona reaches out a hand, imagining she can feel those slick, luxurious leaves. Smell the perfume of pale blossoms—

Touch the toe of her daughter's sneaker.

Her eyes fly open. "Sorry," she says, scrambling to her feet. "I was just—"

"Meditating, right?" Barely awake fourteen stares back at her. "We learned that in gym last year. What a waste."

Mona bites her lip. "Actually, I was waiting for you to come help me roll this carpet up, the way I asked you to last night."

Discipline has never been her strong suit, but the rebuke works: fifteen minutes later, the carpet is outside the hallway. Humming to herself, Mona switches on the floor buffer she rented yesterday and gets to work on that abused hardwood. It's strenuous, but the sunlight's encouragement keeps her going.

Surely other women have done this before her . . . maybe on hands and knees, bringing up the shine with their own sweat. She almost regrets not doing the same. Working through lunch without noticing,

Mona has the floor in decent shape by the time Jim returns home—on time for once.

"You did this for a *rental?*"

He is staring at her efforts with amused disgust. Mona forces herself to shrug.

"It needed doing, and I had the time." A spark of irritation flares. "I told you this room was my project!"

He shrugs back, eloquently uninterested, and heads for the kitchen. Remembering tonight's still-frozen hamburgers, Mona hurries after him. Tomorrow, she promises herself, she'll give the floor another coat of wax. It needs to dry overnight anyway.

But next morning, the carpet is back in place.

Mona stares at its glowing colors . . . at the ethereal pale greens of what very definitely *are* lily pads now, complete with buds . . . and wonders whether she dare wake up her daughter. If she did put the carpet back, unasked and unprompted, it would be a first—and if she didn't, who did? Jim has already made it clear that this room bores him. Her son is even less likely than his sister to do anything useful without pleading.

Which means that she herself must have carried the carpet back in last night, despite her earlier decision to give the floor two coats.

Despite not remembering doing so.

Taking a long, shaky breath of humid air (where *is* that damp coming from?), Mona tells herself that the floor looks fine as is. What does it matter how the carpet got back in? Now she can return the floor buffer earlier, save a little money, and maybe even make Jim happy with her.

Heaven knows that hasn't been happening much lately. This summer rental isn't working out the way he imagined it, though she could have told him that it wouldn't. Not with adolescent ideas of vacation having nothing to do with being stuck out in the country, away from their friends and the malls and everything else Jim didn't quite consider. Not with her own lonely uselessness in the air like a poison.

Still, there is the buffer to be returned. And after that, the whole rest of the day to enjoy this room, *her* room, which is finally just the way she wants it.

Or perhaps the way it wants itself.

* * *

One morning early in July—a very sunny morning, too warm by her second cup of coffee—Mona notices something different about the carpet. Padding barefoot to its center, she stares down at the water lilies between her feet.

It's no trick of the light. They are unmistakably blooming.

Mona gasps softly. Then she sinks to her knees and traces the pinkish-pearl of one flower, wondering how she could have overlooked something so beautiful. Surely the pattern has always been this way. She simply has not been paying proper attention, no matter how often she vacuums in here every week.

That, she knows, is what Jim would say—assuming she had the nerve to tell him the carpet was blooming. But she'd have to be awake for that, and lately he's been coming home well after midnight.

At least that's what the kids tell her.

Mona herself has begun taking sleeping pills, though she never did in the city. In the city, she could still talk to her husband, at least on the weekends. Out here, Jim starts getting restless by Sunday afternoon.

His list of chores is usually done by then. He has tried talking to each child at least once, and had at least one argument apiece. She has made something special for Saturday night dinner, just for the two of them, or they have driven to one of the few nearby restaurants. Sometimes—but not recently—they have made love.

She tries to remember when that last time was.

Under her right knee, unnoticed, another water lily bud unfolds.

What she remembers instead is his cell phone's ring on Sunday afternoons. No doubt it sounds the same no matter where he is, but here in this quiet house its single-note tone is a metallic intruder. Not that Jim ever allows it to intrude for long. He always deals with his calls elsewhere: outside if she is in, inside if she is out.

"The office," he murmurs. "Got to take this."

Back in June, he could usually put off whatever the office wanted until Monday. Lately, though, he has been swearing under his breath as he packs an overnight bag. Sometimes Mona tries to help, wishing she knew what to ask. There is always some explanation—a deal-breaking crisis, a foreign client who is only in town tonight—but explanations are not reasons.

Mona could no more ask for reasons than she could tell Jim the carpet is blooming.

Reasons mean risk, because Jim is not a willing liar. Never in their married life has he out-and-out lied to her—only asked very gently if she *really* wants an answer. How much was the garage bill to this time? What was in that thick envelope she had to sign for, the one from some law office?

Are you cheating on me?

Although both windows are latched against the heat, Mona feels the hint of a breeze. Wafting across her forehead . . . across her sweat, which broke just thinking about reasons . . . it carries the deep green coolness of a pond. She closes her eyes. Now there is a scent as well: exotic as jasmine, comforting as vanilla.

Her fingers curl into the nap of the carpet. She sways on her knees. All around her, thick luxurious petals of cream yellow and pink and purest, pearliest white unfold and sway also.

The breeze that has finally found them finds its voice.

Unfaithful, whispers one cream-pink petal tongue. *Unfaithful* . . .

It is not a hateful whisper, only an infinitely sad and knowing one. Soon it is joined by a dozen others—soprano and deep-toned suffering alto, old and young and wearily middle-aged. Richly scented sympathy blows through them all, cooling Mona's face as the tears she has been holding back for at least a week begin to flow.

Unfaithful.

It is the voice of every friend she wishes she still had. It is affirmation—not only of her fears, but of her right to them. It is the unmistakable knowledge that other women have suffered here as she is suffering now, pouring out self-doubt and misery like rain into these watercolor depths.

And the carpet remembers. She can sense that, too.

Swaying, weeping, and remembering, Mona kneels in the center of the water lily room for hours. She does not watch her tears as they drop into—not onto—the carpet, nor notice how very bright and lush its blossoms have become. Only the noon sun baking in through the windows finally rouses her. Hissing as she unfolds cramped legs, Mona stands rubbing her eyes for a bit.

Then she retrieves her stone-cold coffee and heads for the door, loneliness settling back across her shoulders.

No, she decides, she will not ask Jim about his reasons. Sunday afternoons must remain as they have been all summer, sacred to the unspoken.

As she walks off down the hallway, one cream-pink petal drops from her heel.

Somewhere between July and the depths of August, the kids quit talking to her. At first, it's mostly about their dad: when he does or doesn't come home at night. What her son may have found in one of his pockets while borrowing a twenty last Sunday.

Mona tries to be grateful. She isn't stupid—fading into the background lets a woman notice things—but perhaps her daughter at least is trying to spare her feelings. Or maybe the kids are just scared, the way she was when her own parents divorced. Either way, their silence is understandable. And the room, *her* room, is still a sunny haven in the mornings, no matter how the sleeping pills have started letting her down.

Lately, though, she can't remember the last time either child asked her for anything. Anything at all.

The realization chills her. This is her season. Her last scrap of undeniable value to her children is her willingness to chauffeur them on back-to-school errands: sports physicals, locker supplies, just the right skirt or jacket or pricey sneakers to wear that first day.

But last month was her son's seventeenth birthday. Along with the German chocolate cake and family picnic came the gift he'd been hinting about for almost a year. Not the Corvette he'd dreamed of, of course, but a car nonetheless. One used Toyota's worth of freedom, parked at the end of the drive with its keys on the driver's seat, a birthday card tucked under one wiper.

"From Mom and Dad" in Jim's handwriting.

Since then, shopping bags and fast-food containers pile up in the trash with no assistance from her. Her children communicate mostly through notes on the kitchen table—or in cryptic phone calls that never quite say where they are, or when they might be expected home. Released from their electronic cocoons, they are intoxicated by motion.

Mona, meanwhile, is nearly motionless. Retreating to the water lily room more and more, she sits with her hook and ball of crochet thread, turning out simple white doilies as though she has been doing so since childhood.

The room seems to like them. After she has placed one under each vase and lamp and cachepot of flowers, though, Jim starts to notice. Like small starched spiderwebs, doilies are turning up everywhere, under the most unlikely objects.

"What is this with you?" he asks one Saturday, frowning at the example under his coffee mug. "Some kind of therapy?"

Mona nods. "All my friends are doing it. They taught me."

She waits for him to ask which friends, but he doesn't. This morsel of attention will have to sustain her through another weekend's routines—farmers' market shopping, dinner out, abortive arguments about their son's driving—and the Sunday afternoon phone call. By six o'clock that evening, she is alone again.

By one o'clock next morning, her sleeping pills have failed her completely.

Mona lies adrift in the dark for a long time, uncertain what to do. She cannot stay in this bed any longer. The flat expanse of sheet on her husband's side mocks her like a scar, and the ceiling fan's blades whisper terrible things. Struggling into her bathrobe and slippers, she heads for the door, perhaps the kitchen.

Fat women lose their husbands.

Smoothing one hand across her stomach, she walks downstairs without touching a light switch. There is no need to: she knows where she is going now. Where she has longed to go all this long, miserable weekend.

And what will you do come September, when the water lily room is gone?

Desperation clutches her heart. Jim has been talking about their move back to the city for a week or two now, but she has managed to ignore him. She has gotten so very good at ignoring things that a few dozen cardboard boxes sitting around the house are no challenge. Jim can do what he likes, so long as he keeps them out of her room.

But there is no need for boxes in the water lily room. Very little there will be going back with them, aside from a few doilies and pillows and seat cushions. Not the white wicker furniture she spent so many hours repairing and painting. Possibly not the new curtains.

Certainly not the carpet.

Tonight, she can smell the room's dampness even as she fumbles for the doorknob. It is a subtle, organic scent: not mold or rot, but persistent. Stronger in the dark. The live deep green of it reaches out to her, welcoming her into the only place in this house where she has always felt necessary.

Mona does not remember leaving the curtains open, but she must have. Moonlight spills across the pattern of lily pads and burgeoning flowers . . . so many blossoms, so many shades of peach and pink and cream and purest white.

Keeping carefully to the hardwood at its border, she works her way around the carpet to her favorite chair. Mona cannot say why she avoids walking across. Surely the rich watercolor tones of the background—gray-blue and aquamarine and rippling shadow violet—are only wool. Still, the moonlight picks out depths she has never noticed before, and she does not remember the carpet being quite so large.

A tall brass lamp stands beside her chair, but Mona does not switch it on. Reaching down for her workbag, she finds her hook and thread purely by touch.

Some faint breeze from the nearest window (but surely she closed them both this afternoon?) drifts over the carpet's lily pond, raising its scent of sympathy. Tonight it is headier than ever. Jasmine and vanilla and her best friend's favorite incense—still remembered from heart-to-hearts in college—wrap themselves around her, slowing her fingers.

Unwanted, the breeze whispers through petals. *Unnecessary. Left behind.*

Somewhere outside, a car door slams. A key scrapes in the front door. Two sets of footsteps detour to the kitchen, then creak upstairs stealthily.

Mona's grip tightens on her crochet hook as the petals begin quivering again.

Unloved, they sigh. *Out of place, outgrown.* The breeze hints of lavender, and the musk of old-fashioned perfume. *Only we understand. We remember the lonely mornings, the afternoons drifting like dust—*

Now the voices have faces at last. Gazing into the water at her feet, Mona recognizes each in turn: maiden aunts of palest primrose, neglected wives in peach. Here and there the despairing pink of a spinster daughter, or the crimson of a prodigal unforgiven. And everywhere . . . in every faded hue . . . mothers.

As moisture seeps into the open toes of her slippers, Mona understands that all these women have sat here before her. This room has been their hiding place. Their last chintz-pillowed refuge from an unkind reality.

And something more.

Something the water around her ankles already knows.

Mona stands up slowly, still clutching her unfinished work. The night breeze whips up another chorus as she begins to wade. *Unwanted.*

Her slippers sink down and down, through layered sediments of regret. The footing is treacherous here. Silt swirls around her thighs as something cold—and hard, and round—rolls under one heel. *Outgrown.* Overbalancing, she pitches forward into mooncast shadows, breaking through a mat of lilies which fails to hold her up.

Left behind.

Late tomorrow afternoon, her daughter will find that half-completed doily lying at the carpet's center. Its white is the only brightness left. All the lilies are blighted gray buds, their pads no more than splotches.

She will press the crumpled threads into her father's hand that night.

He will not understand.

THE DEATH VERSES OF YIAN-HO

ONCE MORE, just to be sure.

Andrea glances at the clock on her laptop—thirty minutes until her tutorial with Dr. K, plenty of time—before reopening the file from this morning's e-mail. It is a sample of Asian calligraphy from an unimaginably antique scroll, one of seven owned by the Special Collections library of a small New England university. It has taken some doing to convince the curator that seeing it is essential to her thesis on women's death poems in Japan.

And it is, dear God. It is.

She catches her breath as the image comes up, though she knows nothing of this writing system. These characters were ancient before the first poet in Japan took up a brush. Still, she studies the handwriting carefully, focusing on the last ragged brushstroke of the final left-hand character on the screen. As it stabs into the margin's age-yellowed void, her heart begins to race.

Minimizing the image, she brings up another for comparison: a haiku written near Nagasaki in mid-August of 1945. Then a second, from the Edo period around 1714. Her final sample comes from the Meiji period near the end of the nineteenth century.

In all four cases, the calligraphy is similar. Nearly identical.

And the final menacing brushstroke of that left-hand character is the same.

Andrea glances away from her laptop, twisting her fingers together to stop their trembling. She cannot possibly be mistaken. Not after a whole semester's private study with Dr. K, practicing Japanese calligraphy on brown rice paper until her fingers cramp.

Dr. K believes this is necessary to her understanding of haiku. She has never explained why, and Andrea has never risked offending her by asking. Like the images on her screen, this celebrated haiku poet is a part of her thesis research: living proof of a teaching system stretching back centuries.

Later this afternoon, she will show the evidence to Dr. K for her confirmation. She ought to be elated.

Instead, she finds herself wishing that her desk lamp did not throw so many shadows.

To dispel them, Andrea reminds herself how ground-breaking her thesis topic is. Or at least, it seemed so at first. During some preliminary reading on female poets of various literary periods, she discovered *jisei*: the "farewell poem to life." Fascinated by the notion, she sought out death verses written by women during these periods—and uncovered a curious chain of teachers and students.

Adopting the style of one's teacher—even her diction or word choice—is not unusual, as Andrea knows from her own forays into poetry. What she found in these works went far deeper.

> *silence, cuckoo*
> *this floating world*
> *still mine*

That verse from the Edo period had been her first clue that these poets shared something unusual. Even in the hedonistic climate of that time, life was regarded (in death poems, anyway) as a transient thing. Yet the woman who wrote that believed otherwise, and said so in characters so forceful they had nearly torn the fragile paper.

After her death, the woman's student—previously known for moon-viewing verses of remarkable delicacy and lightness—had turned to themes which got her expelled from one group of poets after another. Her own death poem came only three years after her mentor's.

> *weak vessel*
> *cracked by moonlight—*
> *a raven's cry*

In that short time, however, she had acquired a student of her own. That student's work also changed radically following her mentor's death. And so it went, forward and backward, from the present and Dr. K to a certain court lady of the Heian period.

Andrea shuts her eyes, almost wishing she had stopped there in the late eighth century, safely in Japan. If only she had not traced her court poet's own mentor back to China and the flourishing T'ang Dynasty, then enlisted specialists at other colleges as the trail grew cold.

In the end, even they could not help her, despite more research fees and favors than she could easily afford. The trail did not end in China. Instead, it vanished into a region of Asia mentioned by only the oldest sources: the plateau of Leng.

Further than that, none of these scholars had been prepared to go. Leng was probably a fiction, and a distasteful one at that.

If she insisted on wasting her time, however, she might try the Special Collections at Miskatonic—

Andrea's computer now contains several months' worth of e-mails from the curator of those collections. He is a knowledgeable and friendly soul, though reluctant to send her too many images at a time, or to answer her questions in as much detail as she requires. In the past couple of weeks, this reticence has increased.

There is very little documentation concerning the court city (imperial residence?) of Yian-Ho, I'm afraid, he wrote ten days ago. *The Seven Cryptical Books of Hsan have quite a good history of Leng, including the scandals at court, but the original Chinese translation is antiquated. I really can't recommend an available English translation. We've got the de Marigny, of course, but that doesn't circulate. Not sure whether it mentions poetry or any circles of poets.*

Andrea sent back four words: *Could you please check?*

By the next morning, she had her answer. The court at Yian-Ho did indeed boast a circle of elite poets—and a notorious one, at that.

Talk about the Hellfire Club! I've included a few pages from the de Marigny translation of the historical bits. Reads more like sorcery than literature: ghoul-cults and corpse-eating, experiments with drugs and poisons. And spells. Worse than the Al-Azif, if you're familiar with that.

Andrea was not. By the time she finished the few blurry files her contact had attached, she was grateful. Aside from their dietary habits (which *must* have been mistranslations, surely), the poet-courtiers of Yian-Ho were most noted for their obsession with and hatred of death. Any means to avoid it was worth trying.

Any means whatsoever.

With his typical caution, her contact had not included any spells among the pages she received—only a few poems noted by the mysterious translator de Marigny. No poet himself, he had rendered only one into English.

> *One thousand wine-cups broken.*
> *What do they matter, if the wine endures?*
> *Pour it out to the dregs.*
> *The fate of shards is dust.*

The poets' circle at Yian-Ho had used something akin to haiku names. This one was by Hound, or possibly Servant of Hound. The pages her contact had supplied mentioned a few others, but not what they might have written.

Can you match any of these names with poems? she asked. *In the original script?*

The university owns a copy of the Seven Cryptical Books—actually, scrolls—in the original, but seeing the poems there would do you no good. No scholar alive can read more than fragments of that script. Even de Marigny's translation is assumed to be from a Chinese version.

Andrea had nearly screamed with frustration.

I don't need to read the poems, she sent back. *I need to see their calligraphy.*

The next response did not come for several hours, and was unusually cryptic.

Might be able to help, but must get approval. Need to know why.

At the heart of Andrea's thesis is the notion of poetry as a physical art, passed from mentor to student through years of training. It is an unusual approach, as her thesis advisor frequently reminds her, but studying here with Dr. K has helped her to refine the concept. Hours spent with brushes and inkstone have taught her that muscle memory has a creative component. How better to pass on technique than by practice?

It is the only reasonable explanation for centuries of nearly identical calligraphy and thematic content, yet Andrea felt uneasy explaining this. She had not found nearly enough citations to back up her point, nor any similar cases for comparison. This group of female Japanese (and Chinese, and whatever one calls the denizens of Leng) poets, and no other, passed knowledge along in this fashion.

Lacks academic rigor. Her advisor wrote that in red across the top of one early draft of her first chapter.

What if Miskatonic felt the same?

In the end, she hit SEND and hoped for the best. Two days later—this morning—three images arrived. Each was tagged with a name in English: Yellow Mask, Slayer of Shadows, She-Who-Defies. The images themselves showed two to five lines of characters, presumably poems, from the Sixth Cryptical Book of Hsan.

It took Andrea nearly an hour to compare these with the death poems collected for her thesis.

Despite a gap of centuries, She-Who-Defies matched their calligraphy perfectly.

Now Andrea turns back to her laptop and brings up one final poem, a very recent one. Not a death poem. Simply a haiku photographed from a scroll, blurred a little by the limitations of her cell phone's camera.

> *north wind*
> *the cuckoo's journey*
> *soon, soon*

Dr. K translated that for her last week, after she arrived late for their tutorial and found Andrea gazing intently at her calligraphy. She had no way of knowing that her student already suspected the poem was hers. Nor that her student's phone already held its image.

The last ragged brushstroke of the final left-hand character—

Andrea's laptop chimes, announcing an incoming message. Over the racing of her heart—her office is very quiet so late in the afternoon, at the dim gray end of the fall semester—she recognizes her Miskatonic contact's address and opens it immediately.

I assume by now, it begins, *that you have matched your poet of Yian-Ho. I hope for your sake that this is all you have done. There are aspects of this situation that I had not considered before, and that you do not understand.*

Andrea frowns. This goes way beyond cryptic.

Regarding the photo attached to your last missive, I tend to agree. Your instructor and She-Who-Defies have very similar styles of brushwork.

Whether your thesis's explanation is correct is another matter entirely. There were things done at Yian-Ho . . . experiments, one might call them. De Marigny only mentions the worst of them in footnotes, but suffice it to say that certain great courtiers did not intend to die as ordinary mortals do. They did not practice sorcery and decadence for their own sake, but as means to this end.

One of them may have succeeded.

There is more of this, quite a lot more, but already Andrea is checking her computer's clock. Ten minutes until her final tutorial. For the first time since making contact with the curator of Special Collections, she wonders whether all those other specialists were right. Perhaps she has been wasting her time: these latest e-mails have been veering into folklore, and pretty weird folklore at that.

Andrea did not pay out-of-state tuition to ruin her thesis with unverifiable speculations. It took her long enough to locate Dr. K at this isolated Western university, serving as poet-in-residence for their fledgling MFA program.

. . . strongly advise you not to share your latest discoveries with your instructor. You have sufficient evidence to confirm what you need to. Send her e-mail later if you must, but do not bring up the subject in person. I cannot stress this enough.

I hope you will forgive me, but I have taken the liberty of obtaining your cell phone number . . .

Andrea groans under her breath. Has she gotten involved with a stalker?

. . . will be calling later this evening to assure myself of your safety. My lack of foresight has created this situation, and I feel entirely responsible.

Deleting the message quickly, Andrea powers down her laptop and slips it into her backpack. Her contact at Miskatonic has a point—Dr. K is unlikely to be pleased about her photographing that haiku without permission—but this is their last tutorial. She will not feel confident unless she *does* share her discoveries, showing her the unbroken chain of teaching and learning.

For this semester, at least, she herself has been part of that chain.

*   *   *

The soft clink of porcelain on a lacquer tray greets her as she walks into her instructor's office. As she has done for each of their meetings, Dr. K is preparing green tea: a strong, medicinal-tasting Sencha. Andrea watches the ritual in silence, dismayed to notice how fragile Dr. K looks this afternoon. And how old. Despite carefully applied makeup and crow-black hair, the woman must be on the high side of seventy.

She has suspected for some time that Dr. K is not well, and that whatever troubles her is both chronic and debilitating. Department gossip says heart trouble. Some in the MFA program are dubious about their prized (and expensive) poet-in-residence surviving her first semester.

Until this afternoon, Andrea has never believed them.

Beyond the bookshelf holding tea implements, Dr. K's large desk is already spread with supplies for calligraphy practice. Relieved to have some other focus for her attention, Andrea greets her and heads for the brushes, eliciting a thin smile of approval.

She returns the smile uncertainly. Despite weeks of effort, her brushwork remains clumsy. Her versions of the Chinese character *yong*—containing all eight strokes required for classic East Asian calligraphy—are straggling and inconsistent. She has no aptitude whatsoever.

Yet Dr. K will not let her stop. Worse, she seems increasingly upset by her lack of progress.

Touching her brush to the inkstone, Andrea takes a deep breath and tries again. Her *yong* still looks like a dying spider . . . but she perseveres, filling an entire sheet of paper before Dr. K arrives with the tea tray.

"So."

Dr. K's face is as wrinkled and inexpressive as a walnut shell. Taking up Andrea's work, she examines it in detail before shaking her head and laying it aside. Andrea expects her to sit down now with her own brush, demonstrate *yong* yet again, and make her fill a second sheet.

Instead, she begins pouring tea.

Though Andrea has finally developed a taste for Sencha, she has never felt comfortable with the handleless, eggshell-fragile cups Dr. K favors. Her tea goes into a plain white porcelain mug, which she bought for her instructor after nearly dropping one of the cups. Dr. K does not approve of this mug, but says nothing as she passes it over.

Andrea inhales the rising steam from her tea. This afternoon, she can smell as well as taste its seaweed-iodine tang.

Dr. K finally sits down with her own cup. "You said that you had something new to show me?"

Just like that.

Andrea takes a long swallow to hide her confusion. Though she e-mailed Dr. K after this morning's discovery, she did not expect or receive any reply. Even at the best of times, Dr. K is not a prompt communicator—and the end of a busy semester is hardly the best of times.

Not that Andrea had been too clear about her discovery, either. Perhaps caution is contagious. Or, more likely, her contact's paranoia is overriding her enthusiasm.

But not now.

After clearing space on the desk, Andrea takes out her laptop and boots it up, turning the screen so that Dr. K can see. Her instructor frowns at her own poem.

"I'm sorry. I know I should have asked first." Andrea hesitates. "But I wasn't sure whether I'd found anything, and I didn't want to look like an idiot if I hadn't."

Dr. K's chin dips. "Go on."

The next image is the death haiku from Nagasaki, mid-August of 1945. Dr. K's eyelids flick down as she murmurs the words.

> *through cracks*
> *in this flawed shell*
> *strange light*

"I was with her when she wrote that, you know."

Andrea feels a flutter of excitement. She already knows who Dr. K's mentor was, of course, but this confirms the link beyond all doubt. The first link in the chain.

"No, I didn't," she says quietly. "Thank you."

"It was just before she died. I was barely twenty, afraid to look at her. Her body was ruined. She had no hair left, no teeth. Lesions all over her skin." Dr. K's eyes clamp shut again. "Still, she asked for brush and paper."

There is a steel thread of pride in her voice.

Andrea points to the final left-hand brushstroke in her mentor's death poem, then brings up the image of Dr. K's own calligraphy.

"There," she says. "Right there. She taught you that, didn't she?"

Dr. K does not reply at once. To cover her nerves, Andrea takes a long swallow of her tea and winces at the aftertaste. Perhaps she still has not learned how to appreciate Sencha.

"I suppose she did." Her instructor's eyes are wide open now, hard and bright. "Will this be in your thesis?"

"I'm not sure my committee will allow illustrations, but I hope so. They explain so much."

To demonstrate, Andrea starts bringing up other examples from her thesis file. She has discussed her ideas with Dr. K all semester, of course, but now she can *show* her how far this chain of female mentorship goes. Back and back . . . Meiji period to Edo, Edo to Kamakura, Kamakura to Heian . . . .then further, into fragile scraps from T'ang Dynasty China.

And further still, into Leng.

Andrea's fingers quiver as she brings up this morning's final image. There are only two lines of characters, in an alien—though vaguely Asian—script. No translation, of course. No obvious signature, either, though her contact has identified the poet as She-Who-Defies. Even if he hadn't, that last brushstroke would have been enough.

Dr. K stares at the screen. Her breath hisses out through her teeth.

"Where did you find this?"

For the first time this afternoon, Andrea hesitates. Naming her contact—or even his university—suddenly seems unwise, though she cannot explain why.

"It's from the Sixth Cryptical Book of Hsan."

Which is the truth, though not the one she senses that her instructor is looking for. Dr. K's eyes are even brighter now. She touches the screen with one emaciated finger, tracing each character on the glass.

> *death is the first lie children learn:*
> *truth is a harvest of darkness*

Her lips move in English-language whispers. The moment her hand falls away from the laptop, Andrea begins typing automatically, taking notes as she has for most of her adult life.

No. Her fingers stumble to a stop. *This is not possible.*

"Excuse me? If that was a translation, there isn't supposed to be . . . I mean, that language isn't supposed to—"

Dr. K refills her mug as she struggles for words. The Sencha is a deep, deep green, the color of ancient jade. The color of the pendant at Dr. K's throat, a curiously carved piece Andrea cannot remember seeing before. It is a crouching hound—or something nearly like a hound—with the folded wings of a bat, but its visage is neither canine nor chiropteran. Twisted around fully displayed fangs, the features are malevolence and hunger incarnate, reflections of some inhuman hell.

"—exist as a living tongue?"

Her instructor's question is barely audible above the pounding of her own heart in her ears. Andrea sips more of the bitter tea before nodding.

"It does not. It has not . . . for millennia."

Dr. K's fingers tighten around the pendant as a spasm of pain creases her face. "Do not worry," she continues after a moment. "I will be better soon."

Her trembling grasp on the jade says otherwise, but Andrea forces herself to focus on their conversation. The mystery is finally unraveling before her, justifying her months of work.

"So how can you read it?" she finally asks.

"Because it is too perfect to die. Too structurally flawless and complex." Another spasm, longer this time. " It is the tongue of undying souls."

Andrea stares at her. This is sounding less and less like a heart problem and more like a stroke—a massive malfunction of the brain. Something is terribly wrong with her instructor. She needs to call for help, now.

But when she tries to rise from her chair, her muscles do not respond.

Dr. K seems not to notice. "What was done after moonset in the deepest chambers of Yian-Ho . . . the greater and the lesser rites of Zin . . . it cannot be forgotten. Cannot be lost. *Will not be lost.*"

The jade amulet slips free of her grip, and Andrea can see its eyes clearly for the first time. Pinpoints of dark fire glow deep in the hound-creature's sockets. They flicker with the ragged rhythm of her instructor's breathing, brightening and dimming in response to her voice. It is no longer one Andrea recognizes.

"Not long now," she says, in the subtle and venomous court-accent of Leng. "I shall move on soon, as I always have. The vessel is at hand and the knowledge is mine. The formulae of Hsan have not failed, not once in all the lifetimes we were promised for our sacrifices."

Her hand seizes Andrea's wrist, pulling it from the keyboard with a strength no woman of her age—healthy or not—should possess. Her long nails draw pricks of blood from Andrea's skin.

"What the hell are you doing?"

The question takes a very long time to emerge from her lips. A paralyzing chill has nearly immobilized them . . . and that chill is spreading inward, down the column of her spine and through every nerve.

Andrea's glance falls on her instructor's small white teacup.

It is empty and dry.

Dr. K smiles, tightening her grip. "Your body is in no danger, I assure you. Why would I wish to damage it? It is not what I would have chosen, perhaps, but it is strong and young and female. It will recover quickly, and I shall go on."

The pulsing of the amulet's eyes is more irregular now. The hand clamped on Andrea's wrist has gone deathly cold. Mustering all her strength, she tries once more to tear herself away from whatever her instructor has become.

Or always was?

As her hand thumps weakly against the desktop, Dr. K barely notices.

"The chain you have discovered will be unbroken. Your work will continue, though perhaps not as you intended. Your thesis committee can never see these writings, of course, but your truest destiny will be achieved."

She gasps audibly as another spasm crosses her face. "The wine . . . of my spirit . . . shall endure."

More words emerge from her lips after that, but Andrea understands none of them. No one living could, not even her contact at Miskatonic . . . though that scholar would give his heart's blood to hear them. They are the purest expression of a tongue more ancient than any devised by mankind: the whole text of certain spells from the Second Cryptical Book of Hsan, which pertains to dominion over life and death.

The chill has claimed her body completely now. Deep as winter, as space between unknown stars, it holds even her mind immobile as myriad voices flood in.

All are feminine, pleading for their own lives in the languages of Leng and T'ang-dynasty China, Heian-period courtiers and noblewomen of the samurai. A young poet of Edo weeps as the moon she loved fades from her vision forever. Another student shrieks and claws at her mentor's radiation-seared skin . . . *her* skin—

"Better now."

The voice is her own, yet not her own.

And she cannot feel her lips moving.

Fighting free of the shadows still clinging to her consciousness, Andrea pries open drooping eyelids. Her vision is blurred and growing dimmer. Yet surely those are her own features barely an arm's length away, shifting through each of Dr. K's characteristic expressions—or lack of same—like a woman trying on new dresses.

Settling into a thin smile, the lips press together as hands she also recognizes as her own lift the jade amulet's silk cord from around this neck. This wrinkled, sagging neck, too weak to support its head.

"That was . . . cutting it close." The smile fades. "A bit too close, though no harm done. The formulae of Hsan work swiftly, so long as the materials are compatible and the spirit is strong."

Andrea feels a hot weight in the center of her chest. Something there is fluttering . . . struggling . . . failing with every moment. Every beat. Shifting the weight of this slumped flesh, she strives desperately to rise, but strong young hands push her back into her chair.

Then they move to her laptop's keyboard and begin deleting files.

When they have finished—when the laptop is dark and silent as the shadows gathering again around Andrea's mind—the hands flex themselves on Dr. K's desk. Reaching out for paper, brush, and ink-stone, they begin to write the Chinese *yong* over and over again. Though none of these characters look at all like dying spiders, they continue until an entire sheet has been filled.

The knife smile returns. "Good enough."

That burning weight in Andrea's chest (*oh God* not *mine*) is a clenched fist now. Its fluttering has nearly ceased. Shifting one leaden foot the smallest fraction of an inch, she tries for the last time to stand.

This time, her own clear blue eyes only watch the body as it fails.

"It is fortunate," muses her voice from very far away, "that crema-tion is so popular in this country."

Then that voice falls silent again, forever. The second to last sound she hears is the dance of bristles on brown rice paper, the most recent death haiku of She-Who-Defies.

The last is a cell phone's despair in the depths of her backpack.

Then silence.

TWENTY MILE

THE DEVELOPER'S SIGN by the front gate took Cassie like a punch in the stomach. Phil had told her about it, but seeing it was something else. Something that clenched her fingers white on the steering wheel. Made her swear all the way down that long dirt road, because cussing was better than crying and that asshole Phil was *not* going to see her cry.

Twenty Mile Rural Properties—Your Piece of the West.

Your overpriced shred, anyhow. And none of it mine. Maybe Twenty Mile had never really been hers, but it had still been in her family. She'd worked up here every teenage summer, helping her aunt with cooking when she had to and riding fence as much as she could.

Now there were no cattle left to fence in. No branding crews to cook for. Just miles and miles of dry grass and brush, stuck full of orange plastic flags flapping in a Wyoming wind. The kind that meant thunderstorms coming—maybe a bad one, since it was barely past mid-June.

Good thing she didn't have much further to go. After driving almost nonstop from Denver, even staying under the same roof with Phil sounded better than another three miles up to Bear Lodge, Montana. So long as Phil hadn't shut off the electricity and sewer yet, staying at the ranch was bound to beat accommodations there.

Of course, there was still the problem of talking to her cousin. She and Phil hadn't spoken since the memorial service back in January.

The one that had left him the last heir to Twenty Mile.

Strictly speaking, of course, the service hadn't done that. A drunk in a 4 × 4 had, on a twisting road in a snowstorm. Her aunt and uncle and Phil's two brothers—plus their wives, one with a baby on the way—had been returning from a neighbor's holiday dinner. All in one van. One target.

When the Barrett family lawyer called Phil in L.A., only her aunt had still been alive. He'd flown in just in time to say goodbye in ICU.

By the time the will cleared probate, Twenty Mile was already history.

Raindrops spattering her windshield told Cassie she'd better stifle her grievances for now. Not easy, when the very emptiness of the landscape kept reminding her why she was here. She'd just come to collect a few things her aunt had set aside for her—things Phil had "forgotten" to send down for months—and close the door on too many memories.

By the time she pulled into the graveled front drive, it was raining steadily. The clouds were darker than early dusk could justify, and thin lightning stabbed at the distant hills. Grabbing her windbreaker from the back seat, she pulled it over her head as she ran for the porch.

There was a scrap of paper taped to the front door.

Cassie read it, reread it, then tore it off and threw it into a nearby lilac bush. She tried the door anyhow, but found it locked. *"Shit."*

She was just turning around when bootheels sounded on the porch steps. "Cassie? Cassie Barrett?"

Glancing back quickly, she saw an older man in jeans and a work shirt. The band of his battered straw hat held a single feather.

"Nobody else, Frank," she said, smiling in recognition. "What are you still doing around here?"

"Closing up. Selling out." The Crow looked tired and disgusted. "Your cousin wanted somebody to stay through the summer, at least until that developer brought her people out from California."

His expression hardened. "I'm not staying much longer, though. You'd better not, either."

"Doesn't look like I'm staying at all—at least not tonight. Phil went to Sheridan for another business meeting. He was supposed to be back by now, but his note said . . ."

"He didn't know when he'd be back." Frank's face creased in a leathery smile. "Or if he'd be back tonight at all."

Oh, great. "Let me guess. Our lady developer is good-looking, or at least built." Frank's smile widened. "So, Phil being Phil, he's off getting a little extra profit on his deal."

"One of them is, anyhow."

For the first time all day, Cassie laughed and meant it. Frank Yellowtail did that for people. He'd been the foreman at Twenty Mile for as long as she could remember, and his dry humor hadn't dulled with the years. Even these days, with jobs almost impossible to get here in reservation country.

So why was he planning to leave the ranch early?

When she asked, Frank's face closed up. Stepping onto the porch out of the rain, he took off his hat and just stared at her.

"What happened?" she asked. "Did Phil finally piss you off, or what?"

Frank shook his head, suddenly uncertain. She couldn't recall him *ever* looking that way. "Come on, spit it out. If Phil's done something, I'd better know. If it's something else . . ."

"Thought you'd remember. You were here often enough when it happened—just about branding time, usually. Every year."

He hesitated. "Only this year, there's no stock for it to happen to."

It was probably just the damp, but Cassie suddenly felt colder. She hadn't thought about the ranch's weird little secret in years—not since the '80s, anyhow, when that "harvesting" documentary had convinced her how bogus the whole cattle mutilation thing was. UFOs? Uh-huh, right.

Besides, what happened to cattle at Twenty Mile didn't look like the photos she'd seen in books.

Frank was right, though. Whatever it was did seem to happen every year at least once. At least it had when she was here, though her cousins had tried to keep her from finding out. And her uncle refused to let anyone call the vet when a carcass turned up.

"Oh, I remember, all right." She frowned. "But if Phil's sold off all the stock, then it couldn't . . ."

Something in Frank's eyes stopped her.

"Your cousin made a bad mistake," he said. "I tried to talk him out of it. Tried to get him to sell this place as a working ranch, but he wouldn't listen. The developer promised more money than any rancher could."

"And money's always been the big thing with Phil. I know."

Frank shook his head. "No, you don't. You don't know anything about what happens here every summer, and someone in your family should before it's too late."

He broke off abruptly, glancing up the road as though expecting Phil's car any second. Cassie looked, too, but all she saw was rain and darker clouds and thickening dusk. The lightning in the hills was getting closer.

Just the way it did every year, before the really bad night storms started. The ones that meant a missing cow or steer next morning, and her uncle walking in with his Don't Ask face.

Cassie took a deep breath, hearing her own heart above the rain pounding the porch roof. "So tell me about it."

"Not here."

Given Phil's temper, it made a lot of sense. Cassie nodded. "I've got to drive up to Bear Lodge anyway, and I'm starved. Meet you at the Lazy B in an hour?"

Thanks to the slowest desk staff of any Motel 8 in the country, it took her nearly two hours to get to the cafe. Frank's battered green pickup was still in the parking lot, though, and his face as she walked in looked more worried than annoyed.

"Any problems on your way here?" he asked, between bites of rhubarb pie.

"I didn't meet Phil on the road out, if that's what you mean."

His expression said it wasn't, but the arrival of a waitress forestalled questions. Cassie ordered herself a cheeseburger, side salad, and iced tea, then peeled off her windbreaker and slid into the booth. One foot kicked something lumpy under the table.

"Sorry." Glancing down, she saw a worn Army surplus carryall. "What's in that?"

"Evidence. I packed it to show your cousin, back in January. He said he didn't have time."

Knowing Phil, that wasn't all he'd said. Her cousin had moved off the ranch right after college and never looked back. Anything or anyone that interfered with his plans for success in L.A. (where he alleged-ly worked for an investment firm) got shoved aside.

"Well, I do," she said, wondering how soon she'd regret this.

Frank had never talked much about his ancestry or his culture, but this whole scenario reeked of superstition. Old native curses, or the Crow equivalent. The folded leather packet he dug out of his carryall didn't help.

But when she untied the rawhide thong, she found a stack of Po-laroid photos.

"I'd look at these *before* I started eating, if I were you."

It was good advice. Each picture showed a different carcass—some steers or bulls, some cows or heifers—cut up just the way she remembered. Unlike the well-publicized mutilations in Kansas and Minnesota in the 1970s, whatever got at Twenty Mile stock didn't limit itself to easily detachable extremities. Or even sex organs.

Instead, each animal had suffered a slightly different surgical fate. Some had their heads fully dissected with meticulous care, but nothing else touched. Some lay within a perfect circle of their own intestines. One cow had been found with her entire reproductive system laid out in some kind of pattern—one Cassie didn't recognize, though she was no stranger to comparative folklore.

"So what do you make of this one?" she asked, flipping through the remaining photos in search of similar designs.

The Crow foreman shrugged.

"I don't. Neither did my father, and *his* father was *Batce Baxbe* . . . what you'd call a medicine man. A man of power. Both of them lived in this area almost all their lives, and neither one ever saw anything else—even in a vision—that looked like that."

He glanced at the other Polaroids on the table. "Or that, either. Or *that*, though Grandfather fasted for weeks after it was found. He was afraid it meant something terrible, and wanted to know what."

Cassie picked up the black-and-white photo. It was one of the old-est, faded and badly stained. A label on the back read *20 Mile / June 22 / 1959. 2? 3?*

She was just about to turn it over when her dinner came.

Frank scooped up the Polaroids as the waitress set the food down. Cassie didn't ask for them back. She'd seen enough of the last to realize that 2? 3? meant that the photographer wasn't sure how many cattle had been involved.

There *was* a very distinct pattern to it, though. One she'd rather consider without a cheeseburger in hand.

Turning her attention to salad instead, she ate in silence while Frank dug a black loose-leaf binder out of the carryall. It bulged with photocopies and typed pages, some of which threatened to fall out as he opened it.

"Most of this was my father's work. He interviewed as many of our elders as he could, looking for memories of this area before reservation times. That's around 1870."

"But Twenty Mile wasn't even a ranch then!" said Cassie. "There weren't any cattle to . . ."

"The land was still here. There were buffalo on it. And Crow horses, until the government shot them all in the Twenties."

Frank paged past photocopies into yellowed typescript until he found one section marked with a paper clip. Reversing the binder, he pushed it across the table to her. "This is what I wanted to show your cousin—this and the photos, especially the bad ones." He indicated several lines highlighted in yellow. "I even marked up my father's transcript to help him understand."

Too bad Phil only understands money.

Still, curiosity started her reading. Back in the late 1940s, Frank's father had interviewed one Mary Iron Elk, who had a real imagination for an elderly Crow. Her description of a certain thunderstorm she'd seen as a small child camping with her family sent cold spiders down Cassie's spine. The camp had been on Twenty Mile land, of course, but that wasn't what made her reread so carefully.

Too many details sounded familiar. How coyotes hadn't howled for several nights before the weather turned violent—or afterwards, either, until the strange storms passed. How Mary Iron Elk claimed that she could *feel* the thunder underfoot at the height of the tumult.

And, of course, what her family had found next morning, less than a mile from where they'd slept.

Cassie looked up sharply from the page. "It happened to buffalo, too?"

"Buffalo and horses both. Buffalo if they were available."

"You mean the biggest animals around?"

Frank's nod suggested another question, but she wasn't about to ask it yet. Not sitting here in the old familiar Lazy B talking about events even UFOlogists would dismiss.

Instead, she made herself start on her burger while she still had an appetite left.

She also read on, checking out other highlighted sections. Phrases like *In the longest days. When the earth speaks to the sky. When the earth speaks to the sky, and the sky answers.* And then, on another page even further back, one phrase underlined in faded red pencil: *The Ones Who Come.*

She coughed as a bite caught halfway down. "Did you underline this, Frank?"

"My father did." He looked intensely uncomfortable, but Cassie waited until he went on. "It was something he heard several times, but only from the very oldest people he interviewed. Men so old they were living in visions."

"So he never was sure what it meant?"

"Something like that." Another silence, stretching until she flipped back to his own highlighting. "The *longest days* are around the summer solstice, of course. *When the earth speaks to the sky* . . . is that tremor that sometimes comes with the thunder."

"Or before the thunder."

Frank looked at her with surprise and relief. "You've felt it?"

She nodded. It was another thing she'd learned not to mention at Twenty Mile—at first because her cousins laughed at her, later because her uncle didn't. She'd probably felt an aftershock from some West Coast quake, he said, and what was she doing up that late anyhow when she had chores in the morning?

"The sky answers in the lightning and thunder," she said. "That much makes sense—but how does the earth 'speak' in the first place? And why haven't more people noticed? Bear Lodge isn't that far away."

Frank looked grim and reached for the binder.

"My father wondered that, too. He spent a lot of time mapping individual incidents—where people saw and felt what as well as where carcasses were found—and he came up with this." He turned to a photocopied map of the Twenty Mile area. It was peppered with pencil marks, but a single red pencil circle enclosed them all.

There was a blue ink X near the center of that circle. A little square had been drawn in pencil beside it, almost touching it.

Frank touched the square with a fingertip. "You know what that is, don't you?"

"The house." She frowned. "But there wasn't anything else there before it was built. I've seen old pictures. No rock formations, no trading posts, nothing." Her attention shifted to the X. "So what's that supposed to be?"

He didn't answer immediately. He just let her study the map for a while before he put it and the binder away.

"It's the epicenter, isn't it?" *Epicenter* felt like a good safe scientific word. Epicenters were only points—mathematical centers of events. They weren't really things in and of themselves.

But Frank shook his head.

"It's more like an actual source. Or a focus. And it's underground—a long way down, but reachable." He hesitated. "I'll take you there tomorrow, if you want to see it."

His eyes met hers directly. " I think you should."

The slick red vinyl booths of the Lazy B seemed to close in around her, trapping her in a situation—no, a reality—she felt ill-prepared to cope with. Frank Yellowtail had never given her any reason to distrust him. Nor had he ever shown any sign of an overactive imagination, let alone the superstitious paranoia of the past several minutes.

Maybe it wasn't paranoia. Maybe it was early Alzheimer's. Frank wasn't young—and when he had been, he'd spent some wild years on the rodeo circuit. It could be another kind of brain damage from landing on his head too often.

Or maybe there *was* something under the earth of Twenty Mile. If Frank was right, it had been there a long time, killing buffalo and horses and cattle at a very specific time of year, in a gruesome and distinctive way.

And her cousin Phil hadn't even cared enough to hear Frank out.

"I don't know," she finally said. "What good could it do?"

The Crow foreman shrugged.

"Maybe he'll listen to you. Or maybe he won't, but at least *you'll* know. And if it's ever your decision to make ... about the land, I mean ... maybe you'll make it differently."

More spiders skittered along her spine. Phil never listened to anybody.

And if she understood the rest of what Frank was saying, she didn't want to.

"I've got one more piece of evidence," he continued, when she didn't answer. "It's not something I can show you in here, though."

He lowered his voice. "Did you ever see one of the carcasses up close?"

"Yes."

"Then you'll know if I'm telling the truth."

Cassie nodded, suddenly repulsed by her own half-eaten cheeseburger on its greasy plate. Signaling for their checks, she paid them both and hurried out of the Lazy B.

Outside, the rain had finally stopped. The air was still damp and clammy, though, charged with the dark energy of storms to come. Cassie felt goosebumps starting on her arms. When Frank came out of the diner, she was glad to follow him to the island of security light where he'd parked his truck.

Unlocking the passenger door, he took another packet from his glove compartment. Its leather wrapping looked old and badly stained, but a few worn beads decorated its rawhide thong.

"This was my grandfather's," Frank said, handing it to her. "He kept it because he hoped it held power against The Ones Who Come. Before he died, he told my father he'd been wrong."

Cassie's throat tightened. "Is this your evidence?"

Frank nodded.

She made herself open the packet—and bit her lip as she saw what it held. One large furry ear, a buffalo's by the size of it, still attached to a neat circle of hide. No bloodstains. No signs of violence at all.

"Turn it over."

Her fingers were trembling too much. Frank finally did it for her, revealing the underside of the ear's attachment. Not tanned hide, or dried sinew and flesh, but tiny rust-red crystals glittering in the light.

She poked at the ear with a fingertip. It still felt soft and flexible, almost warm.

Absolutely fresh.

"Oh, shit." She barely managed to hold onto the packet until Frank could take it from hers. "This *is* from Twenty Mile, isn't it? But if it belonged to your grandfather, it must be . . ."

"Over a century old." He wrapped up the ear quickly and put it away again. "Are you going to be all right?"

Depends. She started taking deep breaths, trying to bring herself fully back to the present. Out of the memory coiled like a rattlesnake at the back of her mind. *Crystallized blood.* Just the way she'd seen it sparkle in a heifer's gaping belly one morning at dawn, when she'd been out riding fence before breakfast. Alone.

Her cousins had told her the rest later. How one of them, on a dare, had stolen a piece of intestine from a kill he'd found years ago. How he'd kept it in his closet for a good six months before their mother found it and made him throw it away. It hadn't rotted.

After that, their dad made them help him bury kills like that. Even coyotes and magpies wouldn't touch the meat.

"I think so," she finally managed. "I guess I just hadn't expected that kind of evidence." She hesitated, gathering her courage. "And what did you mean about your grandfather being wrong about 'power'?"

Frank stared at her. "It has to do with visions. Most whites don't believe in—"

"I don't know what I believe in right now."

"After that bad kill in 1959, Grandfather began fasting for a vision. He kept the ear by him as a focus. Some link to The Ones Who Come, so that his vision would help him understand them." Frank's expression hardened. "Fight them."

"And?"

"He dreamed . . . a great darkness. And strange stars in that darkness, though he could never say what made them strange. He only knew when he woke that The Ones Who Come couldn't be touched by this world's medicine. They had nothing to do with this world, or its spirits."

The black overhead was suddenly much too close. Cassie shivered in her windbreaker.

"You still haven't told me what The Ones Who Come *are*. And I don't know what this epicenter's got to do with them. Or the mutilations."

She glanced down, away from the sky. "But I'll come take a look at it with you tomorrow."

"Thank you." Frank put the carryall in his truck, shoving it far under the passenger seat. "Development or no development, what happens on that land isn't going to stop. Someone in your family needs to understand that, before . . ."

She didn't ask before what. She just nodded and told Frank to call her in the morning. Today was June 19th, one day from the solstice.

And her gut said no coyotes sang tonight in the hills outside Twenty Mile.

The buffalo was a cow. Or it had been. Now it was sexless meat in the short prairie grass, its uterus wound into a fleshy flower blossoming from its open mouth. A long slit in the side revealed an artfully arranged cornucopia of organs glistening with dark crystals.

Only the animal's eyes marred the effect. Glazed with agony and panic, they stared up at the stars in dumb accusation.

Then it wasn't a buffalo staring up any more, but a Hereford's red and white mask.

Then it wasn't anything bovine at all.

Just female.

Frank had told her to meet him at ten, but Cassie had been up since four, drinking bitter black coffee from the lobby to keep herself from slipping back into sleep. And dreams.

The Crow's face as he walked out of the bunkhouse said she hadn't been the only one.

"Are you ready to go?" He looked less than ready himself. "The entrance is only a few miles out, but this may take a while. Time seems to . . . . change, down there. Especially when Their coming is this close."

She wondered down *where,* but kept her mouth shut. Frank did the same as he started his battered pickup. He'd insisted on hiding her VW in the barn nearby, just in case Phil got back before they did. No sense making him more suspicious than he was probably going to be anyhow.

Unlike most June mornings here, humidity was practically gluing her to the seat. The sky was hazy rather than clear blue, with a few clouds already massing over the hills.

Her ears strained for echoes of thunder as they drove off-road through the brush, past most of the ranch's outbuildings into a no-man's-land between living space and grazing land. Even during her teen summers, no one had come here often. Now it felt even emptier than the rest of Twenty Mile—aside from one corrugated metal shed that looked decades old.

"OK," said Frank, stopping the truck beside it. "We're here."

While she fumbled with her seat belt, he dug two flashlights out of his carryall and handed her one. "I checked the batteries myself last night, but I've got extras if we need them. Sing out if your light starts to fade. The dark down there isn't friendly."

Down where, dammit?

Her answer came when he wrestled open the shed's sliding door. There was nothing inside but a hole—a long, slanting hole with hand-holds of scrap pipe driven into the earth. Frank switched on his flashlight and stuck it through his belt before starting his descent.

"It's not really that far down. It just feels that way because of the angle."

Lovely. Cassie gritted her teeth and started down behind him, wishing she'd brought gloves. Who knew what biting, stinging, generally disgusting critters might have moved in? She'd already been warned that the dark wasn't friendly.

"Not like that," said Frank, when she finally asked. They were standing at the bottom of the handholds now, with a tunnel—underground riverbed, maybe?—still slanting ahead of them. "Nothing much lives down here. Or ever has."

She glanced at the smooth walls: no cobwebs, no burrows. The silent air smelled of nothing but earth and time. Though the ceiling was too low for them to walk quite upright, Frank scuttled along at a brisk pace. Cassie's back and shoulders soon began to ache, but she didn't care. It took her mind off the fight-or-flight alarms pinging all over her nervous system for no good reason.

None except the realization that they were headed back toward the main house—and the blue X on Frank's map.

The epicenter.

When a sickly glow appeared up ahead, a part of her wasn't even surprised. Gripping her flashlight tighter, she waited in the dimness while Frank moved on, scouting a cavern ahead for something she wasn't sure she wanted to ask about.

Whatever it was, he didn't find it. "Come on in," he called back to her. "I was right—Their time is very close, but we're safe for now."

Stifling serious doubts, Cassie stepped inside and felt her breath catch. The cavern's interior looked almost slick, as if it had melted once . . . and that glow emanated from the wall to her right. Or rather, from something sticking out of it: a rough, curved object which might have been stone except for the shadowy colors flowing under its surface.

Colors like nothing in nature.

"What is it?" she breathed, staring. "It looks like part of a meteorite, except—"

"So far as we know, it *is* a meteorite. Or at least something that fell from the stars. Nobody my father spoke to even had an ancestor who'd seen it fall. It's so far down, I can't begin to guess at when that was."

Frank hesitated. "Most of the time, it doesn't look like this. It just looks like a big rock buried in the earth."

Cassie barely heard him. Staring at the meteorite—or whatever it was—she'd started noticing other things about it. Like a subliminal humming that ran directly through her bones. And the way those shadows writhed beneath the surface, as though they were cast by something deeper in the rock. Something with many long fine extensions that coiled and twisted in the color currents, reaching up ever closer as though . . .

"Get away from there!"

An arctic shock ran through Cassie as Frank grabbed her shoulder, pulling her away from the wall. By the time she caught her breath, he'd dragged her outside into the tunnel.

"You almost touched it," he said in a tight whisper. "It . . . They
. . . wanted you to. You can't go back in there."

As if I'd try it again in this lifetime!

She took a few deep breaths to keep herself from heading right
back down that tunnel as fast as she could go—away from whatever
she'd nearly met and far away from Twenty Mile. Just thinking what
her relatives had been living above all these years made her queasy.
How could they have ignored it? Maybe they didn't know about the
meteorite (if it *was* a meteorite), but they'd known about the mutilations. And the silent coyotes, and the weird storms, and the tremors
that came before the thunder.

"Because it's good land," Frank said, before the question was half
out of her mouth. "Rich grazing land, and it always has been."

He hesitated. "A great chief said once that Crow country was good
country because the Great Spirit 'had put it in exactly the right place.'
When our people first came here and found . . . *that,* too, they tried to
understand it. To make it a helper like Grandfather Sun or the Morning Star, and gain its medicine."

He turned his flashlight's beam back on the floor of the cave. At
first, all Cassie saw was a scattering of beads and bright stones. Offer-
ings to something the first Crow had tried to worship.

Then Frank's light found the dull ivory curve of ribs.

"One or two young men tried to seek visions here. They came
down when they felt this place's power most strongly . . . the worst
possible time."

He switched off the light again, but not quickly enough. Its beam
caught the dark glitter of crystals streaking the bones. A second cold
shock galvanized Cassie's spine.

"I want to leave. Now."

Frank didn't argue. As they hurried back down the tunnel, though,
he kept up a steady stream of talk—warnings, memories, scraps of legend. Verbal force-feeding, she guessed. His last chance to tell her about
Twenty Mile, because he had no intention of staying there any longer.

He didn't want her staying, either. "Whatever Phil says, get away before sunset. Before the thunder. Get him away with you if he'll go . . .
but don't let him slow you down. This storm's going to be a bad one."

*   *   *

Her watch showed well after four when Cassie returned to the house, though she didn't feel as though she'd been gone more than an hour. Phil still wasn't back. Digging a novel and a candy bar out of her glove compartment, she settled on the porch to wait, trying not to notice the bruised color of the sky. Or the wind's wet-earth smell as it rattled the old roof.

By the time Phil's rental car finally pulled into the drive, it was nearly six o'clock.

Her cousin wasn't alone, either. A redhead in a white suit sat beside him, leaning closer than just business would excuse. As she swung long tan legs out of the passenger side, Phil hurried to help her.

Then he glanced toward the porch and scowled. "Your stuff's in the living room, Cass. Just give me a minute, will you?"

She gave him five to get his California developer out of earshot. Then she yanked the sticking screen door open, praying for the thunder to hold off a little longer.

Phil emerged from the kitchen with a beer while she was rolling up the last of three worn Navajo rugs. Her cousin hadn't bothered to bundle them for her. Nor had he wrapped up the half-dozen Tiwa pots waiting beside them, though it was easy enough to find old newspapers and a liquor box.

Then the first tremor came, right through the floor and stronger than any she remembered. Cassie almost dropped one of her pots.

Phil didn't seem to notice. "Find everything all right?"

"I think so." She hesitated. "Did Frank talk to you about . . . ?"

"Frank Yellowtail's a crazy old man. A troublemaker." The false twilight hid his expression, but Cassie could still hear it. "Has he been bothering you with that damn notebook?"

"No, he's been *showing* me his father's notes. And all the Polaroids, and . . . and that buffalo ear. The one with the crystallized blood, just like all the kills around here have."

Her stomach tensed with sick fear, but she made herself keep talking.

"Did he tell you how long it's been happening? Centuries. Always at this time of year, always the biggest animals available—buffalo, then cattle. There aren't cattle here anymore. You sold them off and now what do you think's going to happen?"

Phil took a long pull on his beer and shrugged.

"That's really what this is all about, isn't it, Cass? I sold what's mine to sell. You and your folks didn't get the cut you wanted, so now you want to screw things up. Scare off development so I can't make *my* money."

Another tremor came. Traveling up through her legs as she knelt on the floor, it reminded her hindbrain of thin strong tendrils that twisted in currents of color.

Tendrils like cold stinging knives. Like scalpels.

And God oh God They didn't even kill first before They did it, They just paralyzed the meat and went right on doing whatever They wanted, whatever They'd come here to do . . .

She hadn't remembered her whole dream after all. Not until just this minute.

Scrambling to her feet, she started packing wrapped pots into the box she'd found.

"I don't want your money. I just want you and that developer out of here, before something happens. There's nothing else bigger around here now, can't you understand?"

"Yeah, I understand." Her cousin took another swallow of beer. "Either you're lying out your ass, or Frank's got you *buffaloed* with his mystic Indian shit."

Cassie just stared. She could remember a younger Phil telling her about kills he'd helped bury, about his dad never letting anyone call the vet. Phil had seen a lot of things. He was sucking down that beer like mother's milk, but it wasn't enough. Right now maybe even the development money wasn't enough . . .

"Phil? Is she still here?"

The redhead's voice came from somewhere up the stairs—the bedroom stairs—to Cassie's left. One glance at her cousin told her she'd be wasting breath from here on out.

There were things even evidence couldn't compete with.

"She's just leaving," Phil called back. "Won't be a minute."

Draining his beer, he set the can on the floor and finally helped

Cassie pack the last of the pots. Then he opened the front door while she struggled with the carton. "I'll bring out those rugs for you," he said. "No sense making two trips."

It was the nicest *get off my property* she'd ever heard. Cassie made herself thank him as she hurried her pots outside. By the time she'd gotten them safely stowed, all three rugs were waiting on the porch.

And the front door was locked.

A third tremor—followed by thunder and lightning much closer than before—sent her running for her car with the rugs. Shivering, she locked all four doors, shoved her key in the ignition, and got the hell out of Dodge.

Twenty minutes later, the rain began in earnest—not gradually, but as though something had split open in the sky. What she could see of that sky between the laboring wipers was dark purple and twilight gray, punctuated by lighting that made her consider heading for a barrow pit on purpose.

When the earth speaks to the sky, and the sky answers.

It was answering so loudly and so often, she barely heard her cell phone under the seat. Cursing, Cassie pulled over onto the shoulder as quickly as she dared, hoping nobody rear-ended her in the process. Visibility was rapidly approaching zero.

"Hello?"

"This isn't funny, Cass. Why'd you do it?"

"Do what?" She frowned. Phil sounded half drunk, half seriously scared. "I only took what was mine and got out. What's your problem?"

"Car won't start. Looks like somebody tore out the coil wire. Plus slashed all four tires, just in case . . ." His voice broke up as thunder growled overhead. ". . . called out to the bunkhouse, but Frank's not there. His truck's gone, too."

Cassie's throat clenched.

"He told me he was leaving this afternoon!" she shouted back over the storm. "Don't know where he was headed, but I'm guessing Bear Lodge."

Her cousin's response nearly melted the phone. Hanging up, she sat staring out at the weather.

Frank had stranded Phil and the developer. She knew that beyond question—and worse, she knew why. Whatever The Ones Who Come were, he was mortally afraid of them. Of what might happen if They found nothing at Twenty Mile. How much further out would the mutilations range? For all she knew, Frank might have relatives nearby, on the reservation or in Bear Lodge itself.

But Phil was a relative, too. She didn't have many left.

Breathing deeply to steady her hands, she pulled her VW back onto the road, then into a cautious U-turn. The rain was coming down faster than her wipers could handle, but she switched to high beams and drove anyway. It was early yet. Barely sundown.

When the rain turned to shimmering, twisting sheets ahead of her, she gripped the wheel harder and tried not to notice. Tried not to imagine twining shadows where there could be no shadows. Tried not to see the wet highway ahead as a slick black mirror.

Then her cell phone rang again, sending her fishtailing across the road before she managed to pull over.

"Dammit, Phil! Do you know what you almost made me do?"

"This isn't Phil, Cassie." Frank's voice was a static-haunted whisper. "Did you get away from Twenty Mile?"

A sick sense of unreality washed over her. "Yeah, but I've got to go back. Phil's stranded—something happened to his car." *Or someone.* "I don't know how bad the storm is at the house, but he sounded—"

"Stay away from there. Just turn your car around and keep driving . . . please." His voice was scarcely audible, faint and old and tortured. "Do you think I wanted to do it? I had no choice!"

There were no words for that kind of necessity. And the rain was turning stranger now: she could almost see a *ropiness* to it in the distance, a hint of form inside those twisting sheets. Not shadows any more, but solid presence. Presences. Tall knots of wind-whipped shadow and color and energy . . .

"Are you all right?" crackled Frank's voice. "Answer me, girl! Answer me and get out of there!"

She barely managed the first part. The second was worse: slewing around on that wet black highway without losing control and without checking her mirrors. Or her back windows. Without looking anywhere but straight ahead into the rain.

Into the lightning answering the tormented earth and what came out of it.

Numbing her mind to a gray blank, she aimed her car down the road toward Sheridan and simply drove, not looking closely at anything at all. Not hearing the thunder. A dozen meaningless signs flashed by.

Then the little box she'd thrown on her passenger seat started shrilling again. When it wouldn't stop after a very long time, she turned it on with one hand and pressed it to her ear.

After a moment, she shut it off again.

Quickly rolling down one window, she dropped it out into the rain and kept driving.

EXPERIENCING THE OTHER

YES, I'M SURE it's not blackleg." Reaching across Dr. Saunders's desk, Cassie grabbed the Polaroid photo he was examining and laid it alongside the casebook of cattle mutilations he'd opened earlier. "Take a look for yourself."

Pulling a large magnifying glass from a drawer, Saunders did. As his frown eased, Cassie stifled a sigh. The fact that Saunders—the U. of Wyoming's resident UFOlogist (and tenured anthropology prof)—knew to ask about blackleg wasn't a good sign. Like the gruesomely illustrated book before her, it meant the man had been doing his homework.

People who did that expected results.

The famous '70s cattle mutilations in Minnesota and had ultimately been laid to rest by veterinary pathologists. A bovine bacterial disease known as blackleg attacked the same parts missing or damaged in "mutilation" finds: eyes, lips, and sex organs, mostly. It didn't account for carcasses drained of blood, or the surgical skill of the excisions, but such discrepancies were easy enough to gloss over. The public had a short memory.

Lawrence Saunders didn't. How he'd found out what happened around the summer solstice every year on Twenty Mile ranch, Cassie still wasn't sure—but some time last fall he *had*, and he'd been badgering her ever since.

"So is this a typical instance of the Twenty Mile phenomenon?" Saunders tapped the black and white Polaroid. "Something like this happens annually?"

Leave it to a true believer to pick the most extreme example. This particular phenomenon had happened in 1959, with either two or three cattle involved. Whether they'd been bulls, steers, or cows was anybody's guess. The applicable parts were all missing, and not because a coyote had gotten there first.

Coyotes wouldn't touch a kill like this. No scavenger would.

Cassie swallowed hard, fighting memories. "It's a yearly event, but generally only one animal is . . . taken." She forced a wan smile. "Sorry to disappoint you."

Please be disappointed. Please be so damn disappointed that you throw me out of your office. Tell me I've wasted your time or lied to you or anything you want, but cancel this morbid little field trip of yours.

Saunders looked at her curiously. He was a tall, balding man in his fifties, with the wiry build of an excavator—and the most intense blue eyes she'd ever seen.

"Disappointed? I consider reluctance a near guarantee of authenticity." The smile he gave her never reached those eyes. "You've been reluctant from the first, Ms. Barrett, though I'm not sure why. There'll be no damage to your property . . . aside from what you assure me would happen anyhow . . . and my offer is more than generous."

Cassie had to admit that it was. The several thousand dollars Saunders' study group was willing to pay for authenticity would just about fix Twenty Mile's tax problems, which was the only reason she was here.

Her cousin Phil had never paid the taxes at all. During the year or so after he'd inherited the place, he'd sold off its livestock and arranged to sell the ranch itself to a California developer. Where all the cattle money had gone, neither Cassie nor her lawyer had been able to discover—and the development deal, of course, hadn't gone through.

Not after summer solstice two years ago, when there hadn't been any stock around for what happened at Twenty Mile to happen to.

When the earth spoke to the sky, and the sky answered.

"I've got no problems with your offer." Glancing out his office window, Cassie saw that the clouds had darkened. Laramie's near-daily summer thunderstorm, right on schedule. "I just don't think going phenomenon-hunting up there is a terribly good idea."

"Why not? If I understand the evidence you've provided," he glanced at the pile of Polaroids and their accompanying binder, "we should be in no danger at all. There are cattle in the area, aren't there?"

Cassie nodded reluctantly. The small herd of Angus her neighbor had run at Twenty Mile these past two summers should have made her feel better . . . certainly their grazing fees did. Unfortunately, she could still remember most of the police report she'd read two years ago, after the authorities wouldn't let her see Phil's body. They'd sent Frank Yellowtail, the ranch foreman, to the morgue instead, then called California to have someone come out and identify the female real estate agent Phil had been with that night.

In the end, they'd still needed dental records to be sure.

"Of course there are," she finally said. "It's a working ranch."

"Which is what will *make* the experience." Saunders was on his feet now, blue eyes sparking. "Experiencing the Other is the goal of all anthropology, paranormal or not—but to find the Other in our everyday world is almost unheard of."

"Thank God," Cassie muttered under her breath.

Saunders ignored her. "This is just the chance my study group's been waiting for. I've been preparing them for years . . ."

"Preparing them for what?"

"To experience the Other with a truly open mind. No cultural preconceptions. No judgments. Just a totally receptive skull-vessel into which knowledge from Outside can flow unimpeded."

Cassie stifled both her gag reflex and a shudder. Though she'd attended UW years ago, she'd never taken any of Saunders's classes—but she knew people who had, and he hadn't changed much. Still the same soft-cum-squishy science approach, the same reek of New Age psychology. As an undergrad, she'd laughed and figured he'd done too many alternative chemicals in his youth.

Now she knew better. Not about the chemicals, maybe; but about Outside.

That was why she had to live up on Twenty Mile now, try to make it a working ranch again even though she'd only spent a few teenage summers there. Something from Outside had come to that part of northern Wyoming a very long time ago. Something that survived as the ranch's dirty secret, killing cattle the way it had killed buffalo before. The way it killed whatever was biggest and handiest once a year.

"I'm not sure that approach is a good idea, either." Cassie could feel her cheekbones heating up. "Sometimes the Other . . . isn't what you think."

Saunders laughed. "Isn't that the whole point?"

No, the point is that journal article you're going to write about Twenty Mile. The one you promised to write with or without my cooperation, only if I didn't cooperate you couldn't say where you'd be doing your research. Maybe wherever you heard about the mutilations to begin with. Somebody with access to state police files or the FBI or God knows.

The faint beginnings of this afternoon's storm rumbled through Saunders's open office window. Cassie rubbed sweating palms against her jeans.

She hadn't always been afraid of thunder.

"I guess so." She started gathering her evidence from his desk. The Polaroids went back into their folded leather packet, tied up with a rawhide thong. The massive black loose leaf binder—crammed with photocopies, maps, and typed transcripts dating back to the 1940s—got compressed as much as possible, then joined the photo packet in a worn Army surplus carryall.

"I'll be wanting copies of some of that material later," Saunders reminded her.

She considered holding out for a little extra in exchange for the copies, but decided against it. She felt sick and ashamed and scared enough already. No better than her cousin Phil, profiteering off Twenty Mile instead of taking care of the place.

Only remembering the latest IRS letter waiting at home got her through the next few minutes in Saunders's office. She confirmed his group's time of arrival, handed over driving maps, laid down a few rules about gates and garbage, then excused herself as quickly as she could.

Saunders didn't seem to notice. He was already on the phone as she left, effusing to one of his study group.

It was sprinkling by the time she left the A & S building. Cutting across Prexy's Pasture to the distant lot where she'd barely managed to squeeze in her aging Jeep Wagoneer, Cassie grabbed the strap of the carryall and ran. It felt good to run, almost like escaping.

Until another grumble of thunder reminded her otherwise.

Scrambling into the Jeep, she placed the carryall carefully in the passenger side footwell before digging out her cell phone to call Frank Yellowtail.

"It didn't work," she said as he answered. "I showed Saunders everything: your father's notebook, the Polaroids . . ."

"*All* of them?"

"Not last year's. Don't worry."

Bad as 1959 had been, at least that image was only black and white. What she'd found riding fence last year had been immortalized in full color, thanks to Frank's determination to continue his father's work. The expensive film worked too well: she could have done without capturing *every* nuance of her discovery.

If humans had done it, she'd have called the heifer's slaughter an act of violent frustration. Intestines—and other, less identifiable parts—festooned the barbed wire for yards, ending with the gutted carcass draped elaborately over a post. The interior of that carcass flashed bright rubies of crystallized blood.

"Maybe I should have sent it along too," said Frank, after an uncomfortable silence. "If that wouldn't make somebody stay home, I don't know what would."

"You don't know Saunders." *And what if it* was *an act of frustration? What if They weren't satisfied with cattle any more?* Cassie stifled sudden panic. "Anyhow, he and his study group have no intention of staying home. They're determined to 'experience the Other'—his exact words—and figure Twenty Mile's the perfect place to do it."

There was a very long pause on Frank's end.

"What's the matter?"

"Just the thunderstorms, I guess. And the coyotes."

The ones that hadn't howled in the foothills last night, and wouldn't be singing tonight either. Or at all until *it* was over. "Let me guess," she said. "Jupe and Juno are being squirrely, too?"

Barely a year old now, the Rottweiler siblings had been a gift from an elderly neighbor who couldn't handle them as puppies—never mind the black and tan monsters they'd grown into. They'd been a ton of work to train, but Cassie loved the massive dogs and trusted their instincts.

"They don't like the storms any better than I do." Frank hesitated. "I know it's a long road up, but I'd get home as soon as I could."

Next morning, zombified from the cross-state drive and a short lousy night's sleep, Cassie sat hunched at the breakfast table getting the rest of the bad news.

The IRS had called while she was in Laramie. Frank hadn't been around either—he'd been out with a fencing crew—and the message they'd left on the house machine had been just short of threatening. No matter how stupid and dangerous Saunders's little field trip was, she literally couldn't afford to stop it.

Besides, today was June 20th. There was no time to stop it.

Frank had also gotten a thick letter from his niece down in Taos yesterday. Though the girl was as Crow as Frank himself, she'd married a Northern Tewa guy last summer and now lived and worked on Taos Pueblo, leading visitor tours.

Frank had written to her over the winter while he'd been reviewing his father's notes. He was the third generation in his family to investigate what Saunders called "the Twenty Mile phenomenon"—and what the very eldest elders on the Montana reservation had known as The Ones Who Come. Frank's father had underlined that phrase in red pencil after interviewing several men and women who remembered pre-reservation times.

When buffalo around here suffered the same fate this ranch's cattle now did.

Those interviewees were all dead now, but The Ones Who Come weren't. Cassie had found that out for herself the night Phil and his developer girlfriend died, on a slick black stretch of highway between here and Sheridan. She'd been turning back for the ranch, reluctant to abandon Phil no matter what an asshole he was, when she'd seen something else in that sheeting rain. Or *somethings* . . . all tall and ropy and wind-whipped, twisting with colors nature had nothing to do with.

"So what did your niece have to say?" she finally asked, shaking the memories. "Did she get you the information you wanted?"

"More or less."

Frank looked as though he wished he'd never asked. After handing her the overstuffed envelope, he left to go get more coffee. Too shaky to need a refill herself, Cassie extracted the wad of folded papers, laid aside what looked like a personal letter to Frank, and started reading.

Frank had wondered if The Ones Who Come were unique to Twenty Mile, or whether any Southwestern tribes knew of something similar. His niece hadn't turned up anything at Taos Pueblo. During a recent visit to the Anasazi ruins at Bandelier National Monument, however, she'd stumbled across an intriguing petroglyph.

The glyph in question—a long twisted snake with an outsize head—was listed in a few references as Awanyu, or Father Awanyu. Further cross-referencing linked Awanyu to the feathered serpent common in Toltec, and later Aztec, art. Quetzalcoatl was its usual god-name.

Frank's niece (a frustrated anthropologist, apparently) hadn't left it at that, though. Tracking the Quetzalcoatl legend even further into the past, she'd come across a deity revered in both Mexico and certain remote parts of the Southwest. The Yig-cult was pretty much history now, but she'd found it mentioned in reservation agency reports from the early 1900s. It involved snake worship, guarantees of good harvests and hunting in exchange, taboos against harming reptiles—and a marathon drumming ritual which peaked at the autumnal equinox.

Equinox to solstice wasn't far enough. As for Yig himself, Frank's niece had thoughtfully included a photocopy. The original had been drawn in pencil by an elderly Pawnee in September 1902, trying to explain to a government agent why silencing the drums would be a really bad idea.

Frank's niece didn't say whether or not the agent had listened, but the sketch's thick twisting lines gave Cassie chills.

When Frank came back to the table, she had all the papers back in their envelope. He took it without a word. Then he drained his coffee in a few swallows and stood up briskly.

"I thought I'd start with putting a new padlock on that shed. Not that I don't trust the old one, but . . ."

Cassie nodded grimly. "I hope you got a heavy one that's not easy to pick. Saunders seemed a little too determined to have his experience—and I doubt he'd let a lock stand in his way. Not if something interesting was on the other side."

Frank's expression froze.

"Sorry," Cassie muttered, rising to clear their dishes away.

Neither of them needed reminding about how *very* interesting the shed in question—or at least the tunnel it concealed—was at this time of year. She herself had only been down there once. She almost hadn't come up again.

Located just outside the house environs in a no-man's land neither cattle nor people claimed, the corrugated metal outbuilding protected what Cassie called the epicenter of Twenty Mile's problem. Frank didn't call it anything that she knew of. He'd just taken her there two years ago, to show her the piece of Outside lying under this land.

Her land, now.

Shadowy alien colors flowing . . . squirming . . . under the surface of what should have been stone. What should have been just another chunk of meteorite, one more falling star over some ancient prairie, but it wasn't. Those colors didn't just flow, they writhed. And they hummed—right through your bones and up your spine, keening to something primal and terrible at the base of your brain . . .

"Cassie?"

Still clutching the stack of breakfast plates, she came back to herself with a start. Frank was staring at her. Even Jupe and Juno whimpered softly from their places under the table.

"Just thinking about that new lock. Excellent idea." She took a deep breath. "I'll start with the guest rooms upstairs, if we've got enough clean sheets. If not, I guess I'll start with laundry."

"We've got a couple of spare bunks in the bunkhouse, too." Frank still looked worried. "I just hope they'll stay put tonight."

"I already told Saunders I'd do the fence line and creekbed tour in the morning. All the usual sites—at least the ones you remember, or your father mentioned in his notes. Told him they could even bring cameras if they wanted to."

"Do you really think that's going to work?"

She'd never lied to Frank Yellowtail in her life, and this morning was no time to start.

The foreman smiled reassuringly. "Me neither."

*   *   *

There hadn't been enough clean sheets. There hadn't been enough clean anything. And the bedrooms—a whole big family's worth, not counting her own—all needed airing, smelling seriously funky even though mildew wasn't a Wyoming problem.

The way the air felt this afternoon, Cassie was surprised that it wasn't. Despite having every window in the house open, humidity still stuck her short dark hair to her forehead and temples. This morning's unusually hazy skies had clouded up right on schedule, and she could feel a thunderstorm's sullen energy building in the foothills.

Jupe whined at her from the foot of the bed she was making up. He hadn't left her side since breakfast—just as his sister Juno was sticking close to Frank, wherever he was at the moment.

"Good boy," she said, scratching his blocky head with one hand as she reached for the feather pillows on the floor. "Won't be much longer now."

Cassie wasn't sure whether she meant her unwelcome visitors, or the even more unwelcome annual visitation. She longed to tell him everything would be all right, but Jupe probably knew the truth better than she did.

At least this was the last of the rooms she had to prepare. Saunders was only bringing six people with him—two men, four women—and she'd managed to round up enough beds and cots to avoid using the bunkhouse. No sense mixing up this mess with the ranch's real business, or crowding her neighbor's wranglers. Said neighbor had been upset enough last June when one of his purebred Angus had gone missing.

Still, missing was better than what he'd have found if Frank hadn't spent most of that hot morning digging a very big hole with the Bobcat.

The telephone ringing downstairs nearly shot her out of her skin. Taking the steps two at a time with Jupe galumphing behind her, she reached the living room just in time to hear Saunders's voice on the machine.

" . . . just at the front gate now. We'll see you at the house!"

Judging by voices in the background, Saunders had several people with him in his vehicle, and they were all in high spirits. Excited, curious, utterly open-minded spirits.

Spirits which might be a real pain to keep indoors tonight.

Heading for the kitchen, she got a big pitcher of lemonade out of the fridge, put it on a tray with plastic glasses, and carried everything out to the porch. *Helloooo dude ranch. All that's missing is me in a ruffled gingham apron, and a chuck wagon ride before dinner.* Still, comfortable people were—she hoped—cooperative people.

A first spatter of raindrops pinged on the porch's tin roof. Glancing out from under it, Cassie saw thin streaks of lightning above the distant foothills, thunderheads clustering above and getting darker every minute. The sky closer in was the purplish-green of a fresh bruise, which usually meant a really nasty storm on the way.

Or another midsummer's eve at Twenty Mile.

Diesel fumes drifted toward her on the saturated air. Frowning, she glanced up the front drive—where an RV larger than some family trailers was making its way in.

Cassie swore quietly. Saunders hadn't mentioned this behemoth to her in Laramie, of course. As it wheezed to a stop in front of the house, she struggled to keep her expression pleasant.

Then the professor himself emerged—fairly vibrating with excitement—and all bets were off.

"What *is* this?" she said. "I just finished getting your rooms ready!"

Oh, great. No how was your drive, how about some lemonade, come in out of the rain. Just past the door screen behind her, she could hear Jupe whuffling uncertainly. She'd meant to shut him up somewhere safe before everybody arrived, but now she'd just have to hope the patched wire mesh held. Or that True Believers were also dog people.

Fortunately, Saunders seemed oblivious. Glancing up at the threatening skies, he smiled broadly.

"Excellent," he said, before dashing for the shelter of the porch. "This is the start of the phenomenon, isn't it?"

Cassie nearly dropped the glass of lemonade she'd been pouring. "More or less. It seems to be starting a little early, though . . ."

She glanced at her watch. Almost six o'clock. *Damn.* She'd lost track of time getting all those beds made, and now it really would take some doing to convince this group not to go storm-chasing.

"Actually," she corrected herself, handing Saunders the glass, "you're right. If it's going to happen tonight, this is probably the beginning of it." She looked past him at the others emerging from the RV. "There's plenty of time for lemonade before you get unpacked, though."

Saunders took a long swig and looked puzzled. "Unpacked?"

"We haven't got RV hookups here"—*at least I hope we don't anywhere*—"and I've already made up your rooms. I've got hamburger patties and all the fixings ready to go, too. Why be uncomfortable after a long drive?"

"I wasn't planning on it." Motioning to the group straggling toward them, he called out, "There's some good lemonade up here before we go on!"

Cassie's stomach clenched. *Go on?*

Before she could even start asking, the porch filled with excited, thirsty people. Saunders made introductions, though she was only able to fix on random details and impressions.

The other two men of the group looked like professionals—not business types, though—but only two of the four women did. One of the ones who didn't was very young, maybe somebody's daughter, and the other turned out to be the owner/driver of the RV. She was painfully thin, prematurely gray, and walked with one leg stiff . . . either crippled or prosthetic, Cassie guessed. The RV had a blue and white placard in the window.

Saunders laid an arm around the woman's shoulders as Cassie poured her a lemonade.

"Our benefactor," he explained, smiling down at her. "Without her dedication to the search for experience—unbiased experience of the Other—I doubt our little group would even exist. Certainly we wouldn't be enjoying your hospitality today."

The thin gray woman's face flushed.

"The search is its own reward," she said, "though I know you'd find a way no matter what." Dark intense eyes burned in a narrow face. "The Outside is very close here. I can feel it."

Cassie murmured something polite and turned away, biting her lip. The check Saunders had handed her the minute he arrived suddenly felt dirty in her pocket. How the weasel had done it, she didn't know—didn't want to—but he'd found himself and his gang of True Believers a real sugar mama. Disability case with a big out of court settlement, she guessed.

Not that she'd ever ask. The IRS didn't care.

And neither should you. Still, she felt her hands shaking as she poured out the rest of the lemonade. Anger, guilt . . . and something else as well. The sky beyond the covered porch was purplish-black now, the lightning closer. And the thunder when it came didn't sound like it had yesterday in Laramie.

"You folks ought to stay here tonight," she told Saunders as he stood staring out at the rain. "Camping out could get you all electrocuted, and there'll be nothing to see before morning anyhow."

He gave her a quick tight smile. A fanatic's smile.

"You think so, do you?"

Digging in his windbreaker pocket, he pulled out a penciled list: the locations of every kill on the Polaroids she'd showed him. She hadn't realized Frank's father—and Frank after him, evidently—had put quite so much information on the backs. Enough to let Saunders figure out just where the most kills had happened over the years, and rank the top five locations in order of frequency.

He'd circled number one and added a little sketch map.

Cassie swallowed hard. If this was their camp site, it wasn't nearly far enough away from the house—or at least that shed Frank had bought the new padlock for.

"The RV's got its own generator," Saunders went on, "so we're all set. It'll give us a place to prepare for our experience—and wind down afterwards."

"Prepare?" She wasn't about to ask about *experience.*

"Breathing exercises. Guided meditations. I've been fine-tuning our techniques for increasing cognitive receptivity. Methods for bypassing preconceptions of reality . . . achieving true openness to the Outside."

I just bet you have.

Cassie had her own suspicions about Saunders's methods, but

finding sniffer dogs on her doorstep wasn't her biggest worry. UFOlogist or not, this man had no clue about the Outside. He hadn't seen what it could do to living flesh—bovine or human—without thinking twice about it, assuming The Ones Who Come thought at all. She wasn't even sure what they thought *with*.

"Dr. Saunders," she finally said, dry-mouthed, "please don't go out there tonight. There is no way for you or anybody else to 'prepare.' I've been out in one of these storms myself, once, and I ought to know."

"Which only proves my point. You had the experience—and you came through it safely."

I wasn't being stupid, either.

Relieving Saunders of his empty glass, she added it to the stack she was collecting and turned away without another word. The rain was coming down harder now. And something—almost a throat-clearing sound—had worked its way into the thunder, prickling short hairs at the nape of her neck.

The thin gray woman was the last to leave, smiling beatifically at Cassie and waving as she climbed into the RV.

Cassie was still hunting glasses when Frank drove up with Juno. The young Rott scrambled out of the pickup's passenger door the moment he got it open, almost knocking her over with anxious affection. Grabbing Juno's collar, Cassie hauled her inside to join her sibling before giving Frank the bad news.

The foreman just shook his head. "Idiots."

She was about to agree when she felt the porch vibrate underfoot—a minor tremor, but answered by an impressive clap of thunder.

When the earth speaks to the sky, and the sky answers.

"Is that the first one?" she asked, when she got her voice back.

Frank shook his head. "I felt one about a half-hour ago, but I wasn't sure. Seemed too early." He glanced past her at the screen door and the two panting dogs. "Have you filled the hurricane lamps?"

Cassie nodded. Twenty Mile's electricity was reliably unreliable in thunderstorms.

"I'll be at the bunkhouse, but you know how the phone is out there—and cell phones don't seem to work any better when the weather's like this."

His expression turned even grimmer. "And whatever you do, stay inside. This is shaping up to be a bad one."

The lights went just after nine. Groping for the matchbox on the coffee table in front of her, Cassie lit the nearest oil lamp, then checked the shotgun on the floor. Two shells already loaded made her feel a little better. So did having Jupe and Juno nearby, though she wasn't completely convinced that either firepower or Rott power could stop what this storm was calling out of the earth tonight.

As another tremor started, she took a deep breath and tried not to wonder too much about where they came from. What so many tremors, so close together and so strong, might mean next morning.

Maybe there'd been worse thunderstorms at Twenty Mile in years past, but she couldn't remember the seismic part ever being this bad. Not even two years ago. It was as though the rules had changed somehow—or something critical had been knocked out of balance. Something that a few more butchered Angus wouldn't fix, and she didn't want to consider the alternative.

Reaching for the very large, very strong rum and Coke she'd made herself some time ago, Cassie took a long sip and barely resisted taking a second. Her imagination didn't need lubricating. Not with all the night noises of an old ranch house being magnified by this storm—and by her own memory of what the earth harbored.

Frank had told her once that the Crow believed their sacred tobacco had come from the stars. Or that one of their first ancestors had planted a star to grow it, she couldn't remember which. The sick truth was that something from the stars *had* planted itself here.

And once a year, it didn't stay planted.

She was going for that second sip after all when the floor vibrated underfoot. Without warning, Jupe threw back his massive head and howled, a deep painful sound torn from his body. Juno joined in on the chorus about a half-octave higher.

As the granddaddy of all tonight's tremors knocked Cassie sprawling across the coffee table.

The hurricane lamp beside her swung crazily in its frame, but stayed lit. Cassie stayed where she was for a moment, breathing fast and sweating hard, then pushed herself up and wrung rum and Coke out of her T-shirt.

She waited for the answering thunder, but it didn't come. Jupe and Juno stopped howling abruptly. Even the steady pounding of rain on the roof died away as she started lighting every lantern in the house, every candle she could find. Pushing back the dark didn't push back the silence, though. If anything, the cheerful flames intensified it.

This isn't how it happens. Heading for the kitchen to get a dishrag, Cassie felt her thoughts spiraling wildly. *These storms just don't stop. The sky keeps answering the earth all night long, then you find something butchered next morning.*

A furtive rattle came from the back door in the kitchen. She froze, listening for whatever breath of wind was causing it.

Then she tossed her rag in the sink and ran hell for leather back to the living room.

And the shotgun she'd left loaded on the floor.

Juno was already sniffing around the front door, her hackles raised high. Jupe paced from window to window, grumbling and snarling. Cassie's hands tightened on the stock of the gun.

There is no wind out there. The storm's over. She took a deep breath, willing herself back to reason. *Someone just wants to get in, and they don't feel like knocking.*

I've got to convince them that would be a real bad idea.

The front doorknob was rattling as she approached it, hard enough to shake the deadbolt. Cassie pointed the shotgun shoulder-high at the door and cleared her throat.

"Get the hell out of here!"

The knob rattled again, more violently.

"I've got both barrels loaded with 00 buck, aimed straight at your chest. You come through this door, you die. You try it, and I'll shoot through the door."

There was an almost tangible hesitation on the other side, and the sound of considerable weight—feet?—shifting on the porch's creaky boards. The rattling stopped. Juno still stayed close to the door, though, keening deep in her throat like her brother. Glancing back quickly, Cassie found Jupe at her back, eyeing the door as well.

"I mean it! Get the hell gone or I shoot!"

Silence. No creaking porch, no shifting feet. It was as though a burden had lifted from the air itself—sudden emptiness in place of a presence she wasn't sure she wanted to understand. The dogs' hackles were down now, and Jupe was licking bits of foam off his muzzle.

When her cell phone started squalling from the couch, Cassie nearly dropped the gun she was still clutching.

"You all right?"

Frank Yellowtail sounded as though he'd been running. Cassie frowned, relief and embarrassment washing over her.

Let me guess," she said, mentally cussing herself. "You just came out and tried to check on me here, at the front door." No response. "And I yelled a bunch of stuff, threatened you with the shotgun?"

Another long moment's hesitation.

"Cassie . . . I haven't been near the house tonight."

The smell of fresh-brewed coffee filled the kitchen, coaxing her exhausted brain back to life. Or some semblance of it. Slumped in her chair with both elbows on the table, Cassie wondered if Saunders and his True Believers felt as bad as she did this morning. Between tremors and prowlers, she'd almost forgotten about them last night—but they'd certainly gotten their money's worth out there, probably more than they'd counted on.

Maybe they'd settle for that and just head home today. Not likely, knowing Saunders. According to their agreement, she still owed his group a tour of the most likely "phenomenon" sites this morning.

If last night's storm was any indicator, she might as well skip breakfast.

Cassie's hands clenched around her mug. The more she remembered about that storm, the less she wanted to. That last tremor had felt a little *too* final: one huge convulsive effort as though something somewhere had just died.

Or been born?

Some analogies you really shouldn't draw on an empty stomach, black coffee, and no sleep. Setting down the mug with unsteady hands, Cassie wished Frank hadn't driven back to the bunkhouse last night after helping her search for that prowler. There were plenty of spare rooms here, but he'd insisted on going back to get started with branding this morning. Thanks to the whole Saunders fiasco, they were already days behind—and Frank wasn't the kind to let a neighbor down.

Once she finished this sick little scavenger hunt, Cassie meant to go help out herself. Muddy, bloody, and exhausting as branding was, it was at least firmly rooted in the real. She could use a dose of that.

She was contemplating a little more coffee when gravel crunched in the drive outside. Jupe and Juno, always enthusiastic greeters, galloped out to the living room in fine voice.

Then stopped short right in front of the door, bristling and snarling.

What the . . . ? Cassie hurried to peek through the nearest set of curtains. As she'd expected, it was the study group's big RV—with Saunders at the wheel this morning. As he climbed out and headed for the porch, Jupe growled deep in his throat and planted his front paws on the door, clawing frantically. Juno nearly climbed over her brother trying to do likewise.

"Knock it off!"

The usually obedient Rotts ignored her. Both dogs sounded desperate to get through the inch-thick solid wood, and Jupe was starting to froth again.

Ignoring cold spiders down her spine, Cassie repeated the command. Juno finally sat, growl turning to a deeply unhappy whimper. Jupe's feet came down from the scarred door, but he still stood snarling at it as Cassie walked quietly back into the kitchen.

The doorbell was ringing as she opened one drawer and took out a snub-nosed revolver. Slipping this into the back waistband of her shorts, she flipped the tail of her camp shirt over it.

Even as she headed around front to talk to Saunders, Cassie couldn't say why she'd done it. Keeping guns around if you were a woman living alone made sense. Illegal carry because your dogs were having fits was something else again.

But before last night, she'd never—ever—heard either of them howl.

"Good morning!" Lawrence Saunders stood on the porch looking at her curiously. The RV's engine was still running. "I was beginning to think you weren't home."

"Just out doing chores," Cassie lied. "Ready to go looking for a carcass?"

In the space of a heartbeat, Saunders's vivid blue eyes shifted. Changed.

At first, she tried to blame the morning light. Some weird interaction between contact lenses (*but hadn't he worn glasses before?*) and haze in the air and sunshine. Then those colors—not blue, not anything even remotely pupil-colored—started squirming, flowing and twisting over each other in tendrils that wrapped around (*just around, dear God, not around and clear through*) Saunders's eyeballs.

Then she blinked, and the blue was back. That same clear, direct, fanatic's gaze.

"I don't think we'll be needing that tour after all," said Saunders. "We've had our experience, thank you."

Perfectly normal words. Nice level tone of voice.

But she couldn't help noticing how they didn't quite sync with his lips.

Easing her gun hand behind her back, Cassie forced a smile. "Then I guess this is goodbye, Dr. Saunders. Will you be needing copies of those documents I showed you in Laramie?"

Something shifted again behind the blue. "That won't be necessary."

His lips weren't synching with the words at all now. As Saunders headed back to the RV, Cassie wrapped her fingers around the grip of the revolver. She kept them there as the vehicle drove away—though she seriously doubted even hollowpoints would do much good.

When she eased the back door open again, expecting to be greeted by frantic dogs, she could hear the phone ringing in the living room.

"Cassie? Cassie, where are you?"

"Here at the house." Now it was her turn to sound breathless, after a flat-out run from the kitchen. "Saunders didn't want the morning tour after all."

Frank made a faint relieved sound. "Have they left?"

"Just now. I watched them up the road." Stifled panic threatened to choke her. "What are you checking up on me for, anyhow? I thought you were with the branding crew."

"I'd planned to be, but I . . . found something on the way. You need to meet me at the tunnel shed, Cassie. Now."

Frank's faded green pickup was parked outside when she got there. Frank wasn't sitting in it, but she didn't notice that right away.

She was too busy staring at the peeled-back ruin of the shed's sliding door. The heavy corrugated metal looked as though it had been torn from its frame by an explosion—or maybe a tornado. What remained curled uselessly like a used toothpaste tube. The brand-new lock Frank had just put on lay several feet away from the door, still intact.

Nobody had tried to pick it.

Whatever had happened to the door had happened from inside.

Breakfast turned to lead in her stomach as she went back to her Jeep for a flashlight. By the time she'd steadied her hands enough to aim its beam into the tunnel the shed concealed—*had* concealed—Frank was calling to her from down below.

"What the hell happened?" Cassie called back, negotiating the scrap-pipe handholds at a reckless pace.

She didn't get an answer right away. Even when she'd reached the bottom of the long slanting hole to crouch beside Frank in the tunnel itself, he didn't seem to be in a talking mood. Instead, he headed further into the tunnel before she'd even caught her breath.

Cassie scrambled to rejoin him, but Frank knew this smooth-walled tube in the earth a lot better than she did. His people had either made it or found it—she'd never been sure which—a very long time ago, and some had made it their business since to keep an eye on what waited at the end. As her neck and shoulders started cramping, Cassie slowed down and concentrated on sweeping her flashlight beam across the floor as she proceeded. Whatever Frank had found down here, she sure didn't want to be tripping over it.

The air smelled strange, too. Not just earthy and stale, but vaguely chemical—nothing she could identify. Something like sharp ozone ran through it, though.

Ozone and death.

Frank waited for her at the mouth of the small cavern that lay at the tunnel's end. As she approached, he switched his flashlight off and told her to do the same.

"I thought you told me last time to never, ever . . ."

"I don't think it matters now." He sounded tired and sick. "Go ahead, just for a second."

When she did, the dark closed around them like a fist. Cassie switched her light back on quickly. "So what was that all about?"

Then it hit her. Two years ago, this cavern—or the star-thing inside it—had emitted a sickly bluish glow. Now there wasn't even a glimmer.

Aiming her flashlight into the cavern, she trained it on the wall where a large meteorite had once been embedded in the rock. Twenty Mile's own piece of Outside . . . except that it wasn't *a* piece anymore. Just pieces. Only a deep depression rimmed with jagged glassy shards remained in the wall. The rest of the meteorite had blown violently outward, shattering itself to shrapnel.

But that shrapnel hadn't done what lay on the floor a few feet away.

Staring in spite of herself as her flashlight's beam jittered over the patches of crystallized blood—the bizarre alien patterns twisted from human flesh and bone—her gaze fixed on an odd-shaped cylinder of taupe plastic lying apart from the mess.

The search is its own reward.

The Outside is very close here—I can feel it.

Turning away, Cassie clenched her jaws and swallowed hard. Frank caught her flashlight as it slipped from her fingers.

"I couldn't tell," he said, "but I think it's just one of them."

Cassie nodded. "The one they couldn't use, maybe." Bile rose in her throat. "Or didn't need any more."

Frank stared at her as she described her encounter with Saunders. Then past her, at the shattered remains of the meteorite in the cavern. A shadow crossed his lined face.

"Before the Yig-cult died, believers claimed that rattlesnakes were children of Father Yig—embodiments. My niece says that even now, some folks in her part of the country won't kill a rattler."

His dark eyes hardened. "The Outside is going to get in however it can."

PARADIGM WASH

Slumped at the kitchen table, Cassie Barrett scowled at her plate. Not that there was anything wrong with Sloppy Joes, mind you. What was wrong was eating them three nights in a row, because she was too worn out and it was too late to figure out anything else. Also too hot for July in northern Wyoming, even with a box fan stuck right in front of the kitchen window.

Jupe and Juno, sprawled nearby like twin Rottweiler rugs, grunted agreement. Twenty Mile had been home for these past two years, but it sure would be Home Sweeter Home with a little A.C.

Meanwhile, Frank sat at the other end of the table with his long plaid sleeves snapped at the cuffs, reading the day's mail and drinking hot coffee by way of dessert.

Cassie grimaced and reached for her Coke. "How can you *do* that?"

The question was rhetorical: Frank Yellowtail was born to do it. The sixty-something (seventy-something?) Crow had been foreman at Twenty Mile forever, or at least since she'd started working here summers as a teenager. Her uncle's family had owned the place then.

Two years ago, she'd inherited by default. Since then—for reasons she avoided dwelling on—she'd spent almost every waking hour making it back into a working cattle ranch.

A little over a month ago, those reasons had ceased to apply.

She still needed her neighbor's grazing fees, but Twenty Mile's dark secret was no longer her problem. It didn't matter whether or not something bigger than a human was available for the taking each summer solstice. Thunderstorms no longer haunted her dreams.

But a sense of being trapped did, even after she got up in the morning. Sighing, she finally picked up her fork.

"Dinner's not that bad." Frank Yellowtail glanced up from his letter. "At least, it wouldn't be if you reheated it."

Rather than taking his advice, Cassie pushed the plate away. "I don't need another Sloppy Joe. I need a cheap vacation!"

Frank's expression sharpened.

"Are you serious?"

"About a cheap vacation?" Cassie frowned. "Sure. Assuming I had time to check ticket prices online, or some idea of where I wanted to go—"

"How about New Mexico?"

"Sounds hot, but . . ." Her frown deepened. "You want to tell me what this is about?"

Frank nodded, but indicated the microwave. After Cassie's dinner was warm again, she returned to find several pages by her place mat. She riffled through them for the signature.

"So your niece in Taos really is an anthropology major?"

Frank nodded. She wasn't surprised. During their most recent troubles here, the girl had provided reams of information on snake-cults in Mesoamerica and the Southwest, including the worship of Yig.

"Grad student," said Frank. "She's mostly doing distance courses, since she got married last year, but her advisor got her into this two-week field school. Zia House, down by the Four Corners."

Cassie had taken a few anthropology courses herself at the University of Wyoming, but Zia House didn't sound familiar. She risked a guess.

"Anasazi sites?"

"Zia House specializes in Chacoan projects." Frank smiled at the look on her face. "Sound interesting?"

So far as she was concerned, Chaco Canyon was the Holy Grail of Southwestern archaeology. Its mysteries had fascinated her since college, though she'd done more PBS viewing than serious reading.

But if Frank was talking cheap New Mexico vacations—

"Are you telling me this field school is still open?" Snatching up the letter again, Cassie started reading more carefully.

Then she stopped, her grin fading. "They lost their accreditation? How?"

"Keep going."

Cassie started on dinner as she read. Zia House had been a well-regarded regional school, focusing on outlier sites north of the canyon. Dr. Magda Hudson, its long-time director, was a veteran of the 1970s' Chaco Project. The school had located several peripheral ruins since. Hudson wrote up her field notes promptly and published frequently—as did many of her graduate students, past and present.

Until last year.

The Zia House field school met between the end of summer term and the beginning of the new fall semester. Each summer, Hudson prospected alone for likely sites—and early last June, she'd hit pay dirt. While investigating a cave (or possibly an Archaic-period shelter) in the wall of a small wash, she'd found stonework lining its entrance. It resembled simple Chacoan, but with some startling differences.

She'd devoted last year's field school to preliminary work on this prize, calling it a "unique addition" to the canyon's known outlier communities. Her university didn't object. Hudson's instincts were usually good, and grad student labor was a time-honored academic tradition.

Early one evening, Hudson had taken two of those students on a mapping expedition deeper inside the cave. Hours later, bloody and incoherent, she staggered back to Zia House, scared some late-night TV addicts silly, and collapsed.

She had been alone.

Cassie whistled softly under her breath. "And they never turned up?"

"Not that anybody knows of." Frank looked dubious. "The university sent some people out the next day. Hudson showed them piles of fallen rock and a drop-off at the end of one tunnel. Claimed that the victims hadn't heard her instructions and took a wrong turn."

His expression darkened. "No bodies were ever recovered."

"So why didn't the police check things out?"

"According to Julie, the locals—including the one local cop—avoid that area. Ghost Wash, they call it—and they won't go near the cave, especially at twilight or dawn. Since neither victim had family making a stink, the university finally gave up and went away."

It made an ugly kind of sense. Cassie nodded. "And that's when Zia House lost its accreditation?"

"It's officially on hold, pending some explanation of the disappearances—though how that'll ever happen, nobody knows." Frank sighed. "It doesn't help that Hudson's colleagues aren't convinced about her find."

"Mind telling me why this field school is still being held? Or why your niece decided to bother going?"

Another sigh, deeper. "It's all in the letter. The short answer is that Magda Hudson has tenure. The university can't fire her outright, and they've got too much invested in Zia House to let it sit idle. Besides, Hudson's funding some of this year's work herself. Family money. She believes in the site."

"And your niece?"

"With accreditation problems, most regional students won't be attending. That money's gone, so the university isn't giving any of its own refunds if they cancel. Julie's advisor didn't find out until too late—or so she says."

Cassie rolled her eyes. "Of course."

"With the regional money gone, though, the program's hurting for cash this year." Frank's work-worn hands gripped his coffee mug. "That's why they're allowing a few 'qualified amateurs.'"

And you know I've had the classes and would love a chance at Anasazi fieldwork.

But that wasn't the whole story, of course. Family meant a lot to Frank Yellowtail. He didn't want his niece down there alone—and besides, she owed him. It couldn't be easy being foreman at Twenty Mile these days. Still, he'd hung in here, trying to help her straighten out the God-awful mess her cousin had left.

And the other mess, too. The one that wasn't their problem any more.

Cassie nodded. "Would I need a transcript?"

"Might not hurt, though I'm guessing the university won't be too picky. As long as you've got the check for room and board—"

"Plus some extra to order books. *And* the time to read them, get up to speed on Chaco." She sighed. "Know where I can find a few twenty-five hour days?"

It was close to sunset when she turned into the unpaved drive. Bone-weary after two days on the road, Cassie turned off the engine and sat, reluctant to open her door to the August heat. Her aging Jeep's A.C. hadn't been making much difference, but even those few degrees mattered.

Several other vehicles already occupied the dirt yard she'd parked in. Directly ahead of her, a rambling two-story structure painted white (though not recently) bore the words "Zia House" on a wooden plaque by the front door. Above this hung the most garish painted cow skull she'd seen since Santa Fe.

She slipped one hand under her seat before getting out. The item Frank had insisted on rigging straps for still hung securely concealed.

Road medicine, he called it. Trouble if she got pulled over, she called it—but two days alone on some of the most desolate highways outside Wyoming had given her a certain appreciation.

"Cassie Barrett?"

A copper-skinned young woman in jeans and a tank top emerged from the house. Cassie climbed out quickly.

"You're Julie Valdez?"

The girl nodded. Flipping back a waist-length braid of black hair, she started helping Cassie unload her gear, looking a little sheepish as she did so.

"I'm sorry Uncle Frank made such a big thing about you coming down. I just wanted to help the school break even. He'd said something once about you and the Anthro department in Laramie—"

"I've got my transcript, don't worry."

Cassie knew she sounded abrupt, but she did *not* want to discuss UW's Anthro department. Or at least one professor and his study group.

She wondered if their RV had been found yet.

Taking a deep breath, she made herself start over. "Sorry . . . I guess I've been driving a little too long." She glanced around the dirt yard. "Am I the last one here?"

"I think so—aside from Dr. Hudson. I haven't seen her myself yet, but a couple of her teaching assistants said she's been camping at the site for about a week. She's supposed to come in tonight, but nobody knows when . . ."

Julie glanced back over her shoulder. "Thanks for coming. I didn't want to tell Uncle Frank, but I wasn't crazy about being here alone after last year."

Cassie nodded, frowning. "So what *did* happen last year? I mean, I read most of your letter, but—"

"That's the problem. Only Hudson really does know, and nobody's sure what she told the investigators."

Julie's mouth tightened. "Knowing her, not much."

The two women headed inside. After dumping her baggage in an upstairs bedroom, Cassie returned to the kitchen, where an impromptu buffet spread across every available surface.

Grabbing a plate and silverware, she headed for a slow-cooker at the end of one counter. Despite the weather, hot food sounded good. Baked beans, she hoped, or—

"Better read the sign," said a male voice behind her.

Cassie flushed. A neatly lettered card in front of the cooker read HUDSON: PRIVATE.

Caught with one hand on the lid already, she took a peek. The savory aroma of hominy, chilies, and meat drifted out. "Posole is private?"

"No, but 'authentic ancestral Puebloan' food is—the chilies are hard to find, and wild-grown herbs cost a mint."

The speaker was about Julie's age, tall and lanky. "At least, that's the official story," he continued. "Hudson makes up a fresh batch every few days—for her health—but it's off limits to us peons."

Cassie dropped the lid back on. "Thanks for the warning." She eyed the rest of her options: sandwich makings, fruit, chips, cookies, and the remains of a bucket of chicken. "Is this typical?"

Her rescuer shrugged. "I only got here yesterday myself, but I don't think so. Some guy called McAllister is supposed to be bringing supplies from town—"

"And he's late." Julie appeared in the doorway. "Cassie, meet Mike

Fletcher. He took some classes with me last year. Mike, Cassie's the 'qualified amateur' I was telling you about."

Cassie shrugged and smiled. "Amateur, anyhow."

Helping herself to cookies, Julie headed back into the dining room. Cassie fixed herself a plate and followed, acutely aware of Mike watching her.

Only about a half-dozen people still sat at the long table. Most had already finished eating and were busy with notebooks or laptops. They greeted her politely, but nobody seemed to be talking much.

Seating herself opposite Julie at one end of the table, Cassie glanced past her at the old-fashioned glass display cases lining the walls. Pottery, effigy vessels, beads, and other artifacts filled most of them.

"All from Zia House sites?" she asked.

"Most of them, anyhow." Julie pointed to one case near the door. "That's got a few things from last year's dig, if you're interested."

To Cassie's disappointment, though, the case was nearly empty. Aside from a few potsherds, there were only two objects: a thumb-sized piece of carved turquoise, and a frog amulet of jet with turquoise eyes. The frog looked right—she'd seen one like it in a Southwestern art text—but the other object was unfamiliar. Had she been reading the right books?

"It's not locked," said Julie at her elbow, "but you'll need to wear these."

Pulling on the light cotton gloves she handed her, Cassie picked up the turquoise carving. At first glance, it resembled a Zuni fetish: a coiled serpent with a finely carved head, partly open mouth, and thin lines spiraling down its sides. Not what she'd have called Anasazi, but—

Taking a second look at the head, Cassie felt her breath catch. There was something not right, or at least not completely reptilian, about it. Something almost human about the curve of its skull, the way its mouth opened.

And the ornamental lines looked more like vestigial limbs.

Setting the figure down, Cassie drew a long shaky breath. The frog, at least, ought to be safe enough. According to that art text, there was one like it in the park museum at Chaco. Picking it up carefully, she laid it in her palm.

Definitely toad rather than frog, its jet surface was carved in lumps and bumps that shone greasily. Unlike the little snake-thing, there was nothing even vaguely humanoid—or even terrestrial—about its contours. The more she stared at it, the less she could imagine human hands creating such a bloated, twisted image to be adorned with sacred turquoise.

Yet it did remind her of the amulet in her book. Maybe she was just road crazy after two days on bad coffee and fast food—

"Try turning it over."

Mike's voice, far too close beside her. Cassie took his suggestion without replying.

Line after line of etching covered the amulet's belly. Too purposeful to be mere decoration, the writhing, jagged glyphs looked like nothing she'd seen in any museum. Certainly nothing Mesoamerican.

Besides, the Chacoan culture hadn't been literate.

When she pointed this out to Mike, he just shrugged. "All I know is what I've been told, and I was told that came from Ghost Wash last year." He smiled thinly. "Maybe we've got ourselves a whole new—"

They were interrupted by the front screen door banging open. As Mike faded back to his seat, Julie gestured to Cassie to shut the case.

Moments later, a wiry older woman with an excavator's tan appeared in the doorway.

"Is McAllister back yet?" she asked.

Students glanced at one another, visibly unwilling to get the man in more trouble than he already seemed to be in.

"I'll take that as a no."

Before anyone could respond, Dr. Magda Hudson headed upstairs. A few minutes later, she reappeared with her short hair soaked and a bowl of posole balanced on a metal clipboard. Propping the clipboard in front of herself, she ate in a swift, businesslike fashion.

By the time she finished, every seat was taken.

"Well," she said, crumpling a paper napkin, "it looks as though we've got a full two weeks ahead. More work to do, and fewer hands to do it . . ." She glanced around the table, frowning. "Which will make our days longer, but we'll manage."

Her frown deepened as she returned her attention to the clipboard.

"I'd also like to remind everybody that the university will be sending out inspectors at some point during this session. I doubt that we'll be given much warning."

Talk rose around the table. Most of the students sounded worried—except for Mike, Cassie noticed. Grim satisfaction tightened his lips.

Hudson let the clipboard drop from her grasp.

"We must take this as an opportunity," she told her silenced audience. "This outlier is very likely unique—a fresh perspective on the Chaco Phenomenon. I'm sure those of you who've seen the artifacts will agree."

Across from Cassie, Julie nodded nervously.

"What we have here is, in fact, an entirely new paradigm . . ."

Mike rolled his eyes. Cassie tried not to notice.

". . . which may well rewrite the literature of our field. I expect each of you to keep that in mind, particularly when the inspectors are here. No slovenly note-taking. No excavating outside your assigned area. And absolutely no freelance exploring."

Her dark eyes hardened. "This school can't afford another accident."

You mean you can't. Judging by the renewed buzz, Cassie guessed that almost everyone had suspicions about last summer. She wondered if any two theories agreed.

She also wondered why Mike was here at all.

"I want everyone awake, fed, and ready to work by six tomorrow morning." A chorus of groans responded. "McAllister will be driving the supply truck out, so there's no excuse for getting dehydrated or running out of artifact bags. Let's try getting things right this year."

Before anyone could protest, Hudson pushed her chair back and stood up.

"I'll be upstairs doing my notes. When McAllister gets back, tell him to come see me."

As she left, Mike rolled his eyes again and lowered his voice. "Welcome to Paradigm Wash," he told Cassie and Julie. "The few, the proud, the utterly confused."

His face went grim. "But something happened out there last year, and nobody's told the truth yet."

Bumping along the wash behind McAllister's faded red pickup next morning, Cassie wondered why Hudson had gotten everyone up so early. They certainly hadn't avoided the heat. By noon, she suspected, they'd be heading back to Zia House to collapse under the nearest swamp cooler.

It didn't help that her Jeep had been conscripted to haul a half-dozen people to the site. Most were still waking up, but a couple of Hudson's teaching assistants had downed enough coffee for gossip.

The subject, as it had been last night, was Daniel McAllister.

". . . about one A.M., and he just left the boxes on the floor. Eggs, milk, everything. Hudson wound up putting most of it away herself, and she was—"

"Did they get into it again?"

"Big time. It's going to be an interesting two weeks."

At least she could read between the lines now. Until one night on a rural New Mexico road, Daniel McAllister had been *Dr.* McAllister, tenure-track professor of archaeology and a Chaco Project colleague of Hudson's.

A few too many beers on the way back from a dig site changed all that. The elderly driver he'd broadsided came from a local pueblo. McAllister did five years for felony manslaughter, bargained down from vehicular homicide by a lawyer who cost him every cent he hadn't already been fined. Bankrupt, bitter, and permanently scarred, he spent another few years in menial jobs before the university made him caretaker for Zia House.

No one was sure how he'd gotten the position. Opinions ranged from compassion to suspicions that the former professor "had something" on either the university or Hudson herself. There had never been much love lost between those two, but their relationship had deteriorated in the past year.

Just what I need to be thinking about this morning.

Cassie quickly returned her attention to the landscape. Even in early morning light, Ghost Wash lived up to its local reputation. Aside from clumps of aggressive shrubbery clinging to the shadows of rocks, little grew and nothing moved out here.

And if the site itself really was a Chacoan outlier, she'd been reading the wrong books.

Dug into soft stone halfway up the wash, Hudson's so-called cave looked darker and deeper than any archaic shelter. Worn remains of stone steps led up to its mouth. The steps themselves were carefully roped off, but she could see eroded carvings on the broad sandstone slab which served as a threshold.

Emerging from her Jeep to help offload supplies, Cassie was astonished by the silence of the place. The still, bright air seemed to absorb human voices—not that her fellow students were particularly chatty. Once out of the vehicles, most either headed for their assigned areas or joined in with the unloading. Hudson went directly inside the cave, alone.

"She's copying inscriptions in there," Mike explained later, as they knelt on opposite sides of a remarkably unremarkable patch of dirt. "No cameras. No video. Doing it all the old-fashioned way, as if this was the Valley of the Friggin' Kings in the '20s."

Cassie peered at him from under her hat brim. "Is that a problem? Other than the fact that there shouldn't *be* inscriptions, I mean."

Mike just stared at her.

Embarrassed, Cassie resumed work with her very small brush. God, it was hot. Hotter than she'd ever imagined for New Mexico, and why had she been partnered with Mike anyhow? The guy was just plain uncomfortable to—

"It's a problem because everything she's done out here is a problem."

His voice was a near-whisper now, though no less caustic. "This site's been weird from the first. Nothing I've seen from last year looks Anasazi, let alone Chacoan, and caves weren't used much in outlier communities anyhow."

Cassie nodded, glad to have her own observations confirmed.

"You saw the glyphs on the black stone frog, right? Well, that same stuff is all over the walls just inside there." Mike jerked a thumb toward the cave opening. "There are more carvings, too, farther inside. Like that frog or toad or whatever the hell it is, but bas relief and much larger. Toads, and snakes . . ."

Cassie bit her lip.

". . . and something I'd swear was a squid, at least in the face. Hudson thinks it might be Moche influence."

"So late?"

Mike shrugged. "It's her brand-new paradigm, not mine."

Suspicion sparked in Cassie's mind. Aside from Hudson herself, nobody from last year's field school was here this season. She'd heard as much last night. How could Mike possibly know what the cave looked like inside, let alone what Hudson thought about its decorations?

He scowled at her question.

"Because my roommate sent me copies of his notes last year. Notes and sketches. He'd been helping Hudson clean off the carvings inside—"

"And he was one of the students who went missing?"

Mike hesitated, then nodded.

"He didn't have family—none he ever mentioned, anyhow—and the whole thing just got swept under the rug. I wrote the university a couple of times; never heard back. Never even found out what to do with his stuff."

"So, naturally, you signed up for Zia House yourself this season?"

He nodded again, his expression unreadable. When he picked up his brush, Cassie realized the conversation was over. Turning back to her work, she tried to avoid glancing up at the cave entrance. Part of her still wanted to believe this was a nice normal outlier.

But the artifacts she'd seen last night wouldn't let her.

They worked on for another sweaty, miserable hour before Hudson emerged from the cave. She was carrying her equipment bag and folding stool. Heading for the supply truck, she soaked a bandanna with water from its five-gallon tank and wrapped it around her head.

Then, without a word to anyone, she climbed into her own vehicle and left.

Cassie watched the dust swirling down the wash in her wake. "So," she asked Mike, "do you think she'll be back any time soon?"

He shrugged. "Watch McAllister."

Both of them glanced toward the red pickup. McAllister sat near it on a folding chair, doing paperwork. As the dust settled, he put down his clipboard and took out a cigarette, lighting up with obvious satisfaction.

Cassie grinned. "Is that a no?"

All around them, teams were putting down their equipment, getting themselves water or midmorning snacks. She headed down for a drink herself, bringing a second cup of water back for Mike.

He was heading for the cave's steps when she caught up with him. "What do you think you're doing?"

Mike took the water, but kept walking. Cassie glanced back. Nobody seemed to be following—or objecting, either. Maybe everyone else had already managed a peek.

Or they were more afraid of Hudson than Mike seemed to be.

The eroded sandstone carvings shimmered in the heat as they approached. Cassie knelt to examine them more closely, frowning as she recognized the coiled serpent from the artifacts case. It stretched full length here, like a petroglyph of Awanyu or maybe Quetzalcoatl—

"Hurry up, dammit."

Mike sounded more urgent than angry; more nervous than either. Scrambling up behind him, Cassie tried to stifle her own unease. She knew—or thought she knew—what that snake glyph represented. The Yig-cult had nothing to do with Chaco. It was ancient past ancient, and even Julie's research last year hadn't found its Mesoamerican roots.

Not as though any of that would matter to Mike.

Cassie knew obsession when she saw it.

Reaching the cave entrance, he slipped around the ropes and inside without a backward glance. She followed more slowly, wishing she'd thought to bring a flashlight. She'd expected at least a little sunlight to filter in, but somehow it didn't.

Taking a deep breath, she dug out her Jeep keys for the mini-light on their ring.

A few yards ahead, Mike turned on his own flashlight. Pocketing her keys again, she forced herself to join him. Though caves gave her bad feelings for good reasons, now wasn't the time.

Mike shone his light toward the ceiling. "Check it out," he whispered.

She glanced up. The stone overhead seemed to writhe in the unsteady beam, its deeply cracked surface carved into coils and tendrils and other . . . extensions of living creatures. Impossibly living. Neither deep earth nor deep ocean could have spawned such things, not on this world. Yet they gave no sense of being figments of some ancient imagination.

Glancing farther down one wall, she saw the glyphs Mike had mentioned. Lines and lines of them cut deep, unmistakably the same kind she'd seen on the toad amulet.

Not Mayan. Not Aztec. And something about their shapes almost discouraged translation.

"You're right," she said, when she could breathe again. "This site is weird."

"Oh, yeah," Mike said softly, moving forward into the darkness. "This is exactly what he wrote me about last year—that, and those big bas-reliefs. If I remember his notes, the first one should be right—"

His beam found it before either of them were ready . . . assuming anyone could be. Cassie had seen plenty of grotesque art in archaeology magazines—Aztec priests of the Flayed One, Moche blood-drinking ceremonies, graphic self-mutilation by various Mesoamerican elites—but it all faded before what stared out at them now.

It wasn't a squid, no matter what Hudson thought. Nothing like certain grisly murals in the Temple of the Moon.

Those, at least, had been created by humans.

Beyond this bas-relief loomed the shadows of others her mind was already refusing to see. Most particularly, it was refusing to appreciate the skill required to transform a mere bulge in the wall into the hulking mass of a toad-thing squatting above its—

"You all right?"

Mike's hand closed on her shoulder. With a start, she realized that she'd been standing there frozen, eyes tightly shut.

She managed a nod. "Mike, we need to leave. Now."

"Don't worry, Hudson won't find out. Even if she did, she can't risk booting anybody this year. We're shorthanded as it—"

"That's not what I meant."

He stared at her, confused.

"I know this stuff's pretty sick, but I figured you could handle it." His tone made her wonder how well *he* was handling it. "Julie told me you'd studied Aztec temple complexes—good old twenty-four-seven blood sacrifice . . ."

His voice trailed away as he realized she wasn't laughing.

So how do I explain why we've got to get the hell out of here? With sweat still trickling down her face, Cassie knew she couldn't. There was no way Mike could understand what these carvings were—at least what they suggested—because he was tone-deaf to the Outside.

She wished she could remember the feeling.

"Just tell me what you're looking for," she finally said.

Mike hesitated a moment, then nodded. "Fair enough. What I want to find shouldn't be that much farther in."

He started walking again, swinging the flashlight's beam in long arcs along the floor. "In his last letter before he disappeared, my roommate said Hudson was planning some preliminary mapping down a spur tunnel. He and another guy, one of her T.A.s, would be helping. Neither of them knew what she was looking for, but she'd said something about light."

"Like sunlight coming through a crack?" *Please, let it be that simple.*

"Colored light. The locals told her about it when she first got here, said that's why they call this place Ghost Wash. On moonless nights, the light even leaks out into—"

He stopped as his beam found a chalk mark on the floor. Beyond it to the left was a narrow opening in the cave wall.

"That's it. Come on."

Cassie grabbed his shoulder. "What about the drop-off? You saw what the ceiling looked like back there. Hudson said a collapsed ceiling caused—"

Mike snorted. "She lied. She lied out her ass, and I'm going to prove it. There was no accident. She took those investigators somewhere else, showed them a cave-in and made them believe it."

"You still don't like the looks of this place any more than I do."

When he didn't answer, Cassie swore under her breath. They weren't getting out of here until Mike had a good long look down this tunnel, whatever it was.

As he moved past her into the darkness, she dug out her Jeep keys again.

At first, the going was easier than it had been in the main cave. Except for the occasional glyph, the walls of this spur were unadorned and looked almost natural. The ceiling had some nasty cracks, but at least it wasn't carved.

Then she glanced down at the floor.

Several yards ahead of them, thin translucent coils seeped out across the rough stone. The substance was smoke-like, ebbing and flowing at random. Unlike mist, however, it had a color. Or it was developing one.

"Mike!"

He stopped so fast, he almost dropped his flashlight. "Now what?"

Cassie just pointed, letting him see—hoping he *would* see—how a shimmering blue light had begun spreading. Like the mist itself, it seemed to rise from just beyond their limit of vision down the tunnel. As though some inexplicable illumination waited down there, growing stronger—

Cassie's fingers tightened on her mini-light. As it flared to life, she spun and ran back the way they'd come.

Mike caught up just inside the cave entrance.

"What the hell was that about?" he demanded. "We nearly found it! The weird light all the locals told Hudson about—that's got to be where it's coming from."

Cassie blinked, recalling another cave where something from Outside had fallen long ago. There had been light and colors there, too—spiraling, swirling, strange beyond description.

"You're probably right," she said.

Then she walked out into the clean midday sun, determined to stay clear of Hudson's find from now on.

Next morning, Cassie requested a different field partner. Julie was happy enough to work with her, though Cassie had to lie about her reasons. Not that much of a lie—working with Mike *did* make her uncomfortable—but she wasn't about to tell Julie what he'd been looking for in that cave.

Julie figured that she knew anyhow, and glared at Mike every time he crossed her path.

Cassie tried to ease her own embarrassment by reminding herself that Frank Yellowtail had asked her to keep his niece out of trouble, not get her into it.

Hudson never said anything about the unauthorized cave visit, but Cassie suspected she knew—and guilt made her clumsy. After she nearly dropped a potsherd tray during an after-dinner sorting session, Hudson sent her to the kitchen to transcribe a stack of her own notes at least two inches thick.

By the time she'd finished, the rest of Zia House was quiet and dark. Powering down the laptop, Cassie stood, stretched, and turned for the fridge.

Then froze as she heard footsteps heading for the front door.

Was Hudson planning another after-hours mapping expedition? If so, was she alone? Cassie heard only one pair of feet, but someone else might have been sent out earlier, while she'd been typing.

The screen banged shut a few moments later. Switching off the kitchen light, she waited one breathless minute before heading toward the living room for a clear view of the front drive.

And of someone climbing into a fully loaded off-road pickup.

Cassie didn't need to see his face. Mike drove his pride and joy to the site every day. Cursing under her breath, she waited until his taillights had vanished up the dirt road before slipping outside. Her Jeep keys were still in a pocket of the camping vest she'd treated herself to before this trip.

When she switched on the ignition, though, only the starter sounded. No engine turn-over—not even its usual grudging effort.

With a bad feeling in the pit of her stomach, she popped the hood and climbed out to check the problem.

Her coil wire was missing.

Cassie stared, too disgusted to start swearing again. *Of all the arrogant, pig-headed . . . !* Mike was obviously headed back to that cave tonight, and he didn't mean for her to stop him. How he even knew she'd try was a mystery, but obsessive idiots were mysterious to begin with.

Closing the hood with more force than necessary, Cassie locked her useless vehicle and started back towards the house. If Julie was still awake, maybe she could borrow her Honda—

A light snapped on inside the big travel trailer parked near the drive. Daniel McAllister emerged moments later, heading toward her at a brisk walk.

Damn.

"Having car problems?"

"Obviously." Cassie hesitated. "I mean, somebody stole my coil wire. Unless you can do something about that, I really need to—"

"Throw your life away?"

His expression was unreadable, but McAllister sounded serious. "You were going after Fletcher, weren't you?"

"Mike? Only to keep him from doing something stupid." *And why do I think you already know that?* "Now I've got no chance of catching him."

McAllister shrugged.

"Doesn't matter. Fletcher's determined to find out what happened to his roommate—he told me himself earlier tonight. When I tried to convince him otherwise, he stormed off."

He hesitated. "I'm guessing he will find out. If he's lucky, he won't survive it."

Despite the night's lingering heat, a chill streaked Cassie's spine.

"I pulled that coil wire myself," he admitted. "I'll put it back in the morning."

Flaring anger drove her chills away. "I need it back now if I'm going to stop him. Mike has no idea what's in that place—"

"And neither do you, though I'm guessing you understand something about it." McAllister stepped closer, trying to read her face. "I saw you the other day, just after you'd come out. You were scared down to the bone."

"So what if I was?"

"So you showed one hell of a lot more brains than Fletcher did. Maybe you've seen something like this before."

When she didn't answer, he went on.

"I'll give you back that coil wire, but first you need to know what went on last year. What Hudson's so-called outlier is, and where it leads. If the Binger monograph is accurate . . . and from everything I've seen, it has to be—"

"*What* has to be?" Cassie wished she had a breathalyzer.

McAllister frowned.

"This isn't the place for that conversation." He glanced up sharply at one bedroom window, probably Hudson's. "If you'll come back to the trailer, I can show you the monograph—and a few of last season's artifacts, the ones she won't display. I'll tell you what happened out here, and you can make your own mind up."

This last sounded hesitant, as though he expected her to bolt. Or maybe yell for Hudson, though that was the last thing on her mind. Everything she'd heard about McAllister suggested he was strange— possibly still alcoholic—but the guy kept himself to himself.

Tonight, though, he wanted to talk.

Cassie figured she'd better listen.

McAllister's trailer was the old-fashioned kind, with the galley up front as she entered. The smell of coffee and recent cooking greeted her, but not a whiff of alcohol. A light burned over the built-in dinette. As Cassie seated herself, McAllister reached into his tiny fridge for two cans of Coke, passing one to her.

"Thanks."

It was all she could do to get the word out. Up close and well lit, her host's face wasn't a pleasant sight. A puckered scar dragged down the left side from temple to jaw, and his tan only enhanced the effect.

McAllister did a good job of ignoring her discomfort. Instead, he offered a worn manila envelope.

It bore a single line of typescript: BINGER, WESTERN OK 1928.

"You're welcome to borrow it," he said without preamble. "In fact, I'd strongly suggest that you read it tonight after you leave. It won't make you feel any better about that 'outlier,' but it may answer some questions."

Cassie frowned. "I thought that's what you were going to do."

Instead of answering, McAllister tipped out the envelope's contents: a thin, scholarly-looking pamphlet. The yellowed cover bore a title, but no author's name.

Cassie's frown deepened.

"An Ethnographic Analysis of Certain Events Associated with Earthen Structures in the Vicinity of Binger, Western Oklahoma in the Year 1928?"

McAllister gave a lopsided smile. "Makes you wonder why the author didn't come out and say what he meant—until you read it, that is."

Cassie opened the brittle pages at random. The text was faded, in a cramped old-fashioned typeface, but one phrase jumped out at her: *Yig, Father of All Serpents.*

"See something familiar?"

She was reluctant to admit it, but Cassie finally explained.

To her surprise, McAllister just nodded. "I figured you'd had some experience."

He slipped the pamphlet back into its envelope and handed it to her. "I don't know who wrote this—he made damn sure nobody could find out—but it's my understanding that he was an ethnologist specializing in American Indians. He published this privately, several years after the event it describes."

"Why privately?"

"Because no university press would touch it. Maybe because he still had a career to worry about, although I doubt it." Regret clouded his eyes. "Anyhow, the point is that these 'earthen structures'—only one mound, actually—are related to Hudson's so-called outlier."

Cassie's hands tightened around her Coke. "And you found this out how?"

"Same way you did. I went inside, more than once." He took a long pull at his own drink. "But after that night last season, when she . . . Well, I haven't been back there since."

Cassie hesitated. This whole conversation had that bad déjà vu she'd come to associate with the Outside. The information was coming too fast, and she wasn't ready for it.

"Why don't you start by telling me what that 'outlier' really is? If I knew that, maybe the rest would make more sense."

McAllister nodded. "Good question. You won't like the answer, though."

"Try me."

"It's a gate—or maybe a door—to somewhere else. Deep in the earth, but not *of* it, and older than anything you can imagine. Older than surface life on this continent." He hesitated. "Maybe this world."

Cassie swallowed hard. Though she desperately wished she could blame his wild, half-familiar theories on liquor—*maybe vodka, you can't smell that*—her own experience rejected such comfort. This landscape was empty enough to harbor almost anything.

And she didn't like the implications of *surface life*.

"How'd you figure this out?"

"It started when I was still with the Chaco Project. Every so often, I'd find things I couldn't explain—small artifacts, mostly. Metal ones, but no metal I recognized. Sort of dark and mottled."

He hesitated, pressing the cold can to his forehead.

"Turns out it's also magnetic, though the metallurgical lab I sent a sample to couldn't tell me any more than that. All I got from those tests was grief."

"How so?"

"Magda Hudson saw the results. We were sharing an office and mailbox at the time. She just assumed anything in that box was hers to open, no matter whose name was on the envelope."

He scowled. "First she demanded to know why I'd spent Project funds for the tests without filing the required paperwork. Well, I most-ly hadn't thought about it—but I also wanted to keep things quiet until I knew what I'd found. Some of the sites I'd been checking hadn't been cleared yet, and—"

"You were already in trouble?"

"Independent initiative is not an archaeological virtue. At least, not with federal money involved. I was following up a few local leads." He looked at her closely. "You do know what some Navajo clans say about Chaco?"

"I read a newspaper article once about how they thought it was an evil place. A sorcerer's nest."

"Exactly." McAllister smiled again, grimly. "Except that nest is ages older than the Chaco Phenomenon, and the sorcerers—if that's what you want to call them—came from the stars. From places we don't even have names for."

He tapped the monograph in front of him. "I didn't know any of that then. Hadn't even found this, let alone read it—but I'd already seen plenty. I'd been in the tunnels under a few kivas, the ones all the books say were for ceremonial dance. That's where I found most of those metal artifacts . . . and other things."

His smile faded. "There's a reason tourists aren't allowed in those deep places any more."

Despite the trailer's inadequate swamp cooler, Cassie shivered.

"So what's this got to do with what happened out here last season? How does Hudson finding out about some lab tests almost thirty years ago equal two missing grad students?"

McAllister stared at her like a man surfacing from a bad dream.

"The short answer is that she hijacked my research, after insisting that I explain everything—everything I knew then, anyhow—and show her the artifacts I'd had tested, along with my interview transcripts. At the time, she said I was chasing superstitions. But afterwards, when I wasn't around . . ."

One fingertip traced the scar on his face. "I didn't get the chance to clean out my office. Hudson volunteered to do it for me, and the university let her."

Cassie could fill in the blanks for herself. Hudson had been looking for her brand-new paradigm long before she stumbled (*was it really accidental?*) across that "outlier." When McAllister went to prison, she'd looted his unauthorized work, planning to pass it off as her own when the time came.

And now she thought it had.

"That still doesn't explain the grad students. Even if the outlier really is a gate to—"

"*K'n-yan.*"

The syllables hissed between McAllister's lips, sounding more alien than ancient.

Cassie blinked. "Where?"

"Underground. The monograph doesn't say how far, but it's possible to reach the place on foot. This cave is only one of multiple gates—the mound outside Binger was another—but they've all got one thing in common."

She didn't feel like asking.

"Those who go through them," he continued, "come back changed. Maimed, mad, or both—if they come back at all, that is."

He tapped the monograph again. "Whoever wrote this didn't go that far into the mound himself. Most of what he knew about K'n-yan came second-hand from a manuscript. A message left by someone else who wasn't as lucky." Beads of sweat broke on his forehead. "Whatever Hudson knows, she probably found out on her own."

Maimed, mad, or both. Dr. Hudson looked healthy, though she did obsess about her diet.

"And the grad students?" Cassie asked.

"Casualties of research." He hesitated. "That night, when she came back out of there . . . she wasn't alone. One of her students was still alive. When she got to Zia House, she found me, told me to go pick him up and find an emergency room."

He ran a shaking hand across his brow. "As if that would have helped."

"Where was he?"

"Just outside the cave entrance. There was no moon, but that awful blue light—have you seen it?—was pouring out. No trouble finding him." He wiped again. The shaking was worse. "But moving him—"

Cassie swallowed hard. "Spinal injury? Broken bones?"

He didn't answer her right away. Instead, he got up and went into the back of the trailer. She heard a door slide open, some digging around, then the door closing again. When he returned, McAllister handed her a shoebox.

"Open it."

Two sets of odd, double-looped devices (*handcuffs?*) lay inside. Their metal was strange, too: dark and mottled, the way he'd described those small artifacts he couldn't explain.

"These were on his arms and legs. What was left of them. God help me, I used them to lift him onto an old blanket, so that I could drag him back to my truck. I didn't dare try carrying him."

Cassie bit her lip. "And the emergency room?"

McAllister shook his head. "He died out there. I don't think he ever knew me, and he certainly couldn't have told me what happened. His mouth . . . nothing worked any more." He paused for a shaky breath. "Me taking him into town was out of the question. A felon showing up with a body—Hudson knew I'd have to deal with it on my own."

His eyes were hard now. "I got him as far away from that damned place as I could manage, way up in the hills. Piled rocks over him to keep the coyotes off. Hudson handled the university, and nobody else ever came out. The locals won't, and he had no family—"

"Was he Mike's . . . Fletcher's . . . roommate?"

"Could be." McAllister frowned. "Hudson picked two who wouldn't be missed, that's for sure. Once that so-called investigation ended, it was like neither of them had ever existed."

"Except for Mike."

He gave her a hard look. "Promise me you won't go looking for him."

When she didn't answer, he went on. "Fletcher's dead by now, if he's lucky. Once you've read the monograph, you'll know why. K'n-yan is older than Chaco, Mesoamerica, or humanity. The ones down there might look like us—if it suits them—but they aren't *like* us. Those things they call gods brought them down from the stars so long ago, they've even forgotten—"

"Gods?"

McAllister's gaze sharpened. "You saw them inside the cave. On the walls, on the ceiling—Yig and Tulu and the oldest one of all, He of Tsath . . ."

As his voice trailed into some dark silence, Cassie got up to look for her missing coil wire. When she found it on the counter by a bag of chips, she collected both it and the Binger monograph and headed for the door.

"I'm sorry," she made herself say, "but I've got a lot of reading to do. Thanks for the Coke."

The former archaeology professor didn't get up. "It's just too hard to believe, isn't it?"

Remembering other night skies, Cassie shook her head.

And left quickly.

Mike Fletcher wasn't at breakfast, though everyone else was trying not to notice. Not with Hudson at the head of the table with a massive mug of coffee and her posole, scribbling in her field notebook and apparently ignoring them all.

Cassie knew better. Bleary-eyed after too many hours reading in the deserted TV room, she'd stumbled over Mike's duffle and backpack in the upstairs hallway this morning. Before she could ask questions, Julie had pulled her back into their room.

"Mike took off last night," she said. "Didn't bother packing, just grabbed a few things and drove off in that truck of his."

Her expression darkened. "Must have had one hell of a fight with Hudson. He's never liked her—but I sure hadn't expected this."

Cassie rubbed her eyes, trying to focus. "This what?"

"Didn't you hear? Hudson came storming up here at oh-my-gawd-o'clock, woke up all his roommates and made them pack his stuff. Said she wasn't letting him finish here even if he did come back. McAllister's supposed to put his luggage in the shed after breakfast."

Cassie couldn't manage more than a few sympathetic noises. Her mind was too full of what she'd just read, and profoundly wished she hadn't.

Thanks to the monograph's unknown author, she knew now what might have happened to both grad students—almost certainly to the one McAllister found. Tsath in K'n-yan, decadent and terrible . . . the *curious diversions of the amphitheatre* . . . dead-alive *y'm-bhi* corpse-slaves . . . the hollow-eyed acolytes waiting with their knives . . .

Had Magda Hudson bartered two lives that night to save her own?

And if so, with whom—or what—had she struck that bargain?

Just as Cassie realized that even toast was a bad idea, Hudson looked up from her notes. Her mouth was set in a tight line.

"We will not be going to the site today," she said. "As some of you may be aware, there was a serious breach of the rules last night. Unauthorized entry into the structure itself . . . the responsible party endangered not only himself, but this entire program."

Hudson's eyes glittered in the morning light.

"As a reminder of the importance of proper procedure, we will be spending the day processing and cataloguing potsherds. I will also be examining all your field notebooks."

Disgruntled murmurs erupted up and down the table. Even Hudson's teaching assistants looked surprised, though they at least tried to hide it until she left. Then they shrugged, swore, and went to fetch the potsherd trays, leaving the others to clear away mostly uneaten breakfasts.

"Thanks a lot, Mike," Julie muttered to Cassie as they collected coffee mugs. "Just when you think things can't get any weirder—"

"Have a little faith. The day's just starting."

Her confidence was rewarded by a phone call after dinner. Hudson took it in the kitchen with the door closed, but everyone in the vicinity knew—or could guess—what had happened.

University inspectors were headed for Zia House.

Most of the students retreated to their rooms early that night. Concealing the Binger monograph in her field notebook, Cassie headed for the TV room instead. Finding it deserted as she'd hoped, she eased the door shut and continued reading.

Her attention was quickly drawn by a series of marginal comments in pencil. Beside speculation on the dietary habits of the (possibly mythical) residents of Tsath, McAllister had written *Cowboy Wash, CO?* Other notes referred to "Turner's book," and still others hinted at the disturbing contents of certain Anasazi trash mounds.

Cassie's teeth found her lip. If she understood the primary text, the beings who had once inhabited the underground world K'n-yan kept and bred somewhat less than human slaves as a source of—

Raised voices outside broke her concentration. Slipping the monograph back into her notebook, Cassie grabbed for the remote on a nearby table. Then she recognized the voices, and froze.

Hudson and McAllister were arguing again.

Curiosity wrestled with conscience and won hands down. Pulling off her sandals, Cassie tiptoed to the door and held her breath. The argument apparently concerned tonight's call—or at least how Hudson planned to handle it.

"They'll be here tomorrow, Magda. Not in a couple of days." McAllister sounded less nervous than insistent. "There's no time to find a convenient rockslide."

Even through the door, Cassie heard Hudson's breath catch. "I didn't say I intended to."

"You'll have to do *something* about this year's—"

"Situation." Hudson cut him off. "An unfortunate situation. One of our students chose to withdraw from field school."

Her former colleague snorted.

"You know why Fletcher went out there last night. I'm guessing he found what he was looking for, poor dumb kid."

"And I'm guessing you've had a few." Hudson's voice was sharp. "I have no idea what you're talking about, but Fletcher was a troublemaker. This school is better off without him."

"Really?"

The silence stretched toward a minute before Hudson replied.

"Let's be clear about one thing, Daniel. You have a decent job here because I made sure you got one. You're unlikely to find another. Unless you enjoy washing dishes or cleaning toilets, I suggest you let me deal with this."

"The way you dealt with last year's 'situation'?"

Whatever response Cassie expected, she was unprepared for what she heard instead.

Hudson laughed.

"Not exactly," she continued, over McAllister's protests. "But I'll go out and make sure everything looks right. *You'll* stay put here and keep the home front quiet. This time tomorrow, it will all be—"

The sound of McAllister's boots retreating down the hallway cut her off. Cassie held her breath, but all she heard after that were Hudson's lighter footsteps.

Then the screen door banging.

And later, much later that night, an ancient pickup heading away from Zia House.

Next morning at breakfast, one of Hudson's teaching assistants passed around her scrawled note. One by one, students stared at it and swore.

"We're supposed to spend the morning *cleaning?*" said Julie Valdez. "After potsherds all day yesterday?"

The T.A. looked uncomfortable. "All I know is what's in the note. Dr. Hudson is already out at the site, but she wants this place looking halfway decent before the inspectors . . . I mean, visitors . . . get here this afternoon. That means trash out, kitchen mopped, everything."

"Doesn't McAllister usually do that?" someone else asked.

Cassie's stomach clenched. McAllister's breakfast cuisine might not be imaginative, but it was reliably decent and hot. This morning, they'd been greeted by cold cereal and bottled juice instead—along with some vile coffee.

Hudson's posole pot had actually looked tempting.

"He's not here either," the T.A. snapped. "Obviously." He paused to sip his own coffee and grimaced. "We're on our own this morning, so let's try not to screw up."

Cassie exchanged worried glances with Julie across the table. Hudson's T.A.s were notoriously crabby, but she couldn't blame this one. His boss had gone off without warning, leaving him to pick up the pieces.

Definitely not a good mental image.

As soon as she possibly could, Cassie headed upstairs. Julie joined her in their room a few minutes later.

"So what the hell's really going on?" she asked.

Cassie told her what she'd overheard last night—omitting her earlier meeting with McAllister and any mention of the Binger monograph. Julie looked as though she knew there was more to the story, but listened politely enough.

"And you think what happened last year . . . might have happened again? To Mike?"

"It's possible."

It was more than possible, but Cassie wasn't sure herself what had happened—and what she suspected was nothing to tell after breakfast. Instead, she reached for the camping vest she'd thrown across a chair.

"So what are we going to do?" Julie demanded. "We can't just sit here on our—"

"No, but we can't both leave, either. Some T.A. would notice for sure."

It was a lame excuse, but Cassie couldn't think of a better one. "Look," she continued, "you're here for credit. I'm not. If I screw up, all I get is a fast ticket home . . ."

If I'm very lucky.

". . . but you could be in real trouble if Hudson catches you out there."

"Right now, I'm not sure I care," said Julie. "If you're right, isn't her career toast anyhow?"

Cassie groaned inside. She knew the sound of stubborn. She also knew what Frank Yellowtail might do if she got Julie involved, and she really didn't want to start looking for another ranch foreman.

"Probably," she finally said. "That's why I need you to cover for me. Get us both packed, if you can. I've got a bad feeling that we're going to want out of here fast when I get back—"

"With Mike and McAllister?"

"Hopefully." *I'm a lousy liar.* "Either way, I'd rather not have to leave without luggage."

Putting on the vest, she fished out her keys and tested the mini-light. It worked fine, but its beam looked terribly feeble.

"If I'm not back by noon," she told Julie, "just get out of here and head back to Taos." Her stomach clenched. "Please."

Then, without giving herself more time to think about it, she slipped out of the room.

Despite the morning heat, cold sweat beaded her forehead as she drove into the wash. McAllister's pickup sat only yards from the "outlier" entrance, looking sorrier than ever. As she got closer, she understood why: it was sitting on its axles, all four tires slashed. Ruined tread littered the dirt, and its plates were gone.

Turning her own vehicle around, Cassie drove back until the entrance was no longer in sight, then coaxed the old Wagoneer as far up into the scrub as it would go.

After killing the engine, she reached under her seat for Frank's road medicine.

The snub-nose .44 in its worn leather holster—only partially concealed by her vest—rode heavily against her thigh as she walked and climbed. By the time she reached the carved steps, Cassie was questioning her own paranoia. She'd done plenty of can-plinking with the revolver, but she'd never aimed it at anything else.

The wash's bright silence felt more breathless than it ever had, though. The way a prairie dog town got, just before that first sharp barking alarm—

Enough, dammit.

The area immediately inside the cave was as dark as she remembered. Pulling out her keys, Cassie switched on the mini-light to search for footprints. Everything looked clean . . . which made it even harder to start retracing the route Mike had taken just days ago.

Those few days ago, she hadn't read the Binger monograph. Hadn't sat with McAllister in his trailer, listening to his take on this place—this gate?—and what might have carved the bas-reliefs waiting beyond her in the shadows. The strange syllables of K'n-yan and Yig, Tsath and Tulu hissed and whispered in her mind as she hurried past, raising hairs on the back of her neck.

McAllister, at least, might still be alive in here somewhere. Why didn't she believe the same of Mike? *One of our students chose to withdraw from field school . . . better off without him . . . found what he was looking for, poor dumb kid—*

So far, though, she'd found no evidence that anyone had come out here at all. No sign of Mike's rig or Hudson's university truck. Nothing but McAllister's junker, which now looked like any other abandoned vehicle and could be explained as such. Whatever cleanup Hudson intended, she must have finished already.

Maybe she wasn't even out here?

As though in answer, a faint tendril of blue light snaked along one wall up ahead. Cassie glanced down. The chalk mark Mike had shown her lay only inches from her boot.

Which means he probably went this way again, if he came back. Before she turned into the narrow side corridor, Cassie slid the .44 from its holster for comfort. However crazy Hudson might be, she was still human—and probably unarmed.

Ahead of her, at the distant end of the corridor, more blue light seeped from what she now guessed was an opening in the floor. A clammy draft rose with it, brushing her face.

Recalling what McAllister had said about deep places, Cassie tightened her grip on the revolver. The draft had a smell to it, now, animal/musky/rotten all at once. She stopped, but could hear nothing: no breathing, no movement. No explanation for the stink.

Sickness rose in the back of her throat. She couldn't recall ever smelling anything so utterly *wrong*. Ranch life was full of interesting aromas, but what was natural (and the worst of it was) smelled natural.

This didn't.

A few yards further along, her mini-light caught the glint of stone chips on the floor. Bending to check, she felt raw edges sharp enough to cut—which suggested recent work. But where?

As she straightened, the screaming started.

It was a mindless, tongueless wail of terror, torn from a throat that might or might not have been human. Garbled words mixed with the shrieking, along with intermittent gasps and the liquid hint of blood.

Cassie froze. Another wail started up at once, directly ahead of her and to the right. Her teeth dug into her lower lip. What the hell *was* this? The pervasive stench she'd noticed earlier intensified as the noise went on—again, emanating from somewhere to her right.

No motion, though. Just the screaming.

You're not going to figure it out from back here.

Gripping the .44, Cassie took a step forward. Then two . . . three . . . and froze again as the shrieking resumed, very close indeed. Biting her lip, she flicked her mini-light's beam toward it with her free hand.

What she saw next made her wish she'd left the damn thing in her pocket. In her pocket in her closet in her room at Twenty Mile, where she should have stayed oh sweet God stayed and been safe, stayed and never seen what had unmistakably been Mike Fletcher. Or parts of him. Those parts required to scream and breathe and scream again, and not much more.

Her light still flickered off the raw edges of the niche he—it—sat in, but those white-blue eyes weren't tracking it. After one hideous moment, neither were Cassie's.

Dead-alive y'm-bhi corpse-slaves . . . cruel perversions of discipline and utility—

Her stomach doubled her over without warning. Barely managing to holster the .44, she clamped her eyes shut and turned away, spewing into the dark.

By the time she straightened again, the screaming had stopped.

And a dark form stood at the end of the corridor, silhouetted by the freakish light.

"Are you quite finished, Miss Barrett?"

As Hudson's voice reverberated, the thing which had been Fletcher began to whimper. Cassie fought back a resurgence of nausea. Switching off her mini-light, she drew a ragged breath and waited.

"Have you found what you came for?"

The question sounded as though Hudson didn't much care what Cassie had seen, or what she might have made of it. Reflexively, her left hand twitched toward the bottom of her vest.

Then froze as she realized her possible advantage.

"Not hardly. Where's McAllister?"

"Safe enough, for the moment." A small, strange sound—laughter?—escaped Hudson's lips. "I'd hate to deprive the amphitheatre."

Maimed, mad, or both. Cassie choked back bile.

"The university inspectors are still on their way." Her voice felt weak and unsteady in the darkness. "They're going to find—that. They're going to figure out what you've done, and when they do—"

"What *I've* done?"

Hudson lunged forward, as though trying to see her better. Cassie edged back.

"You have no idea what *we've* done," Hudson continued. "How we've waited down there since our world changed, since the ice and the oceans drove us back. Tsath . . . great Tsath in the abyss, city of endless dream and nightmare . . . it is all we have known for so very long. Until now."

Cassie's jaw clenched. The reverberations in that voice, she realized, were not entirely due to the tunnel. Multiple voices struggled to speak simultaneously, pitching themselves close to Hudson's ragged alto but never quite getting it right.

"We have attempted travel outside before. Mental projection . . . but there are serious limits. And the primitives in this region get alarmed so easily—"

Ghost Wash. Frank Yellowtail said the locals wouldn't go near this place between dusk and dawn.

"Better to remain hidden. No death . . . no time . . . only the unending curse of ennui, and the need for sustenance." As Hudson moved forward again, the blue light fell across her face. "Fortunately, we have learned to raise a variety of meats. So much more nourishing than the creatures of your surface world. Or at least, those you consider food."

Not going to ask. Not even going to think about it. Pebbles skittered under Cassie's boots as she backed up fast.

"McAllister didn't understand what he'd found." The reverberation eased in Hudson's voice. "Even hints of it unnerved him, so badly he turned to alcohol. Just as well. His weakness gave me—"

Us. The word did not emerge from her lips, but Cassie heard it anyway.

"The opportunity I deserved to make a difference in my field. To be noticed again. A whole new cultural paradigm, after all those miserable years since the Project. The unsuspected origins of the Chaco Phenomenon . . . revealed to me alone."

Ice traced Cassie's spine. "And you paid for it in blood!"

Her voice was loud in the tunnel, but she no longer cared. She knew the Outside when she met it these days. She knew what it did to those it touched—let alone those ignorant or arrogant or just plain crazy enough to try touching it first.

The laughter she heard this time didn't even pretend to come from Hudson.

"What a crude expression, Miss Barrett. Participatory research, please. There was a price, of course, but knowledge always comes with a price."

Hudson's drawn features fell slack for a moment. "Afterwards, it seemed so unimportant. I had my work . . . my true work at last . . . and all the time I would ever need to complete it. It may take years for my paradigm to be accepted, but I can wait. The physical evidence will speak for itself, and all my colleagues' bleating about Mesoamerican influences on Chacoan ritual will—"

But another sound had distracted Cassie. It came from inside that light at the end of the corridor: a scrabbling, irregular rhythm, like something clumsy—*no, definitely more than one*—struggling to ascend from a great depth. The stench she'd noted earlier was much worse now. It too emanated from that opening: a gust like wind from an abattoir, redolent with old corruption.

Then a shape emerged from the light. A long, low shadow, it dragged itself out from the edge with arms that seemed to falter with each effort.

Cassie felt her nerve failing.

"Dr. Hudson," she interrupted, "why the hell are you telling me this?"

But her hindbrain knew already. So did her fingers, finding the holstered .44's grip even as she backed away. The rhythm from below throbbed stronger and louder.

Hudson's mouth twisted in a smile. "Because it doesn't matter. You're never going to—"

"*Run!*"

Daniel McAllister's head and upper torso rose into the light, thrust up by one desperate effort. The rags of his shirt still hung from one shoulder, and his skin shone bare and bloody in that strange illumination. As his arms trembled with exhaustion, Cassie realized both his legs must be broken.

Or worse.

"For God's sake, run!" he screamed again.

As the sounds behind him rose to a crescendo, something Cassie could not see jerked him backwards and down. Still shouting, he slipped into the abyss.

Other shadows—hulking, strangely *incomplete* things—began to appear in the light. Hudson gestured them forward, still smiling. Her mouth was moving, but Cassie no longer paid attention.

Then the .44 was in her hand . . . both hands, as Frank had taught her . . . and her finger found the trigger.

Just as she fired, the Mike-thing's panicked shrieking filled the tunnel.

Her gun bucked high. As the bullet ricocheted from the ceiling, shards of rock showered down and Cassie heard a sharp loud crack. Then another, and another. Cursing, she tried to aim again, but shards were falling all around her now.

With a last look at the dead-alive horde advancing steadily, she holstered the weapon and took McAllister's last advice.

Behind her, larger and larger chunks of the tunnel ceiling rained down—and an ominous rumble underfoot made her wonder what else her shot had set off. At least she couldn't hear any *y'm-bhi* thudding in pursuit. Maybe the rockfall was taking them out, or maybe they were just too slow to keep up with sheer terror.

She had nearly reached the main part of the cave when a female scream sounded behind her. A glance back showed Hudson sprawled on the floor several feet behind her, bloody and pinned by what looked like a small avalanche. One arm reached out, flailing wildly. Cassie's breath caught. For a split second, she stopped and turned.

Until a larger chunk of the ceiling struck Hudson in the head.

Cassie stared a moment longer at the result, unwilling to believe the evidence of her own eyes. Then she began running again, stumbling, half-sick with fear.

The stark sunlight outside felt like another world. Nearly blind from her time in the cave, she squinted downhill—and was unspeakably relieved to see that Julie hadn't listened to her after all. She'd parked her Honda near their former work site and now stood beside it, waving.

Making no move to approach.

Scrambling down the roped-off steps, Cassie ran toward her. As the .44 banged against her thigh, she wondered how she'd ever explain it—let alone the stink of firing it still carried. *Too late to ditch it, though.* Taking a long breath, she forced herself down to a walk.

"Thank God you're all right." Julie stared at Cassie's rock-dusted face and shirt. "When I saw your Jeep up in the brush, and McAllister's truck—"

"Is my Jeep still OK?"

Julie looked startled. "Yes, just locked. But McAllister's going to be . . ."

Her voice trailed off as she noticed Cassie's expression.

"You didn't find him?"

Cassie just shook her head. "Not him or Mike." *Not in any way I'd ever want to describe.* "And there's been a rockslide in the cave—a major collapse."

"Dr. Hudson always said the place was unstable." Julie hesitated, frowning. "She was supposed to be out here this morning, but I didn't see her vehicle." The frown deepened. "If she got caught in that slide—"

Please let me be a good liar just once.

"If she did, I didn't see her. Or any sign she'd been on the site to-day."

She could feel her heart racing as Julie stared at her—but not, she noticed, at the holster half-concealed by her vest. It occurred to her belatedly that Frank Yellowtail's niece might have road medicine of her own.

For one crazy instant, she wished she could tell the rest of it: what had finally sent her running again, crazy mad with terror and disbelief. How one side of Hudson's skull had been crushed by that last rock fall, revealing the gleam of strange metal sunk deep in brain and bone. A slender, worked piece of mottled darkness, like some device she didn't want to understand.

And then, as though it had been dead a long time, how Hudson's body had begun to collapse and liquefy . . .

"You don't look good," Julie said finally. "Come on, let's get out of the sun."

Cassie's throat clenched. "Back to Zia House?"

Julie shook her head guiltily.

"The university guys showed up early, and they weren't in a good mood. They started asking lots of questions—digging through Hudson's records, hassling the T.A.s ."

She paused, wiping her forehead with a bandanna. "Finally, one of the T.A.s noticed they'd bought fry bread along the way. He suggested they have lunch before heading out to the site, and that seemed to calm everybody down. At least enough to let me sneak all our stuff out to my car."

"Lunch?" An awful suspicion crossed Cassie's mind.

"A whole batch of Hudson's posole. She must have made it last night. She's going to pitch a fit when she finds out, but there wasn't anything else." Julie looked even guiltier. "Besides, isn't it supposed to be authentic?"

Tlacatlaolli. Memory supplied the Aztec word even as Cassie's stomach recoiled. McAllister's marginal mentions of "Turner" had provided the first clue—from something controversial that she'd read while preparing for field school. The book's title translated that ceremonial term in plain English.

So much more nourishing than the creatures of your surface world. Or at least, those you consider food . . .

Mesoamerican influences.

Man corn.

Cassie nodded reluctantly. "Not strictly Chacoan; but yes, it's authentic."

Fishing her Jeep keys from a pocket with one trembling hand, she managed to drop them on the ground. Julie handed them back.

"Then we'd better get on the road," she said. "I hear the margaritas of Taos calling!"

Cassie wasn't about to argue.

—In memoriam Zealia Bishop

NIGHT OF THE PIPER

THE NIGHT WAS THE SNOW was the wind, and all of it howled. Barefoot and shivering, she stood alone under a broken moon whose face was not the clean silver she remembered, but a festering wound. Only desolation met her gaze: no huddled cattle here. No snow fences or barbed wire.

Only the wind's madness, and something worse twisting through it.

At first, it resembled the wail of an ancient flute . . . but voiced by nothing human. Nothing her mind could bear. Clutching both arms tightly about herself, she dug her teeth into her lip as a shadow coalesced from the night and the snow. It was a malformed thing, skinny and hunchbacked, and it capered as it played upon its instrument.

More shadows appeared in the distance. Slinking along the ground, whimpering and fawning, they crept toward the piper—and her—with gathering fire in their yellow eyes—

Whuff!

A gust of Rottweiler breath tore Cassie Barrett out of the dream. Gasping, she reached out with both hands and hugged two black-and-tan heads close. Jupe and Juno, still whuffling anxiously, began to lick her face.

Not again. Digging her fingers into fur, she held on tightly. *Oh, damn, not again.*

The gray light of a late November afternoon slanted across her kitchen table. Glancing down at the pile of mail—mostly holiday catalogs—her ranch foreman had just brought in, Cassie noticed a brightly colored flier. More junk. Frowning, she pulled it free and turned for the wastebasket—

Then stopped, her grip creasing its glossy paper.

There on the cover, in Santa Fe orange and turquoise, danced a creature far too reminiscent of last night's terrors. PIPER WITH A PURPOSE, the copy read. *Authentic Ancient Designs for a Stronger Community.*

Cassie flipped the paper over. To her relief, she found no more art, only details. A charity workshop project founded several years ago in the Four Corners area, PIPER WITH A PURPOSE offered job skills training, housing assistance, substance abuse counseling, and other services. Native Americans seemed to be its primary focus, but anyone in need was welcome.

COMING FOR CHRISTMAS! the copy promised. Now opening in SHERIDAN, WYOMING!

Cassie's stomach knotted. Sheridan was where she bought groceries and ran errands for Twenty Mile.

Her foreman glanced up from his own mail. "Something wrong?"

"Just junk."

Of all the people she'd rather not explain bad dreams to, Frank Yellowtail topped the list. Not that Frank wouldn't believe her. The grandson of a Crow *Batce Baxbe,* a "man of power," he had no trouble drawing correlations between the dreaming and waking worlds. Or between this world and other phenomena. The Outside.

In her three years here at Twenty Mile, Cassie had had her fill of the Outside.

Frank continued to look puzzled. Reluctantly, she handed the flier over. She did *not* want to admit to nightmares about Kokopelli, for Gawdsakes—

"You too?"

Cassie stared. Either Frank could read minds—which she couldn't quite believe, *Batce Baxbe* grandson or not—or he was confessing to bad dreams himself. Bad dreams about a tacky Southwestern icon.

Either way, it couldn't hurt to nod.

Her ranch foreman looked both embarrassed and relieved. "Not sure why, but I've had the same nightmare two or three times lately. The thing in them doesn't exactly look like this"—he tapped the flier—"but it's close. Same flute, same hunchback."

Cassie looked at the gaudy Kokopelli again. Did it even have a hunchback? At first glance, no. This was the smooth, cute, sanitized version from every tourist trap in Taos . . . then, a few seconds later, it definitely wasn't.

Blink. Blink. Shift.

She glanced away from the flier in Frank's hand. "Sorry." A hopeful thought struck her. "Maybe they've already got a billboard or something. We might have both seen it on the way into town."

Frank shook his head. "There's no billboard." He hesitated. "Maybe these dreams are what Grandfather used to call 'frostbite.' It happened to him a lot."

"Frostbite?"

"You get frostbite once, cold bothers you more for the rest of your life. You get close to the Outside—"

Cassie nodded, feeling queasy.

"Question is, what's a Kokopelli shop doing this far north? I thought he was strictly a Southwestern thing. Or at least, I hoped he was."

Frank shrugged, shoulder blades prominent under his denim jacket. Then he handed Cassie the flier and turned to leave. He still had horses to feed.

Or maybe he didn't like this conversation any more than she did.

After he was gone, Cassie poured herself coffee and sat down with the flier, Kokopelli side up. Blink. Blink. Shift—

Cursing, she flipped the image over quickly. She'd always found Kokopelli a little creepy, but the rock art image had never actually *frightened* her before.

Maybe anything Anasazi could spook her after last year's field school at Zia House.

Taking a big glug of coffee to banish memories, Cassie started reading. This PIPER WITH A PURPOSE was only the latest in a series of workshops, including one in the Santa Fe/Taos area. Frank's niece Julie Valdez, still working on her Anthro grad degree from the U. of New Mexico, might know something. If PWP was peddling "authentic ancient designs," it could be looking for academic inspiration. An e-mail was definitely in order.

Reading further, she found that PWP also welcomed what every other charity outfit did: cash and volunteers. Cash especially, of course, but extra hands for the holiday season were also needed.

Nothing like on-site research while giving back to the community.

By the time she finished, the windows were dark and both Rotts had joined her, looking for dinner. Cassie laid the flier aside with relief. Protective, intelligent, and uncomplicated, Jupe and his sister Juno deserved all the attention she could give. In her limited experience, dogs and the Outside did not get along—which had probably saved her life at least once.

After their meal, though, she'd fix herself a sandwich and hit the Internet. If she ever hoped to understand why Kokopelli haunted her dreams, she needed to know a lot more about him.

Hours later, she had all the facts anybody could want (and then some) about fluteplayer images in Southwestern rock art. Kokopelli was not one mythic figure, but several: Chu'lu'laneh at Zuni, sometimes; Ghanaskidi for some Navajo; Nepokwa'i for certain Hopi and Tewa. The sleek, genderless gift shop version came from Hohokam ceramics. Otherwise, Kokopelli was very male—with petroglyphs to prove it—when he wasn't shape-shifting into a locust.

Kokopelli was associated with rain, hunting, mist, snakes . . . and, big surprise, fertility. He was a shaman and a trickster, like Raven or Coyote. His image showed up all over the Anasazi regions of the Four Corners area, wherever people had lived.

Nobody seemed to know how old Kokopelli was. Some sources attributed him to the Anasazi or older tribal groups. Others linked him to Mesoamerica, possibly the Mayans.

And not one gave her a clue about her nightmares.

Staring down at the useless pile of notes on her desk, Cassie rubbed her stinging eyes and shut off her computer. If she wanted real answers, there was only one place left to look: at the bottom of her closet, in a box she'd rather forget about entirely.

Tossing boots, an old jacket, and an even older quilt aside, she felt her hands shaking as she hauled it out. According to its logo, the battered container had once held beer. Now it held the legacy of Daniel

McAllister, caretaker of Zia House—and former professor of Southwestern archaeology, contributor to the Chaco Project.

Former living human being. Or at least, she profoundly hoped he wasn't still alive.

Cassie had met McAllister a year ago last August, when Julie Valdez (and her uncle Frank) had convinced her to sign up for a field school in need of extra paying participants. Cassie had had enough Anthro coursework at the U. of Wyoming to qualify—and a fascination with the Zia House specialty, Chaco Canyon.

Frank Yellowtail mistrusted the school. Due to a couple of missing students the year before—and the director's inability to account for them—Zia House had lost its accreditation months ago. Unfortunately, this hadn't happened until after Julie's advisor had signed her up, and the university didn't give refunds. The more her uncle learned about the disappearances, the less he liked the idea of Julie being down there alone.

Even then, Cassie suspected, he'd caught a whiff of the Outside.

She had caught the same scent at that year's work site—which was also the site of last year's troubles. Just a small cave in the side of a wash a few miles from Chaco, but the school's director called it a "new paradigm" in Chacoan outliers.

Within the next few days, that paradigm had claimed two lives: another student, and Daniel McAllister.

She had found McAllister's box in the back of her Jeep while unpacking back at Twenty Mile. C. BARRETT PLEASE OPEN, it read on all four sides in black marker. Taped to the top was an envelope, also with her name on it.

Cassie had detached and hidden the envelope before carrying the box inside. Nearly a week later, she'd finally read his letter.

To Ms. Barrett, with my deepest apologies . . .

What followed was an account of McAllister's unpublished discoveries during the Chaco Project—and for years afterwards, though by then he had neither the academic credentials nor the cash to travel much. During their only real conversation at Zia House, he had hinted at Southwestern links to much older myths: older than the Maya, the Olmecs, or humanity itself in North America.

Maybe on the planet.

In several heavily annotated pages, McAllister laid out the evidence behind these hints. Tunnels under kivas, and the strange metal artifacts that he'd found there. Sketches of carvings from caves—not outliers, no matter what Zia House's director had claimed—where there should have been nothing. Inscriptions in strange, writhing glyphs, though the Anasazi were illiterate. Petroglyphs which tracked neither the sun nor the moon, but the rising of Aldebaran.

Myths from the stars. Mythic beings (gods?) from the stars, cross-referenced to texts Cassie had never heard of. At least she recognized a few names now: Yig, Tulu, Tsath-something-or-other. McAllister had included more sketches. Some resembled petroglyphs, though the articles she'd read on Southwestern rock art said such symbols could never be explained. They were mysteries, fading contacts with ancient spirituality—

What the hell?

At the bottom of the next to last page capered a sickeningly familiar form. Sketched from a petroglyph, it boasted an elaborate headdress of twining, writhing . . . feathers, she hoped. Like most Kokopelli images, this one's instrument formed an extension of its face.

Unlike most, this extension had a life of its own, twisting away from the flutist toward a crudely indicated group of other figures. Some had two legs, most had four. All the four-leggers looked canine.

The two-leggers were cowering away. Unsuccessfully.

Kiva tunnel wall, Casa R., Chaco, McAllister's marginal note read. *Poss. plastered over after creation? Binger p. 58—Nyar'la'a?*

Swearing again under her breath, Cassie laid the pages aside and opened the box. On top of a stack of field journals lay a worn manila envelope marked BINGER, WESTERN OK 1928. Inside that was a pamphlet.

An Ethnographic Analysis of Certain Events . . .

Her mind flashed back to that strange conversation with McAllister. He'd lent her this monograph overnight, telling her it might explain that "outlier" where two grad students—three, by the end—had gone missing. She never had the chance to return it. In the end, she'd just stuck it in his box and tried to forget it.

She couldn't forget her brush with what it described, though. *Tsath in K'n-yan, decadent and terrible*—an underground city older than humanity, populated by the degraded spawn of those beings from the stars. K'n-yan could be reached by many gates. One had been inside a mound in Binger, Oklahoma.

Another had been a few miles outside Chaco Canyon.

Cassie started flipping through the monograph. Page fifty-eight listed several "gods" worshipped in the very lowest . . . oldest . . . levels of K'n-yan. Yig Serpent-Father. Tulu, who resembled the Moche "Decapitator." He of Tsath, a toadlike thing less revered than feared. And, near the bottom of the list, Nyar'la'a: forms unknown, possibly infinite.

Messenger of the exiled gods, the anonymous author had noted. *Bringer of chaos and nightmare. Associations: ritual music, wild beasts, madness.*

She read the entry over again, closed the pamphlet, and slipped it into its envelope. Then she laid the envelope on top of McAllister's field journals, shut the box, and shoved it as far back into her closet as possible.

It was only after that that she noticed McAllister's letter on the floor.

Wincing as her conscience bit hard, she carried it back to her desk. She did not want to finish rereading it tonight. Daniel McAllister had not filled all those pages—possibly on the last night of his life—merely to answer her questions about Southwestern mythology.

He had done it because he had no one else to tell. No one else who shared his experiences with the Outside.

Nobody but the director of Zia House, who had embraced it and been destroyed.

Now the Outside might be sniffing around Twenty Mile again, and she didn't want to think about it. Better to keep on believing that her nightmares (*and Frank's?*) were random nuisances. PIPER WITH A PURPOSE was just another charity project selling Southwestern gifts—

A project out of the Four Corners area. Kokopelli country.

Nyar'la'a.

She didn't even know how to pronounce it, but the word made her skin crawl. Switching on her desk lamp, Cassie turned to the conclusion of McAllister's letter.

Well, Ms. Barrett, that's the worst of it, at least as much as I dare put down. I hope you'll find this useful. I hope even more that you'll never have to, but there are plenty of Magda Hudsons in this world.

She bit her lip. Dr. Hudson was the reason McAllister was dead now. Hudson and her brand new Chacoan paradigm.

Once you've seen these things for what they are, you can't ever look away. At least I couldn't. The world we think we live in now is just a skin—a modern skin—and every so often something else breaks through. Something too ancient to care about us monkeys, even if it bothers to notice us in the first place. Better it doesn't.

I doubt I'll be writing more field journals after tonight, so I'm handing these on. Read them or burn them, but for God's sake don't publish.

His signature was a ragged scrawl. After a few moments, Cassie folded the pages back into their envelope, then shoved the envelope behind the bookcase next to her desk.

But not so far she couldn't reach it again.

This time, there was no moon at all in her darkness. No suppurating sores of stars. There was only the glow of a newly kindled campfire, barely reaching the blackened walls of the cave she stood in.

Even so, pale images were beginning to manifest from those walls. Ragged and primal, more ominous than she had ever imagined petroglyphs could be, they danced in the air for a moment before beginning their slow spiral upwards.

As the flames below leaped to meet them, a too-familiar wailing began.

Pipers all, the maddening notes of these figures rose as they did—swirled as they did, higher and higher, toward some unseen point overhead. Each figure was uniquely malformed. Some capered on two legs only, some locust-like on six, others on writhing tangles of lines. Almost all were hunchbacked. Their instruments—less pipes than appendages—elongated and curled in the firelight, driving her into shadows.

As they reached the very top of the cave, the pale figures began to converge. Writhing limbs wound themselves around and through one another. Headdresses intertwined. The humps and bulges of a dozen bent spines deformed even further, curving as one.

And now, suddenly, that image-cloud no longer gyrated overhead.

The campfire illuminated one figure only: a twisted, still-shifting thing that did not shine in those leaping flames.

Instead, its very darkness diminished all light.

The music of its single pipe rose wilder than ever. Somewhere outside, a multitude of canine throats answered. The cave entrance that had seemed desperately far away before now felt all too near ... too full of unblinking eyes and crouching furred bodies. Belly-crawling like fearful pups, they pressed past her in the shadows, converging at the feet of—

Aroo! Aroo!

Jupe's voice and Juno's frantic tongue woke Cassie almost simultaneously. Reaching out at random, she grabbed Juno's neck and held on as she shook off the dream. Jupe stayed bristling by her second-floor window, howling from the depths of his heart at something outside.

Cassie bit her lip. Releasing her grip on Juno's ruff, she reached one hand under her bed.

The .44's snub nose caught on the carpet for one heart-stopped second, then came away clean. Swinging the heavy pistol onto her quilt, Cassie took several long breaths before getting to her feet and cocking the hammer back. Only then did she tiptoe toward the window, terrified and curious.

Jupe was quiet now, but he hadn't backed off and his hackles were still high. Parting the curtains, Cassie looked down.

The yellow eyes of a coyote stared back.

Wrapping her hands around her third mug of coffee that morning, Cassie slumped in her desk chair, staring at the e-mail on her screen. Julie Valdez hadn't wasted any time responding to the questions she'd sent last night.

Strange you should mention PWP up in Sheridan. We lost a lecturer to them just this past summer—she'd only been with the dept. 3 semesters. Tenure-track, too, but she got recruited and off she went. Said she wanted to do more for her people. Not sure whose rolls she was on, but it must have meant a lot to her. PWP wasn't offering squat for pay.

Like her uncle, Julie didn't mince words.

She said she'd been hired as a creative director, whatever that means for non-profits. She was interested in rock art—did a lot of documentation and photography between semesters. Maybe PWP wanted some fresh designs?

I'm not sure what she's doing up your way now. Nobody here's heard from her for a couple of months.

Cassie's coffee went to acid in her stomach. Relax, she told herself. Quit looking for trouble between the lines.

Still, she scrolled quickly.

I never met the guy who recruited her, but he must have been some salesman. The dept. secretary said he blew in like something out of a Hillerman novel—definitely on the rolls—and claimed he had an appointment. Went up to her office, talked to her for maybe thirty minutes, left whistling. She handed her resignation next day and was gone by the weekend. Didn't even finish out summer session!

I was pissed at her at the time—had to cover one of her classes—but later I got worried. She was always pretty passionate about her work, but that was it. Never drank, never partied. No boyfriend. I finally asked around the dept. until I got her address—a Sheridan P.O. box. No e-mail, even though she had a laptop.

I wrote her a couple of times, asking how the program was treating her. Got one reply on a postcard, then nothing.

Sorry I can't help more. Keep me posted, OK? PWP doesn't sound like a bad program, but I'm not sure what might be going on with this gal. Who knows, maybe she's the director there now. If you're thinking about volunteering, here's her name and address. Good luck!

Cassie took a long sip of lukewarm coffee. Then she wrote the name Julie had provided at the bottom of the PIPER WITH A PURPOSE flier and slipped it into her back pocket.

How do I not need this? Let me count the ways—

But first, she had a call to make.

It took some doing to get away from Twenty Mile unnoticed. Cassie didn't want to lie to Frank: lying to your foreman was a bad idea, and he'd always been able to read her way too easily. Still, it might be better for all concerned (including Julie) if he didn't find out about her going out to PWP—not until she'd started volunteering there.

After that, she hoped he'd understand for the sake of charity. Or curiosity.

Or frostbite.

The wind was screaming by the time she found the turnoff to the workshop. Grabbing the wheel whenever her old Wagoneer caught a gust, she bumped along nearly a mile of dirt track before reaching the site. Aside from another orange and turquoise Kokopelli—on a sign about twelve feet high—it was an unimpressive place, all prefab and trailers. The main facility might have been a tech school once. Several aging double-wides clustered nearby were probably PWP housing assistance.

Despite the weather, a couple of people in heavy jackets sat on the front steps of one of these. When she pulled up to the main building, they disappeared inside.

The brown paper bag they'd been sharing remained behind.

Cassie tried not to notice, though she locked her vehicle before heading inside. The wind nearly tore the front door from her hands— and once she'd gotten it shut, she wondered why she'd bothered. Heat didn't seem to be a high priority. She guessed they were using propane, and hoped to God that their system was maintained better than the rest of the place.

Plywood panels, more or less painted, divided the building's cavernous interior. The front section was office space. From the back came voices and intermittent noise from equipment, manufacturing or maybe packaging. Whatever it was, she wished she had earplugs.

"Need some help?"

A teenage girl edged around the nearest partition. She looked Native American or possibly Hispanic, rail-thin and very tired. Her grubby sweatshirt and jeans hung from her body.

"I've got an appointment to see your director about volunteering," Cassie said. "For four o'clock, but I think I'm a little early."

The girl stared at Cassie for a moment. Then she pointed down the hall (or what passed for one) with a skinny finger.

"Second from the back."

Before Cassie could thank her, she ducked back into her cubicle. Smoke from a freshly lit cigarette rose from behind the plywood. Mentally shaking her head, Cassie headed toward the back, noticing as she did so that some of the partitions featured artwork. Most of it was spray painted, with or without stencils.

Rock art images. Some she'd never seen in any archaeology magazine.

Lots and lots of very strange pipers.

She started averting her eyes, though she knew this was stupid. Sure, a few looked too much like McAllister's sketches, but his had depicted actual rock art. Maybe workshop artists had been practicing newly discovered designs on the walls here. Julie's missing lecturer might have supplied a few.

The second cubicle from the back had an actual door. Cassie hesitated, then knocked.

Strains of a solo wooden flute drifted out to her.

"Come in."

It was a male voice, well-educated and bland. Professionally bland. She pushed the door open to reveal a fully office-sized space, with Navajo rugs covering most of the cement floor. All the walls here were white, more or less. There were only a couple of bookcases, mostly empty aside from what looked like Anasazi artifacts and the CD player emitting the Native American music.

The desk itself sat far to the back in one corner. Like the door, it bore no nameplate—only a cardboard tent with MARCUS GRAY in felt-tip marker. An elaborately carved and feathered flute on a stand completed the desktop décor.

"Ms. Barrett?"

Cassie nodded and took the folding chair in front of the desk. The man watching her reeked of '60s-era social worker. Even in corduroy jeans and a sweater, she felt overdressed.

"I understand you're interested in volunteering for the holiday season?" When Cassie nodded, he drew a yellow pad toward him and began making notes. "Have you done community service work before?"

"Not since Girl Scout cookies."

Gray didn't react. Perfect non-judgmental mode. "How did you happen to hear of Piper With a Purpose?"

She described the flier, willing her hands not to clench in her lap. "I'm intrigued by Southwestern archaeology," she added. "Especially rock art."

Was that a flicker of interest in those faded eyes?

"This workshop is primarily about helping people in the present—answering the needs of the community. Helping our clients make better life choices. Most know nothing about the cultural symbols we use, though many of them come from that culture."

Not up here in Wyoming, I'm guessing.

"However, we do encourage them to explore spiritually." He reached out a hand to the feathered flute. "There's an incredible richness in these ancient cultures. The designs we use help to promote that, bring it into modern awareness."

One finger stroked a feather. "I think our clients are better for it."

The back of Cassie's neck prickled. If she'd learned anything about the Outside, it was that some ancient cultures should stay buried.

"They certainly seem interested," she finally said. "The wall murals I saw on the way to your office . . . I've never seen anything quite like them."

Not since my last nightmare, anyhow.

Marcus Gray brightened. "We're proud of those designs. All authentic—though you won't find some of them in the standard texts. They're recent discoveries from sites very much off the beaten path."

The folded flier in Cassie's pocket crackled as she leaned forward. *Now or never.*

"I heard you hired a creative director some time back. I'm assuming she contributed some of those designs?"

Gray's hand froze on the feathers.

"Dr. Lyn Trujillo, from the University of New Mexico." Cassie's throat tightened. "She's a friend of a friend. From what I hear, you were lucky to recruit her."

Or someone was. The man sitting across from her certainly didn't match the description from Julie's department secretary. He looked about as Native American as Cassie herself did.

So who was the mystery salesman?

"I'm afraid that arrangement didn't work out, Ms. Barrett." Disapproval crept into Gray's voice. "She only lasted a few months here. We can't afford to pay much, and the non-material rewards of the position weren't enough, it seems."

Cassie bit her lip. She hoped she looked embarrassed rather than alarmed.

Or suspicious.

"That's too bad," she managed. "I never met her, but I heard all about her rock art documentation. I was looking forward to seeing what she came up with for you." She hesitated, trying to sound hopeful. "Unless those mural designs in the hall weren't—"

"Some of them."

Whatever enthusiasm she'd seen in those eyes was gone now. Before she could ask more questions, Gray passed her a clipboard. It held a standard volunteer information form and a cheap ballpoint pen.

"Given our holiday rush," he said as she worked through it, "you're welcome to start whenever you wish. We ask for at least two-hour sessions, preferably at least twice a week."

Cassie agreed to start the next day, listed her preferred hours, and handed the clipboard back. Gray didn't rise to see her out.

Strains of his office music—minor, plaintive, disturbing—followed her down the hallway. The lights had dimmed since her arrival. One overhead fluorescent was in its death throes, flickering shadows across the murals. After the first couple of panels, Cassie shifted her gaze straight ahead and walked quickly, telling her imagination to shut the hell up.

By the time she reached her Jeep, she was losing that argument.

Sundown this time of year gave the wind an extra edge. Her numb fingers fumbled her keys into the dirt. Muttering under her breath, she crouched to retrieve them—then sprang up as footsteps thudded toward her from the main building.

"Hey! You almost forgot this!"

Before she could react, the skinny teenage receptionist thrust something at her and ran away, veering toward the cluster of double-wides. Cassie didn't even think about following. She unlocked her vehicle and slid in fast, locking all four doors before driving away at the maximum sane speed for conditions.

Thin snow had joined the wind by the time she reached the highway, snaking across it as she pulled over and flicked on her overhead light. The receptionist's gift—a battered blue spiral notebook—lay on the passenger seat.

Cassie flipped open the cover. *Lyn Trujillo, Ph.D.,* in shaky blue ink. *Her Dream Journal.*

Several hours later, fortified by a few sips from a stiff rum and Coke, Cassie switched on her desk lamp and took a deep breath. Trujillo's journal, she reminded herself, was no different from the serious weirdness McAllister had left her. It might be one more minor artifact, recording somebody's brush with the Outside. It might be nothing at all.

Blue spiral notebooks don't bite.

And even if they did, they'd be outmatched. Jupe and Juno had followed her upstairs after dinner tonight, just as they'd been doing every evening lately. Before that flier had shown up, Cassie had blamed the approaching winter solstice: cold darkness meant hole up with the pack.

Now she wasn't so sure. Maybe Frank's frostbite wasn't limited to humans.

Flipping past the oddly formal title page, Cassie found that Trujillo had started her journal in late August—not immediately after arriving, but while she still might have been in contact with Julie or other colleagues.

Gray says we are all "here"—who knows if he means PWP or Wyo. or this planet—to explore our spirituality, so here goes. For three nights now, I've been having the first spiritual dreams of my life. No clear details, just the sensation of something incredibly old & powerful. Sometimes I see rock art images, but nothing I can draw after I wake up. Not sure why the art's there, but isn't that how it is with dreams? I'm going to leave this journal by my bed from now on. Maybe sketching sooner will help.

Two days later, Trujillo sounded frustrated.

Still nothing. Nothing I can use for my designs here, anyhow. I've shown Gray all the books I brought with me—hundreds of petroglyphs & sketches—but he keeps asking for something fresh. Authentic but fresh. Says to get in touch with my own "deep understanding" of the culture this art came from, though how I can do that when the Anasazi weren't even literate is beyond me.

Gray asked me tonight how my work is coming along. I think he meant my dreams, partly—he asks everybody about their dreams, even the clients. Maybe he's a Jungian or something. Some of the clients really get him going. The stuff they come up with!

There were no entries for several days after that. Then, in the middle of an otherwise blank page, Trujillo had drawn a bowed tangle of lines with a single protrusion emerging from the right side, toward the top. Two more protrusions at the bottom seemed meant as feet.

The scribble was dated September first.

I hope Gray's happy, Trujillo had written on the facing page. *That damn flute tape—he told me listen to it before bed, so I did & what do I get? Same dreams I've been having off & on ever since I got here, but now they've got a soundtrack. Did manage to see one of the glyphs a little better, though. Tried drawing it when I woke up, but it's nothing worth working with.*

Cassie took another look at the scribble.

Then she reached for her rum and Coke, and started flipping pages.

Kokopelli first appeared in the entry for September eighth. Trujillo was complaining about PWP's logo. How, she wondered, could she create anything fresh with the biggest cliché in the Southwest in her face everywhere she went? Admittedly, the items this workshop shipped out bore some very interesting variants—

It was bound to happen, she wrote two days later. *The ancient spiritual presence in my dreams is now Kokopelli. Or something similar, though I've never seen real petroglyphs quite like what I saw tonight. Fortunately.*

There was a bonfire or something—a fire in a cave. Glyphs all over the walls, & they were all Kokopelli & they weren't. There were flutes, & a wind. Then the glyphs started dancing . . .

Please, Cassie thought, let there not be coyotes.

There weren't, but only (she suspected) because Trujillo's alarm had gone off shortly afterward. At the bottom of the page, Trujillo had drawn a whole line of her dancing glyphs: two-legged and six-legged, hunchbacked and not. Almost all had flute-like appendages, and a few looked intertwined.

No need to dig out McAllister's field journals. Cassie had been through most of them by now, and he'd made his own sketches. Images from tunnels running under certain kivas, from the backs of obscure caves and shadowed, inaccessible cliff faces.

Nyar'la'a.

Well, I've finally come up with a few designs Gray likes, Trujillo wrote about a week later. *Says I'm finally in touch with that "deep understanding."*

He's already ordering stencils for stuff like coffee mugs—if I can come up with something really striking, he'll do holiday cards. Or a new cover for those flute CDs the shops in Taos love.

I know I ought to be thrilled—this is what I'm here for, right?—but I'm not. We lost two clients last night. One overdosed & one hanged himself. Same night I dreamed most of this art Gray's so high on—I was working up the prelim sketches when I found out. I wish I'd torn them up, but I needed something for this morning's meeting.

By the end of September, Trujillo's handwriting looked ragged. Her sketching, however, had improved.

Started the pencil work today for that hallway mural Gray wants. It's going to take a couple of evenings, but at least the clients will be helping with the painting. I've cut stencils for a lot of that—Gray's suggestion. Stencils and spray paint, though I hate having paint around. We've got one or two huffers—pretty damaged—& they don't need temptation.

She'd added a couple of images Cassie recognized from her visit to PWP. One, she noted, had impressed Gray so much he was using it for the CD covers.

Not sure it's worth it, though, she wrote a day or two later. *The dreams are getting worse. Sometimes in a cave, sometimes outside, but always the damn flute & the glyphs & now coyotes. They howl like mad when the big one starts assembling itself—no, HIMSELF. Definitely HIMSELF.*

Started work on the mural tonight after dinner.

The rest of the page held sketches, most still similar to those in McAllister's field journals. The last, however, showed HIMSELF in the act of forming. Cassie flipped the page and reached for her rum and Coke again.

The glass was empty.

I told Gray to keep that paint locked up. I've rounded up all the cans now & pitched them—the mural's nearly done & what isn't yet I'll do—but too late for . . . Cassie raised the notebook, squinting, but the name was illegible. *We'll be lucky if the county doesn't shut this place down. Maybe it should. The clients aren't making progress, & the dreams they tell Gray keep getting sicker.*

One girl I work with (good artist, when she's sober) says there's screaming in her trailer almost every night. Nightmares. She wants to leave, but it's too cold on the street in town.

Cassie scanned down the page. Trujillo's handwriting was a mess, but the same couldn't be said for her dream sketches. By mid-October, she'd switched to colored pencils and felt-tip pens.

Sickly green moons. Festering holes of stars.

And rising up against them, twisted and lean and hideous, something which raised its face to those stars . . . tore at them with straining appendages *of* that face—

Cassie flipped past, to the end of the notebook, then dropped it on her desk. There were no more words to read anyway. Trujillo's final entries hadn't even been dated, though she had obviously been trying to communicate something. More dreams? Waking hallucinations?

So much for artistic inspiration at PWP.

Whatever Lyn Trujillo had hoped to accomplish there, Marcus Gray was right. The arrangement had not worked. Cassie was starting to wonder exactly how badly it hadn't—and how that receptionist had gotten hold of something so personal as Trujillo's dream journal.

Three client deaths. At least. And Gray said Trujillo wasn't there any more, the nonmaterial rewards hadn't been enough—

Muttering a few choice words, Cassie dragged McAllister's carton out of her closet and put the notebook inside. Jupe and Juno seemed to approve. Both Rotts settled close beside her chair, sighing themselves to sleep as she booted up her computer.

And began a very difficult e-mail to Julie Valdez.

Aside from her own nerves—and that God-awful road out to the facility—Cassie's first week volunteering went well enough. To her relief, she wasn't asked to manufacture any Kokopelli products, though she'd been told that some were handmade in-house. Instead, she spent her two hours per shift packing boxes for mailing.

The intermittent racket she'd heard on her first visit turned out to be a conveyor belt that carried boxes past the workers, allowing ample time to check packing slips and select items from stock kept on shelves behind them. In theory. In practice, the belt was down more often than not—and even when it wasn't, her fellow workers were none too helpful. Most were PWP clients: recovering addicts, possibly recovering alcoholics, and psychiatric cases.

The few volunteers from town, mostly church groups, never showed up more than once or twice.

There were a couple of staff members as well. They wore denim shirts with the garish PWP logo, and looked more like prison guards or bouncers. Other than fixing the belt when it broke down, they did almost nothing. Equipped with folding chairs, cigarettes, and a cooler full of Pepsi, they just sat and watched the clients.

A few of these—generally the psych cases—hummed along to the piped-in work music. It was always solo Native American flute, like the stuff she'd heard in Gray's office, and it wore on her nerves. After her first day, she kept a pair of shooting earplugs in her jacket pocket.

After her second, she wore them almost continuously.

Cassie drove home dead tired on Friday afternoon, fighting the wind and the road and her lack of decent sleep. She had volunteered for five days straight. For the past four nights, the music she'd blocked at the workshop had returned in her dreams, woven through the voices of coyotes.

She needed a hot meal. And a very hot shower.

The scent of the first—followed by two ecstatic Rotts—greeted her as she walked through the door. Cassie knelt and hugged both dogs, then headed for the kitchen. Frank Yellowtail was already there, settled at one end of the table with the day's mail and a mug of coffee. She poured one for herself and joined him.

Since the dreams had started—or at least, since they'd admitted to them—she and Frank had been eating dinner together often. The idea had been hers, but he'd been more than willing to help out. It was easy enough for her to shove a casserole in the oven or start a pot of soup before leaving for PWP.

Easier than coming home to darkness, anyhow. She suspected Frank felt the same.

Cassie set her coffee down on the *Sheridan Press,* which had been left folded open across her placemat. She frowned: Frank generally lacked patience with news outside the cattle business. Since when had that changed?

The article's terse headline didn't help much. *Woman, 31, Found Frozen to Death.*

Judging from the accompanying photo, it was the kind of story most papers ran this time of year to help the Salvation Army kettles. The sad fact was that transients got wasted and collapsed in alleys all year round.

Lyn Trujillo, a former client of Piper With a Purpose—

"No." Cassie's hands tightened on the paper. She picked it up to examine the photo, then shook her head. She'd never met Trujillo. That blanket-wrapped form slumped against a Dumpster could have been anyone.

I'm afraid that arrangement didn't work out, Ms. Barrett—

"This had to be a mistake." Cassie pushed the article in Frank's direction. "Trujillo was their creative director, not a client! There's no way she could have ended up like . . . that. Julie said she didn't even drink—"

She stopped short at the look on his face. *Damn.*

Lacking children of his own, Frank was a devoted uncle. From past experience, Cassie knew all too well how he felt about her getting Julie involved in anything strange.

"I know," he said. "I called her this morning. We had a good long talk."

Which meant, it turned out, that he knew all about her recent e-mails to his niece. Why she'd really started volunteering at PWP, and what she she'd learned from Trujillo's dream journal. Not surprising that Julie had wanted her uncle's opinion on that. Frank's grandfather had been a powerful dreamer, and Cassie suspected he'd inherited some talent.

Not a good thing, lately.

"If you want to see that journal yourself," she offered, "I'll get it. I should have let you check it out in the first place." To her surprise, Frank shook his head.

"You'd better leave it alone, too. From what Julie told me, nothing in it could make any difference now. Trujillo got too close."

Cassie nodded, wincing at another touch of frostbite.

Frank looked at her sharply. "Maybe you should quit volunteering there."

"Don't you think I haven't already considered it?"

The words burst out with a surprising mix of anger and fear. Staring down at the article to avoid his reaction, Cassie felt a cold certainty: she did have to go back to PWP. Whatever had happened to Lyn Trujillo—and several clients—there wasn't like last year at Zia House. It wasn't something lurking in some remote cave.

Whatever Trujillo had seen in her dreams had a toehold right here.

After a moment, Frank picked up the paper and threw it on the floor.

"I figured you'd say that." His face was expressionless now. "You and Julie, when you get an idea into your heads—" He sighed. "There's something going on out there, all right, and we both know what it feels like. Maybe there's nothing to be done about it, either."

Cassie swallowed the desert in her throat. Frank was making good sense, but he didn't know the whole story. He only knew what Julie had told him.

Not what Marcus Gray had announced this afternoon.

"You're probably right," she finally said, "but I've got to keep going for a while longer. The Little America in Cheyenne just placed a huge order, so there'll be an all-night packing party on the twenty-first."

Frank Yellowtail frowned. Twenty Mile had its own bad solstice history.

"We're going to have a special visitor that night, too," Cassie added. "The director won't say who, just that he's very important to 'the mission of our program.' Like a founder or something."

Frank wasn't frowning any more.

The creases in his face looked more like crevasses.

In the end, they'd compromised. She would cut back on her hours and carry her cell phone whenever she was at PWP. She would also keep her nose out of Trujillo's dream journal. In return, Frank would back her decision to keep volunteering until the twenty-first.

When she asked what "backing" meant, he handed her the keys to his pickup.

"We need to swap vehicles, at least on the days you're going out there."

222 DARK EQUINOX AND OTHER TALES

Cassie blinked. Frank had recently traded off his ancient green monster for a two-year-old Ford half-ton in gleaming black. She'd never borrow it for a grocery run, let alone that miserable drive out the workshop.

"Why?"

"To bring the dogs with me," he said, avoiding her eyes. "If you call."

For a moment, the statement didn't make sense. Then she nodded. "Coyotes."

Though they were smart about them, Jupe and Juno hated coyotes—and most of the "song dogs" around Twenty Mile stayed clear of the big Rotts. Cassie wasn't sure what one coyote under her window and a whole pack in her dreams (not to mention Trujillo's) meant in the waking world.

Still, coyotes did seem connected with whatever was wrong at PWP. And Frank would no more risk the dogs than she would. If he thought they might be useful in a crisis, or prevent one—

Cassie had handed over her Jeep keys. She carried her phone and cut her hours and tried to ignore Marcus Gray's bursts of irritation.

But now, well into the evening of the twenty-first, she was starting to regret her decision.

To begin with, she'd never had to work with *all* PWP's clients before. Not counting yet another church group (which had disappeared within the first two hours), there had to be at least thirty people here tonight. Some looked intoxicated or high or both, though the staff wasn't paying much attention. They were too busy catering to tonight's special visitor.

The guy had arrived around sunset, escorted by Gray himself. Lean and wiry like a cowboy—and busted up like one, too. His back twisted under the flame-colored Western shirt he wore with black Levis and silver-toed boots. His black felt hat—sporting the flashiest concha band Cassie had ever seen—rode low over his eyes, obscuring his face.

Feathers fluttered at the back of his belt. The ornamented flute from Gray's office, or one suspiciously similar, had been stuck through it casually.

Trujillo's recruiter?

Whatever he did for PWP, Gray's mumbled introduction left it a mystery. Cassie hadn't even managed to catch the guy's name above the rumble of the conveyor belt, and Gray hadn't stuck around for questions. Instead, he had muttered something else about a phone call and disappeared—leaving the visitor to account for himself, which he didn't. He seemed to prefer working to talking, which was fine with Cassie.

For the first few hours, anyway.

The belt was running fine tonight, miracle of miracles, but she could still hear the usual work music above it—and she hadn't had the time or privacy to put in her earplugs yet. At least half a dozen people were humming along, some even swaying as they packed the CDs Gray had such high hopes for.

Glancing at Lyn Trujillo's cover art as the jewel boxes slid through her hands, Cassie shuddered. Were there coyotes lurking in that unfocused background?

"Break in five minutes, people!" shouted one of the staff. "Let's get these boxes sealed for the truck."

As the zip of packing tape replaced the belt's rumble, Cassie glanced at the workroom clock. Ten-thirty already. The minor wail of the flute was giving her a headache, setting her nerves on edge and tweaking her paranoia. Glare from the overhead lights threw shadows she couldn't quite account for.

The air smelled funky, too. She wondered again about the heating system and headed outside as soon as possible.

Even the wind had to be better than this.

After detouring around a knot of smokers—not all of them favoring tobacco—near the back door, Cassie worked her way around the building, staying close to the wall. She'd been right about the wind. It was nastier than usual tonight, buffeting what few security lights still worked. By the time she reached the parking lot out front, she was shivering persistently.

Frank's pickup was still safely where she'd parked it, though, in the farthest space from the front door. Relief washed through her. *Why not just leave?* the voice of reason suggested. *Hop in, go home. Bail from this creepy situation.*

Then she noticed another parking space, directly by the door. It was empty . . . except for DIRECTOR stenciled in white paint.

Fishing in her pocket with numb fingers, Cassie grabbed her cell phone and flipped it open. As it sometimes did, the two-word curse of rural America appeared onscreen.

No service.

To her surprise, everyone who had gone on break was actually back when the conveyor belt started up again. Dirty looks directed at the two staff members told her why—or at least how. The *why* of nearly everything about this evening was turning mysterious as the clock's hands crawled toward twelve.

Starting with where the hell Marcus Gray was, on this Very Important Night he'd been ranting about for the past week.

Focus on what's going on here. Now.

Tonight's special visitor wasn't working so hard, though everyone else seemed to be. PWP's clients were packing CDs and other Kokopelli merchandise as though their messed-up lives depended upon it. Some looked twitchy, sweating profusely in the chilly room. Others were zoned out, slaving away in their own private worlds.

The visitor was walking among them now, though he didn't seem to be saying much. Maybe he was whispering. Certainly he was leaning in close, touching some of the women who looked particularly nervous. The teenage receptionist she'd met on her first day here was following him around like a starving puppy.

As the woman next to her reached out for his sleeve, Cassie turned away quickly. The woman's expression when she glanced back chilled her.

Passive. Sheep-like. Glazed.

Meanwhile, Cassie's temples were starting to throb. The work music had grown louder, piercingly insistent, and she was sure now that the heating system had problems. At least the overhead lights weren't glaring any more. They had dimmed noticeably since their return from break, though neither the staff nor anyone else seemed to have noticed.

Eleven-thirty now.

Eleven thirty-five. Was the belt speeding up?

At eleven-forty, the staff hauled open the rolling door in one wall. A large van had been backed up to the other side. With more speed than she'd have thought possible, both staff members and a few of the fitter male clients started lifting boxes onto handcarts for the van. Wind from the open door howled past unnoticed.

By eleven fifty-five, the job was almost done. As a final box went in at midnight, Cassie heard the conveyor belt stop . . . and the work music, more intense than ever, rising to fill the auditory void. She dug in her pocket for her earplugs.

As she palmed them, another sound began, weaving through the flute recording and the wind outside. It was rasping and ancient, yet a part of her recognized it even before she glanced across the room.

Gray's feathered flute wasn't stuck through their visitor's belt any more. He was playing it, his body curved over the elaborately carved tube almost like an extension of the instrument. What came from it was less music than breath: a wordless ritual, an artifact out of time before civilization. Or thought.

Or humanity.

Most of the people around her were already swaying in place. A few moaned. The young receptionist gasped softly, then sidled around her table and began slow-stepping toward the music, head thrown back and long hair streaming.

Moving toward the center of the workroom to join her, their visitor played louder. Other women—then a few men—began to copy the girl's steps. It looked like the most natural thing in the world, a physical evolution of the music.

A ceremony in the making.

Every frostbitten nerve in Cassie knew that much, even as her own body began to sway. Forcing herself down on her knees behind one of the tables, she fumbled with the earplugs she'd manipulated so easily moments ago. One nearly slipped from her grasp—but the effect was astonishing. Cut off from the wail of the visitor's flute, she found herself back in charge of her muscles.

And in danger of being noticed by anyone still paying attention.

Easing back up, Cassie tried to copy the rhythm of those closest to her. Her earplugs hadn't gone in perfectly: enough of the music leaked through to let her follow along, maybe too well. Shuffling and slow-stepping through the dimming light, the knot of PWP clients and staff swept her up. Wind gusting through the loading door pushed them all along, following the flute-player toward the only other door in the room.

Most of them had used it on their way back from break. Now it gaped open onto a pitch-black corridor far longer than any Cassie remembered in this building. As the dancing crowd disappeared inside, she felt the first stirrings of panic.

What had Daniel McAllister said about "many gates"?

Still the visitor with his flute played on, ever-changing yet somehow monotonous. Caught up in the rhythm, the others swayed after him into the darkness, some moaning under their breaths. Ahead—*but how far ahead?*—hints of dim light flickered against the walls.

The scent of piñon pine grew stronger as they approached. Piñon smoke . . . as from a newly kindled fire. Cassie's panic rose even as her feet carried her along. This was nowhere in the PWP complex, she was certain. This was a waking dream, a collective primal nightmare, a footnote from Trujillo's last desperate scribblings.

This was a wound in the modern skin of the world.

Abruptly, the corridor ended in a cave some cringing part of her already recognized. A small central campfire threw shadows on the soot-blackened walls, summoning pale ghosts of petroglyphs. They danced in imitation of the one who capered and piped in the firelight, throwing sparks from the conchas of his hatband and the silver-mounted toes of his boots.

Men and women all around her joined in that dance. Someone even had a hand drum, its soft malignant heartbeat growing stronger as the flames leaped up.

Cassie struggled against that rhythm. Like a swimmer fighting current, she forced herself away, toward the nearest curve of stone. Other bodies flowed into the gap she made. The dance and the music and the flames began to blend, calling malformed petroglyphs from the walls to writhe in the air above their heads.

And as they did—as the shadows writhed with them—the piper's flame-colored shirt turned to actual fire, enveloping him for an instant.

Murmurs of awe and terror rose from the other dancers. Out of that brief conflagration, something taller, leaner, and far less human was unfolding. Still piping, curved over and around the appendage of its instrument, it shook its—*head, surely*—until tatters of black felt and silver fell away.

Cassie pressed herself further into the shadows.

Turned her own head away, but not quickly enough.

"*Nyar'la'a!*" The syllables tore themselves from a dozen straining throats at once. "Nyar'la'a!"

A sudden gust of wind blew through the cave . . . blew *down*, from the distant ceiling which was no longer solid, if it ever had been. Live coals spattered from the fire. Cassie glanced up. Through whatever the smokehole had become, she could see stars.

Too many stars, even for rural Wyoming. Too many stars in very wrong colors, torn by a wind which blew out of somewhere unimaginably desolate, inconceivably cold.

"Nyar'la'a! Nyar'la'a!"

More voices this time—and not all of them human. There were dozens of coyotes somewhere outside this cave, lending their responses to the wind and the chant. The rising, writhing chaos of it all. Biting her lip to focus herself, Cassie picked up the rhythm of the dance again, swaying back toward the corridor which she desperately hoped still existed.

"Nyar'la'a!"

She had almost reached the darkness when something landed on her shoulder. A large, beefy hand—staff, probably—hauled her backwards, toward the firelight and discovery. Cassie grabbed onto a protruding rock ledge, then kicked back with all her strength. Her captor howled. She kicked again, to the kneecap, and his grasp loosened. Twisting away, she bolted down the corridor.

And nearly gagged on the chemical stench spewing into the air behind her.

Glancing back over her shoulder, Cassie cursed and redoubled her speed. There were people coming after her, all right, but pursuit was the least of her problems. Or theirs. Whatever ancient nightmare had manifested itself tonight, it hadn't been real enough to turn gas line into solid rock.

*   *   *

Freezing wind hit her in the face as she jumped through the loading door. Cassie landed hard and scrambled to her feet, intent on getting as far from the facility as possible. PWP hadn't maintained its heating system to start with. A broken line wouldn't help, and if any of that fire in the dream-cave had actually been—

What the hell?

Still several yards from the parking lot—let alone Frank's pickup and some chance of leaving—Cassie stopped dead, staring into the night around her. Pair after pair of narrow yellow eyes stared back.

Associations: ritual music, wild beasts, madness.

Already two for three.

From where she stood, she could see coyotes ringing the area. Lean shadows just beyond the security lights, they sat back on their haunches and watched her, apparently waiting for her next move.

Did coyote packs ever attack human beings?

Moot question. The natural laws of the rest of the world no longer applied out here, and her gut knew it. She had seen things tonight that nothing in McAllister's notes or her own brushes with the Outside had prepared her for . . . nothing wind and sky and earth were meant to contain.

Without warning, the closest coyote threw back its head in song. It was a weird, tormented wail unlike anything she'd ever heard around Twenty Mile, and it penetrated her earplugs effortlessly.

As the rest of the pack joined in, Cassie bolted for the parking lot.

She expected pursuit, strong jaws dragging her down, but it never came. What did was the blast of a propane explosion—then a second, smaller blast as the delivery van's gas tank caught. Running for her life now, she headed for the farthest space out. The comforting bulk of a Ford half-ton . . . if she could only unlock it in time—

Headlights flashed on to meet her.

Jeep headlights.

Frank Yellowtail scrambled from the driver's seat, then reached back inside for a shotgun from the rack. His mouth started moving as

Cassie reached him. Shaking her head, she pulled out both earplugs and gasped her thanks.

"How'd you know to come?" she asked, as he passed her the weapon and headed for the Jeep's back cargo door. "I tried to call you, but—"

"The dogs told me."

Cassie frowned. Rather than asking her for his keys—or just climbing back into her vehicle and getting the hell out of Dodge—Frank was opening the door for Jupe and Juno. Both wore their heavy leather leashes, which he grabbed as they emerged.

And started barking challenge at the coyote ring.

"What's that mean?" she yelled over the Rotts.

"Every coyote around our place started up about an hour ago. The dogs went nuts, started giving it right back—and then they stopped. No more barking, no more howling. No more coyotes. It didn't sound natural, somehow. When Jupe started in on the front door, I thought we'd better get out here."

He glanced down at the furious dogs. "All of us."

Despite the weirdness of the situation, Cassie sighed. That door had taken a lot of abuse in the past couple of years—but the idea of Frank waiting at the house for her call was reassuring. She needed reassuring right now.

Speaking of right now, why weren't they leaving?

Frank pointed past her to the coyotes. "We met more coming in. A lot more than I've ever seen around here—bigger, too. Like wolves."

In the fitful light from the propane fire, Cassie saw his expression change.

"I don't think they're going to let us leave," he said. "Not until this is over."

Cassie wasn't sure what "this" was, but she kept both hands on the shotgun. Things looked pretty much over to her—aside from the damn coyotes, anyway. The main PWP facility blazed like a torch, and the wind was spreading flames to a couple of the trailers. Surely nobody in there was still alive. There wasn't even any screaming, the way you'd expect—

Abruptly, the coyotes fell silent. So did Jupe and Juno, though they stood their ground, the fur on their necks and shoulders bristling.

A line of shadows was emerging from the holocaust of the main facility. Some new and terrible wailing twisted itself into the wind, rising above it tunelessly. Ragged bursts of mad laughter responded.

Cassie's breath caught. At the head of the line, lean and hunched and utterly inhuman, capered the image of her nightmares.

She did not understand how any of those following it—*him, oh yes, him*—could still be alive, or even if they were. Stumbling, dragging ruined limbs behind them, they staggered through the wind and the night like unstrung marionettes. Thick black strands trailed from their leader's headdress. Coiling and whipping in defiance of the wind's direction, they lashed back at random into the line.

Shrieks followed.

Cassie bit her lip, hoping none of them were hers.

The coyotes were on the move now. Whimpering, they broke their ring and belly-crawled toward the piper, flattening themselves at his feet. He danced over them heedlessly. Rolling clear (most of them, anyhow), they trotted along beside the others, causing some of them to flinch away.

Cassie pressed herself closer to Jupe and Juno.

Blink. Blink. Shift.

Shadowy petroglyphs, two-leggers and four-leggers and Kokopelli himself, dancing forever on a kiva tunnel wall no one was ever meant to see. The faithful record of a primal nightmare . . . or a primal memory. Daniel McAllister's sketch from the last night of his life.

The world we think we live in now is just a skin—a modern skin—and every so often something else breaks through.

She blinked again. The line was turning away from the facility, away from the flaming outbuildings and the road. Its leader was drawing farther ahead, and the coyotes with him—yet the others kept staggering along behind, into the snow-flecked void and the shifting wind. It blew from true north now, a Canadian blast carrying the first flakes of a storm.

Jupe and Juno snuffled at her knees. When she didn't move, Frank Yellowtail laid a hand on her shoulder.

"I think it's over," he said. "Let's go while we still can."

The distant shriek of a fire engine punctuated his words. As she loaded the dogs back into her Jeep and coaxed its engine to life, Cassie tried not to think what those would-be rescuers would find in the morning.

What they would not find, she knew, would be tonight's visitor. He, like Marcus Gray, was already on some other road, spreading chaos ancient as the stars she dared not look up at yet. And with every PWP workshop, every coffee mug or greeting card or flute CD, another little piece of this world would fall apart.

Nyar'la'a. Messenger of the exiled gods.

Whatever the message had been tonight, she hoped she never understood it.

THE WIND-CALLER

EVEN THE TUMBLEWEED Motor Lodge's neon cactus wasn't cutting through this blizzard. Leaning forward until her nose bumped her Jeep's windshield, Cassie Barrett strained to read the sign. Was she out of luck?

Unable to see for certain, she cursed and climbed out. The wind tried tearing the door handle from her grip, but a few steps forward relieved her mind. VACANCY. She might actually have a bed—of questionable age and cleanliness—for the night.

Not that she had many choices. Once the Wyoming highway department's snow gates came down, you grabbed what you could. There hadn't been much warning: no weather alerts on the radio, no threatening clouds. All the way up from Denver, the weather had been decent for January.

Then, just outside Warren, it had gone straight to—

"No king-size beds left. No rollaways, either."

Cassie stomped the snow off her boots and stared at the speaker, a lanky kid in his late teens. He was leaning heavily on the check-in desk.

"I just need a room," she said. "For one."

The news didn't seem to cheer him up, but he grabbed a key from the almost vacant pegboard behind him. Cassie sloshed to the desk and dug out her credit card. As she filled out the paperwork, news spewed from a nearby radio. Nothing was moving anywhere near Warren: several big rigs were off the road, power lines were sagging, and the National Weather Service was tying itself in knots trying to explain.

The kid scowled and snapped the radio off. "Idiots."

"So when do they think this is going to clear?" Cassie asked.

233

"They've got no clue." He scowled and handed her a key. "They think they know what's going on, but they don't."

Cassie hesitated. She was too tired for riddles, but the kid's comment sounded like more than the usual Western distrust of government.

"You mean a ground blizzard didn't close that road?"

The young desk clerk looked startled. Then nervous.

"Sure it did. A real sudden ground blizzard. Happens sometimes around here." He cleared his throat. "Anything else you need right now?"

So much for curiosity.

"Somewhere halfway decent to eat. I missed lunch."

"Try Vinnie's. Two blocks down the street, on your right. Nothing fancy, but the food's better than the Flying K's . . . and it's got a bar."

Before she could thank him, the desk phone shrilled. Cassie headed back out to the Jeep with her room key and her questions, hoping the storm had eased in the interim. It hadn't. Snowflakes were spewing down with a vengeance, and the wind howled like a lost thing.

Feeling like a lost thing herself, she regretted driving down to Denver earlier this week. Twenty Mile needed a new baler, though, and the stock show was the best place to get deals. Either she or her foreman had to go, and Frank Yellowtail looked after the place better alone than she could.

Hopefully, he wouldn't have to for much longer.

Even seen from the doorway, Vinnie's was a fire marshal's nightmare. Stranded travelers, truckers, and locals filled up every table and booth—plus all the stools at the bustling bar at the end of the room. Cassie's spirits sank. The two blocks here had felt like two miles, and she doubted pizza delivery was an option tonight.

She was zipping up her parka for the return trip when the hostess took pity on her.

"Mind sharing a booth, hon?"

A head-shake later, Cassie was sliding into a seat opposite a worn and fiftyish woman already drinking coffee. Her boots struck something under the table.

"Sorry," she said, with a quick glance down.

Aluminum crutches. The kind that meant a permanent problem. Her tablemate stopped her next apology with a shrug.

"Don't worry about it." Her wary expression softened a little. "Really."

Not knowing what else to do, Cassie introduced herself.

"Sharon O'Reilly." The woman reached for her coffee. "Get caught by the storm?"

"That's one way to put it."

Despite her heavy wool sweater, Cassie shivered. The woman's words were too close to her own suspicions after calling Frank a few minutes ago. The weather here was news all over the state, it seemed, but the rest of the state wasn't getting it. Just the usual gales and flurries, with nothing in the forecast to suggest any change soon.

"Whatever it is," he'd said, "it's too damn localized. Get home as soon as you can, but don't take any chances. Something about this doesn't—"

"Feel right. I know."

Frank's agreement hadn't helped her mood. Her foreman was the grandson of a *Batce Baxbe,* a Crow "man of power." He generally denied that this affected his view of things—but once in a while he couldn't.

Since she'd inherited Twenty Mile a couple of years ago, "once in a while" was happening more often.

"You have an accident?" Her tablemate gave Cassie a closer glance. "You look pretty shook up."

"Sorry." *God, she needed caffeine!* "I was just thinking how fast that storm hit. Do you folks get many like that?"

Sharon's mouth quirked. "Didn't used to."

Cassie leaned forward, but her question was interrupted by a nervous young waitress with the coffee pot. She poured a mug for Cassie and took her order for a burger, then glanced up sharply at the front door.

"Expecting somebody, Jess?" Sharon asked.

"More like avoiding." The waitress lowered her voice. "Shar, you'd better leave. I was just outside, and I saw your ex headed this way. Didn't look too sober, and after this morning—"

She hesitated. "I could let you out through the kitchen if you want. Might be safer."

Cassie froze in her seat, but her table partner just shrugged.

"What's he going to do . . . kill me?" Her expression softened to concern. "How's your little boy doing?"

Jess bit her lip. "Mom said she'd call me when the antibiotics kick in."

Someone at a neighboring table waved a coffee mug at her, and she hurried away. Sharon sighed. "Poor kid."

Cassie gave her a questioning glance.

"The doctor already thinks it's meningitis. Antibiotics aren't doing shit. If her boy gets any sicker, he's going to need a real hospital—not what we've got here."

As in Cheyenne, or maybe Laramie. Cassie bit her lip.

"Maybe in the morning, when—"

A burst of snow-laden wind from a door near the bar interrupted. Stomping and swearing, a big man in a hunting orange parka blocked the doorway for several seconds before bothering to pull the door shut. Two customers bailed from their stools and took their drinks elsewhere.

Nobody was saying a thing.

And Sharon clutched her coffee like a life preserver.

By the time the newcomer had peeled off his parka and dumped it on one of the vacated seats, none of the bar stools were occupied. Cassie kept sipping while she tried to figure out the guy's popularity. His size and bearing said town bully, though the gray in his thinning hair and beard put him on the wrong side of fifty.

He wasn't aging well, either. His heavy flannel shirt hung on his frame, and he wasn't all that steady on his feet.

"Beer and a shot."

The young bartender hesitated. "Jake, I think you've—"

"Beer. And a shot. Now."

Jake leaned across the bar, one hand slapping down. A long-necked bottle and a short glass appeared promptly. He downed the whiskey, then swiveled on his stool to face the silent room.

"Got a call this morning," he said. "From some Feds. Claim they're concerned about my tax situation. Claim I haven't been answering their letters."

A buzz of whispers rose from a few tables. Non-locals were tucking cash under plates and heading for exits. Burger or no burger, Cassie seriously considered joining them.

"These same Feds were planning to drive out today for a little talk." Jake took a pull at his beer, then grinned. The effect through his beard wasn't pleasant. "Didn't happen, did it?"

Sharon's face froze.

"Not about to happen any time soon, either."

The buzz grew louder. More cash hit the tabletops. More people—including a few locals—slipped out, tightening parka hoods and scarves against the icy scream of the wind.

Jake took another pull at his beer, draining it. Then he hooked one finger into his shirt's open neck and extracted something on a long cord.

"Not about to happen," he repeated. "Not until I find out who."

The statement made no sense to Cassie, but it apparently did to those around her. Their whispering fell away again, into an uneasy silence punctuated by Sharon's coffee mug slipping from her grasp.

Cassie reached to catch it before it spilled. Sharon's fingers were trembling.

Jake ran his finger down the cord, flicking the object dangling from it at chest level. The café's light wasn't good, but it looked like a small whistle or flute—maybe Pacific Coastal, or Inuit. It was carved from some dark shining substance Cassie couldn't identify.

When Jake's fingers lifted the object, the young bartender slid another long-necked bottle across the bar.

"No need for that," he said, the words barely loud enough to carry. "I'm sure nobody here—"

"Some sonofabitch did. Told the Feds something—some damn lie—but *what* doesn't matter. Until I find out *who*, nobody's going anywhere."

Grabbing the opened bottle, Jake slammed down half its contents before dropping it on the floor. No one moved. Then he pulled on his parka and left, letting the side door swing behind him. Wind and snow gusted in before anyone moved to close it.

In the hum of voices that followed, Cassie cleared her throat and looked hard at her tablemate. "I'm guessing that was your ex?"

Sharon nodded.

"You want to tell me what that was all about?"

"Back taxes." She hesitated. "More like no taxes."

Which was part of the answer, Cassie suspected, but not all of it. She waited.

"Jake's never been one to blame himself. Trouble's always someone else's fault—doesn't matter much whose. He's not real forgiving, either."

Sharon rubbed at a pale line of scar tissue on her chin.

"Nice guy," Cassie muttered. "But what's him being an idiot got to do with the roads being closed?"

Sharon's voice dropped to a whisper. "Everything."

Cassie took a long breath and looked around for Jess with the coffee pot and her dinner. Something here was still not making sense—or, just maybe, it was starting to make the kind she didn't like. The kind she'd never suspected before moving up to Twenty Mile.

The kind she didn't seem able to stay away from.

"I'm confused," she whispered back. "Are you saying Jake's lousy temper has something to do with this storm?"

Sharon gave a short nervous laugh. "Sounds nuts, right?"

"Maybe." Cassie felt her stomach clench.

"Problem is, it's happened before. More than once. Come winter, things around here run Jake's way, or—"

Sharon hesitated. "But this time is a whole lot worse."

Glancing around the café, Cassie saw that most of her fellow storm refugees were already gone. The remaining patrons looked local—and very interested in their own business, thank you. Several had migrated to the bar, though the noise level hadn't picked up.

And no one occupied the stool Jake had claimed.

"*No need for that.*" The bartender's words replayed in her mind. *Jake's fingers toying with that whistle or flute or whatever it was, that dark shining carved object on its cord—*

Cassie shivered. Then she found a pen in one coat pocket and grabbed a paper napkin. Scribbling her cell phone number, she passed it over to Sharon.

"I believe you," she said, "but there's a lot I don't understand. If you feel like explaining . . . anything else . . . please call me later. I'm more than willing to listen."

Sharon's look of confusion deepened as she tucked the napkin away. "You sound like you've seen stuff like this before."

"Not quite like this, but I've seen some things." *And I hope to hell I'm wrong this time.*

"Walkin' After Midnight" erupted from her bedside table, shattering the uneasy sleep she'd barely fallen into. Cassie fumbled for her cell and cursed Patsy Cline.

"Sorry to call so late."

Sharon O'Reilly sounded more urgent than apologetic. Cassie switched on a lamp and glanced at the bedside clock: nearly one A.M. *Please God, let the woman be sober.*

"You were right," Sharon went on. "There's a lot you don't understand—but I couldn't tell you at Vinnie's. It's been happening for years. Ever since Jake came back from working on the pipeline—"

"Pipeline?" Cassie's brain wasn't processing yet.

"Trans-Alaska Pipeline. Nineteen-seventies."

All this and ancient history, too. "So what's a pipeline got to do with this blizzard?"

"It's complicated." Sharon hesitated. "Look, there's way too much to explain on the phone. Could you come over?"

"Tonight?"

"Please. What Jake's doing this time . . . it's out of control." Another long hesitation. "People are going to start dying."

Against her better judgment, Cassie wrote down Sharon's address and directions. Then she sat on the edge of her bed listening to the wind scream, wishing the stock show had been anywhere but Denver. City ordinances there meant she'd left Jupe and Juno home, along with the road medicine Frank usually prescribed for her long distance drives.

Not that two Rotts and a .44 might have helped much.

But she'd have settled for even one of them right now.

Crawling along at maybe ten miles per hour, Cassie squinted through her windshield and struggled to stay on the now unmarked road out to Sharon's trailer park. Snow still whipped around madly, and wind whistling through every loose panel in the Wagoneer made her heater useless. Her radio was advising people once again to stay home unless they absolutely had to be elsewhere.

Something had changed about this storm, though. Something she couldn't put her finger on.

Sharon's home stood near the edge of the park, a tired double-wide with a chain link fence and a ramp in place of front stairs. An RV gate in the fence stood open, but only the curtained kitchen window and a single bulb above the door were lit.

Cassie parked near a snow-covered lump of car, bailed out, and hurried for the ramp. The cold here felt even worse than it had in town, a chill like space itself that bit through her down parka in seconds. Glancing up into the night, she almost expected to see distant stars—

What the hell?

Snowflakes were still coming down in thick flurries . . . but not from a clouded sky. Instead, the flakes spewed from some bizarre central vortex, whirling out across Warren like a tornado in reverse. As Cassie watched, the storm began to strengthen as the wind shrieked louder, whipping scrawny trees and skittering trash across the snowdrifts that filled the front yard.

A crack of light appeared at Sharon's front door.

"Get inside! Now!"

Propelled by a gust of arctic misery, Cassie sprinted up the ramp. Sharon yanked the door shut behind her hard enough to make the whole trailer shudder, then shoved a kitchen chair under the doorknob.

"Sorry," said Cassie, shrugging out of her parka.

She wasn't sure what she'd done, though—and Sharon didn't look eager to explain. Leaning heavily on one aluminum crutch, she limped to the refrigerator for a Pepsi. "Want one? I've got beer, if you'd rather."

"Pepsi's fine."

Cassie followed her hostess to the living room, where she chose the last clear corner of a newspaper-covered couch. The other woman eased herself into a old recliner before placing her crutch on the floor with its mate. The metal on both looked dull, their pads mended with tape.

Whatever Sharon's medical situation was, it wasn't recent.

"I wish you hadn't had to come out here." She hesitated at Cassie's expression. "It's not something I wanted to explain at Vinnie's, though. Maybe it's nothing a person can explain."

Cassie nodded, trying to hide her confusion.

"It's OK," she finally said, sipping her Pepsi. "If you say your ex is doing . . . what I saw out there tonight, I'm willing to accept that." *For now.* "Just help me understand why you think it's his fault."

Sharon's mouth quirked. "Nothing's ever Jake Fowler's fault."

Cassie nodded. She'd seen guys like Jake before—though not many, thank God. Time and hard living usually broke them down, but this particular bully might have found himself a compensator.

"Not that he was much different before he went up to Alaska," Sharon continued. "I was just too young and stupid to see it. He was one of the big dogs around here, and I thought we had something. Even after he had to leave town for a while in '74—"

Her voice trailed off in a direction Cassie didn't feel like following.

"She was underage, OK? But one of the cops knew his dad. Told him there were plenty of jobs on the pipeline up north, and Jake caught a bus out next morning. I didn't hear from him for about six months after that."

Lucky you. "So what did he have to say for himself?"

"Well, he didn't apologize, but he actually sent a check. He'd left owing me money—which was nothing new, but paying me back was. Went on and on about how much he was missing me, how he hoped I wouldn't forget him—"

Or else, Cassie filled in.

"—how we were going to be together again just as soon as he got done with the job." Sharon snorted. "Of course, he sort of forgot to mention that the job would last three years."

"So you waited," said Cassie. "And the letters kept coming?"

"Not too often, but yeah. Jake was doing really well, making the kind of money that people here don't. I got to hear all about that, though I figured he was pissing it away as fast as he made it. Turns out he wasn't."

She hesitated. "Then in '76, he got sent way up north, around Prudhoe Bay."

Cassie leaned forward. Why was this important?

"He didn't write for a long while after that. When he started again, his letters were . . . different. He wasn't bragging so much about the money. Said he'd found something else, something better to help him out when he came home."

"Like what?" Cassie heard her own voice tighten.

"That was the weird part. He'd met some old guy up there, an Indian. Like an Eskimo, maybe. Inu—"

"Inuit."

"Jake had no use for Indians. Proved that more than once, in the bars down in Cheyenne. . . . Anyhow, I couldn't imagine him picking one for a drinking buddy. Seems he did, though." Sharon hesitated. "Or maybe the guy picked him."

"What makes you say that?"

"It all seemed pretty sudden. Jake was never great at making friends, but he and this Inuit sure spent a lot of time drinking and talking. Mostly about stuff I never knew Jake cared about."

"Like what?"

"Spirituality, I guess you'd call it. The guy claimed to be a shaman or something. Sounded like New Age crap, but Jake said he'd seen him do things . . . You feeling all right? You don't look good."

Just a little frostbite. That was what Frank's grandfather had called it: that vibe you got when the Outside leaked through, and you already knew too much. Knew because you'd been close before.

"What kind of things?" Cassie finally asked.

"Snow. Wind. Not like they didn't have enough up there, but this old man could bring storms out of a clear sky. Said he had a spirit who 'walked on the wind' . . . and he knew how to get its attention."

Bad, bad déjà vu. "With a whistle, right?"

"Jake called it an amulet." Sharon's forehead creased. "You really believe me?"

"I wish I didn't."

Before Sharon could ask the wrong question, Cassie went on. "I noticed how Jake was treating that thing tonight: like a loaded gun with the safety off." An ugly thought hit her. "I suppose this old shaman just gave it to Jake as a going-away present?"

"He was a little vague on that point. Said the guy had taught him how to use it, though."

Which made sense, though Cassie doubted this particular shaman had been Inuit. Peel back enough layers of anybody's mythology, and you found something older and darker. Maybe older and darker than humanity's bright little moment on this rock.

"Anyhow, Jake came back with his amulet, and some wild stories, and a lot more pay saved than I'd expected. That was in the fall of '77. I was still living at home, cutting hair for a living and bored out of my mind."

Sharon snorted. "Definitely out of my mind."

"So what happened after that?"

"We rented a place together, and Jake went back to the garage where he'd worked before. He wasn't a bad mechanic. His boss was in his sixties and looking to retire—said he'd bring him into the business, then sell it to him outright in a couple of years."

"Sounds like a good deal."

"Not good enough for Jake. Waiting wasn't his thing, and he thought his boss wanted too much. They argued. Then he made the guy a counter-offer just short of insulting, said take it or regret it, and walked out."

Cassie's stomach clenched. *Wait for it.*

"Next morning, Jake didn't go to work. He just dug that amulet out of a drawer and went out back of the house. Stood there staring up at the sky for a long while. Then he blew into it."

Her voice dropped into memory.

"We were living outside town then. Not much there to break the wind—and it started to rise before he even stopped blowing. Awful sound that thing made, too. Hollow and deep and creepy, not like anything else I'd ever heard ... Anyhow, he did it a couple more times and then started praying. I guess it was praying."

Cassie tried to look encouraging.

"It was a cold morning to start with—February, I think—but I swear the kitchen window started frosting over *while I was watching*. I got away from it. Decided to leave early, before Jake caught me watching, and damn near went off the road on the way in to work. It was snowing by then, even though the news hadn't mentioned a storm the night before. Warren got about a foot that day."

She sucked in her breath. "And Jake's boss got his carport caved in with his wife's brand new Buick underneath. More snow than anywhere else in town, right there."

Action A preceding event B—and bully C wanting event B—does not imply the Outside. Cassie was still having trouble with her breathing.

"So what happened with the garage deal?"

"Jake bought it about a week later, on his terms." Sharon frowned. "Who knows what he told his boss, or if the guy even believed him. The man's heart wasn't strong, though, and his wife had been after him to retire. I think they moved down to Arizona."

"And after that?"

"Jake kept on wearing that amulet, but nothing else happened for a long time. He was still the same old Jake, throwing his weight around and running his mouth, maybe a little more than he used to. Drinking more, too. The garage wasn't doing as well as it had before he bought it."

Big surprise there.

"We started ... not getting along so well." Sharon rubbed at the scar on her chin. "I stuck it out for a couple of years, then finally grew some brains and told him I was moving out. He said I wasn't going anywhere, but I went."

She took a long swallow of Pepsi. "Bad timing, right?"

Cassie gave her a puzzled look.

"It was November. Cold." When Cassie's expression didn't change, she went on. "About a week after I left, I was driving home late when a freak snowstorm hit. Not as bad as tonight's, but a whole lot more wind—at least where I was. My car went off the road and rolled two, three times."

Her voice went flat. "Next thing I remember, the EMTs were cutting me out of the wreck. My legs were almost crushed. I had five operations, but my insurance was crap, and don't let anybody tell you doctors don't care about that."

Cassie could fill in the rest. She didn't want to.

"Thing is, I don't know whether he meant to kill me or not. Jake told me a few things about his amulet before I left—mostly when he was drunk—but I'm still not sure how it works."

If it works, Cassie almost said—and then didn't. Her gut was convinced.

"That spirit the old guy talked about . . . Just because you can get something's attention doesn't mean you can control it." Sharon's voice dropped. "I've been keeping track. I'm the only one in town Jake's actually hurt. Usually he just wrecks stuff, though he's shut down a few high school games, too. Didn't like the coach."

She hesitated. "But it's been getting worse, lately. A lot worse."

"Worse how?"

"Used to be, he'd only do his little party trick once every few years. Sometimes he'd just make threats. Any more, though, it doesn't take nearly as much to trip Jake's trigger. He's paying for it, too."

Cassie thought back to the man she'd seen tonight: wasted, shaky, paranoid. The Outside didn't care about humans, and exposure to it wasn't healthy—even for humans who thought they knew what they were doing.

Especially for them.

"Now he gets that call from the IRS or whoever, and it's the last damn straw." Sharon groaned. "Everybody in town knows he doesn't pay his taxes, but who'd be stupid enough to rat him out? Nobody wants the Feds around here—"

Her voice trailed away. After a moment, she pushed herself painfully to her feet and headed back out to the kitchen. Cassie followed. Pulling out a drawer by the sink, Sharon detached a long battered envelope from its underside and handed it to her.

"What's this?"

"Some pictures I got once, while he was really wasted. Don't know why he took the thing off—maybe he'd rolled over on it or something—but there it was on the floor by the couch. I took it away, got a few shots, put it back exactly where I found it. Sent the film out of town to get it developed, too."

Cassie nodded her approval and slid the envelope's contents onto the kitchen table. Five cheap photos fell upside-down.

A wave of cold nausea hit as she turned them over.

Not Inuit, her gut said. *Not Pacific Coast.* And not human, either, though she couldn't tell Sharon why she knew. The answer lay in a glass case down in New Mexico, at a remote field school she hoped had been shut down. The object in question there had been a small froglike image carved of jet, with turquoise eyes. And on the reverse—

Keep looking, damnit. Be sure.

On the reverse had been jagged, twisted glyphs, impossible for a preliterate culture like the Anasazi. Equally impossible, she guessed, for whatever tribe Jake's old shaman had supposedly come from . . . because the glyphs etched into this thing's gleaming surface were the same.

And the same as those on the walls of a narrow cave near Chaco Canyon.

Cassie made herself go through all the photos. Even discounting the glyphs, there was an utter *wrongness* about the thing. Its mouthpiece flared oddly, carved for other than human lips. The complex knotwork she'd taken for Pacific Coastal revealed itself as the elongated and entwined bodies of something aquatic. There were a few eye-symbols as well, primitive and baleful and unlike any "evil eye" protections she could recall—

"You OK?" Sharon asked.

Cassie started—and stared down at her shaking hands. Returning the photos to their envelope, she took a deep unsteady breath.

"Just a little surprised, that's all."

"Right." Leaning on her crutch, Sharon met Cassie's reluctant gaze. "You recognized it, didn't you? Don't know how you could have, but you did."

"I've seen items a little like this before. Not whistles or amulets, but other carved things. Same kind of writing on them, too."

Sharon frowned. "Bad shit?"

"Definitely."

A sudden gust of snow peppered the trailer like a shotgun. In the instant of shock that followed, neither woman spoke.

Then Sharon said, very quietly, "Any idea what to do about it?"

Not a clue. Mostly, what she'd done about it was run. She'd also tried a 12-gauge and a .44, with very mixed results. The Outside wasn't a problem you could solve. It was a reality you needed to avoid.

"Better not to do anything, unless you absolutely have to." Cassie tipped one photo back out of the envelope. "Are these the only copies?"

"Hell, no." Sharon smiled grimly. "I sent another batch to my sister in Montana, in a letter she's not supposed to open unless—"

"Good idea," said Cassie quickly. She glanced at the photo in her hand. "Mind if I take this one with me?"

"Not if it might help. Anything else you need?"

Getting herself in trouble—make that more trouble—tonight wasn't on her agenda, but suspicion still nagged at her. "I'd like to know where your ex lives now," she finally said. "And how to get there."

Color drained from the other woman's face. "You don't want to do that."

"I'm not going anywhere near him," Cassie promised. "I'm just curious."

The storm had weakened again by the time she made it back into town, but she wasn't trusting that to last. Four wheel drive was barely getting her through, and she didn't relish explaining herself to any cop who might still be patrolling. Pulling in close to the chain link at the back of A-1 Auto Repair, Cassie shifted into park and held her breath, peering through the fogging window at a figure just beyond the fence.

"There's an apartment back of the shop," Sharon had told her. *"After I left, Jake moved in to save money."*

One security light on a high pole revealed fluorescent hunting orange sleeves and woolen gloves raised to the sky. As a blast of wind blew the parka's hood back, Cassie caught a glimpse of ragged beard— and Jake's features twisted in a feral scream against the storm.

She eased her window down and strained her ears.

"Ithaqua!" Gray-clad fingers stretched higher, clawing at the night. "Ithaqua!"

Next morning, Cassie woke to the sound of snow against her window. Her radio informed her that all roads around Warren were still closed, with no further comment from the highway department. She called Frank before heading out for breakfast, though she suspected he wouldn't have good news either.

He didn't.

"I don't know what to tell you about your weather, except that we haven't got it. Nobody else in the state does, Cassie." The crackle of a bad connection filled the silence. "Don't suppose you've noticed anything unusual?"

When she finished telling him—and describing Sharon's photo— there was a longer silence.

"Tell me that word again," Frank said. "Slowly, so I can write it down. I may have to call Julie."

He sounded deeply unhappy. Julie Valdez was Frank's favorite niece, an anthropology grad student down in Taos. She'd been Cassie's ticket to that field school near Chaco, and Cassie wondered sometimes if Frank had ever gotten over that. If he was willing to get Julie involved, maybe she wasn't the only one with frostbite this morning.

After that, there wasn't much else to do but trudge over to Vinnie's. The place was crowded again, though mostly with locals. Aside from a radio on the counter along one side of the room, the atmosphere was quieter than it had been last night—and tenser.

As she'd hoped, Sharon sat alone in a booth, both hands wrapped around a steaming mug. Cassie joined her.

"What's good?"

Sharon blinked at her with red-rimmed eyes. "You need a Famous Cinnamon Roll. Jess will be along in a minute."

Since Cassie hadn't gotten much more rest than Sharon had, that was the extent of their conversation until her roll arrived. Redolent of spices and oozing homemade frosting, it covered the plate it came on and looked about the size of her head. As she picked up her fork, though, her tablemate's voice interrupted.

"Wait a sec, Jess."

The young waitress hesitated, then turned back to their booth. It was obvious that she'd been crying, and equally obvious that she hadn't slept lately. Sharon's refill splashed from her coffee carafe.

"Thanks, but that's not what I meant." Sharon lowered her voice. "Is your boy worse?"

Jess dug a tissue from her apron pocket and started twisting it in her fingers.

"Doctor says it's meningitis for sure. He's already talked to the hospital in Cheyenne, and they said get him down there. Like yesterday." Moisture welled at the corners of her eyes. "My baby could go deaf from this. Or even—"

A blast of wind and snow from the front door cut her off. Sharon glanced past her and stiffened, then motioned Jess toward the kitchen. The young woman practically ran.

Cassie felt her first bite go cold in her mouth. "Him?"

The café's abrupt silence was answer enough. Both women kept their eyes on their plates—more or less—as Jake Fowler headed for the counter, brushing off snow in random directions and leaving a trail of slush in his wake. The few people already seated there relocated.

An older man behind the counter offered coffee and a Famous Cinnamon Roll. Ignoring him, Jake planted himself on the center stool and spun to face the rest of the room.

"How much longer is it going to be?"

The words came out in a guttural rasp. Cassie was amazed that he had a voice left: she'd heard him clearly over the wind last night, and he didn't strike her as a quitter.

"How much longer?"

Cassie could hear bills being slipped under plates, but there was no real chance of anyone leaving yet. Not with Jake's scary-crazy glance jittering around—or those fists clenching at his sides.

"Dammit, how much longer are you folks going to be stupid?"

The man with the coffee and roll stiffened. Then he set them down and came around the counter. Like Jake, he looked to be on the wrong side of fifty—maybe sixty—but he'd been eating a lot better, and he was nearly Jake's height.

"That's Vinnie," Sharon murmured.

"Nobody's being stupid," he said, loud enough for everyone to hear. "Nobody called the Feds on you, and Jess's kid might die if he can't get to Cheyenne soon."

Jake's fists clenched tighter. "That's not my problem. It's your problem, all of you." His bloodshot gaze swept the café. "You know what you have to do—"

"Quit being an asshole!"

The café owner's advice silenced the room. Sharon froze in her seat. Even Vinnie himself looked pale, though he stood firm as Jake pulled the amulet from his collar and turned on him, mouth twisting in words Cassie didn't recognize.

A rising shriek of wind rattled the café's doors and windows. Snow scoured its panes. Siding creaked under the storm's renewed force, and somewhere a garbage can blew over. As the noise intensified, a toddler in a high chair began wailing.

Then a sudden spasm of agony crossed Jake's face. Stuffing the amulet back into his flannel shirt, he turned and left without another word.

In that same moment, Cassie heard the wind falter.

Sharon's expression said she'd heard it too. "So what just happened?" Cassie mouthed, taking advantage of the inconsolable toddler. "It was like he suddenly—"

"I don't know."

But Cassie could guess, and it was the first hopeful thought she'd had all morning. As conversations revived at neighboring tables and Vinnie circulated with his carafe, she filled Sharon in on her theory.

"Makes sense," the other woman finally said. "The guy never did know when to stop." She rubbed at her chin. "He was right about one thing, though: I know what we have to do."

Cassie got back to her breakfast while Sharon speculated, trying to quiet her nerves with sugar overload. By the time she'd finished about a third of the monster, though, her tablemate was looking for feedback.

"Sounds a little complicated—and a lot dangerous—but it might work." Cassie frowned. "Or it might not. Even if it does work, there's no knowing what might happen next."

No knowing, but a certain amount of experience.

And in that experience, what happened next was never a good thing. Not in a cavern under Twenty Mile, not in the propane fire that had consumed a charity workshop outside Sheridan last Christmas . . . and not in that damned outlier at Chaco Canyon. There were still nights when she woke sweating and shaking, the last screams of Daniel McAllister echoing in her mind—

"That's why you need to stay clear when it starts," said Sharon. "Jake Fowler is our problem."

Cassie shook her head. "Let me do something."

"Better not to do anything," Sharon quoted back to her, *"unless you absolutely have to."* But she smiled a little as she said it, and Cassie knew she understood her decision.

Or at least saw it in a few of her own.

"So what do you need me to handle?"

Sharon thought a moment, then wrote another phone number on a napkin and passed it over. Cassie took a glance before stuffing it in her pocket: not a call she'd enjoy making, but a stranger's voice made sense.

Then she returned to her Famous Cinnamon Roll. If nothing else, she wouldn't be hungry again today.

". . . I don't know who they've got. I told you, I don't live here! All I know is, he'll be dead if you don't get out here soon."

Cassie clutched the receiver tighter as her hand shook. "They're truckers, OK? Buck knives. Maybe guns. They just want this crazy storm finished." *Breathe, girl. Breathe.* "So are you coming or not?"

The answer wasn't quotable, but at least he hung up.

"How'd he sound?" Sharon asked from the Flying K's office doorway. Behind her, the truck plaza restaurant was crowded but quiet. Cops, long-haul drivers, and what looked like half the town—all waiting in the whiteout dusk for something, anything, to happen.

For this two-day hell to be over.

"Pretty much crazy," said Cassie, "or at least paranoid. Maybe drunk. And his voice is shot."

"You think he believed you?"

She shrugged. Jake had blustered through the call, but her gut said he wanted an end to this as badly as anyone else did. The Outside just plain wore on people.

Or at least it's wearing on me. Cassie rubbed her burning eyes.

"You need coffee," said Sharon. "Come on out, and we'll all wait together." She snorted. "I'm guessing he'll be here any minute. Young, scared, and female is his favorite combination."

Cassie didn't have the heart to tell her that Jake was only part of her worry. She'd made the mistake of calling home again this afternoon, just to warn Frank that Warren might be making the news.

He'd flat out told her not to get involved. Worse, his niece had told *him*.

"Julie didn't recognize 'Ithaqua,'" he went on, "but she did some digging and found another Northern storm spirit, a Wendigo. Algonquin, usually. Likes eating people."

"And walking on the wind?"

Frank hesitated. "She didn't mention that. Just cold and snow and starvation."

Which was less than helpful, though Cassie still wasn't sure how much of it he believed. "I'm not sure I have any choice," she'd finally said. "None of us here do."

Twenty minutes later, the choices weren't looking much better. It was full dark now and the wind was picking up, piling snow into the corners of the front window she'd picked to sit by. Several long-haul guys were having a lively debate—which the police were studiously ignoring—about whether or not to just go get the bastard.

When headlights snaked across the parking lot out front, a muffled cheer rose from the room.

Sharon shushed everybody. "Let him sweat for a minute."

Even in the dimness, Cassie noticed a tight smile stretching her face. Or maybe she imagined it—along with the hard, glittering eyes of the people around her, the cops' hands twitching at their gun belts. Strong coffee and fear stank up the air. Nobody here, herself included, really understood what had been happening in Warren all these years.

Or what might happen here tonight.

Outside in the storm, Jake finally climbed out of his truck. Leaving the driver's door open, he staggered across the recently plowed lot toward the Flying K's main building.

A single light pole near the entrance illuminated his face as he began shouting. The storm took his words, but Cassie could guess: demands, questions, threats. When one gloved hand clutched at his chest, skiffs of snow whipped themselves into miniature twisters as the wind rose even higher, howling renewed vengeance at the building and its occupants.

Sweat trickled down the back of Cassie's neck. Pressing herself into the farthest corner of the booth, she stifled a hollow sense of inevitability.

Even now, he's got Something's attention. He knows some way to make it listen, make it give him what he wants—

Then all the parking lot lights came on at once.

Caught like a deer on the highway, Jake stumbled back. Two police officers emerged from the front door: one with a riot shotgun, one holding a bullhorn. Four other officers were already rising from their seats to follow. Someone even cranked a window part way open, spewing snow into the restaurant but letting everybody hear most of what came next.

". . . so where the hell's that informer?" Jake demanded.

"There is no informer," the cop with the bullhorn responded. "Never was one! You make the Feds wait much longer, it's going to get ugly."

He paused. "Jake Fowler, stand down. You're under arrest."

For what? Sick laughter rose in Cassie's throat. Even now, nobody in Warren was willing—or perhaps able—to say what Jake did. What he'd been doing for over thirty years now, imposing his nasty little ego on people.

The wind tore away Jake's answer, but Cassie could read lips just fine.

So could the cops. As thickening spirals of snow poured past the lights, the officer with the riot shotgun leveled it and stepped forward.

His partner raised the bullhorn. "Both of your hands up! Now!"

A blast of snow and wind hit the shotgun officer full in the chest, knocking him back toward the building. As his weapon discharged uselessly, his partner dropped the bullhorn and went for his own sidearm—only to see it torn from his hand by another gust. The other four cops raced out the front door. Two dragged their fallen colleague to safety, one retrieved the shotgun, and the fourth helped their commander collect his bullhorn and service revolver.

A tactical retreat followed. Cassie groaned and glanced over at Sharon in the next booth.

"*This* was the plan?"

Sharon didn't answer. Beside her in the booth, Jess was clutching her cell phone to her ear and crying softly, shaking her head. The older woman put an arm around her, then took the phone for a moment.

"Not yet," she told someone before handing it back.

Cassie ran a hand through her short dark hair and swore. Along with two police cruisers, various stranded tractor-trailers, and a snow-plow crew, the ambulance with Jess's little boy and his doctor had been waiting behind the Flying K's main building for over an hour. No one had expected this to be easy, but Jake wasn't taking the bait—

"I—tha—qua!"

A good-sized chunk of the truck plaza's sign tore off and pin-wheeled into the restaurant's front windows, slamming hard enough to spiderweb cracks through glass. People seated nearby jumped and scattered. The police commander and his shotgun-toting partner reemerged from the doorway, but stinging gusts blasting into both men's faces made it impossible to see, let alone raise their weapons.

When Jess's cell rang again, Sharon grabbed her crutches and headed for the door.

"We don't have time for this," she called back to Cassie. "He's not going to stop. He'll rip this place apart, and Jess's kid—"

Shrieking wind drowned out the rest. Cassie didn't doubt her, though: Jake's upturned face was a mask of frost and ice and reddened skin, twisted and screaming at the sky. The big red Flying K swung in tatters from its poles, and random snow-twisters the size of small trees were springing up all over the parking lot.

As the restaurant roof began creaking, Cassie grabbed her parka and followed Sharon.

"I—tha—qua!"

Was she hearing the word—*the name*—or feeling it up her spine? At this point, it hardly mattered. Finding herself alone now in the restaurant's entryway, Cassie peered through the mostly frosted glass doors, trying to figure out where the other woman had gone.

Instead, she saw all six cops huddled in a knot a few feet away. One had finally managed to raise the shotgun—but another was pointing at the sky directly over Jake Fowler.

Where a solid mass of clouds should have been—where it had been, minutes before—a slash of starless blackness gaped. Though wind-driven snow spewed from its edges like blood from a wound, its center held nothing but a hideous suggestion of depth. Of space beyond the sky and the night and—

"Give it up, Jake. It's not going to work."

It was the bullhorn's blare, but not a cop's voice. Not even a man's. Cassie's breath caught as she finally located Sharon, some distance away from the knot of uniforms and leaning heavily on one crutch. The other lay abandoned at her feet as she gripped the bullhorn. Her graying hair blew wildly, and she had not bothered with a parka.

"Time's up, loser." A gust tore at her, but she recovered somehow and went on. *"Your tantrums have caused enough misery. You're through."*

Lowering his iced-over, featureless face, Jake turned toward her. Even from where she stood, Cassie could see him stagger with each step, one hand out before him like a blind man. His heavy coat flapped around his chest. Even his jeans, frozen as they were, seemed to hang from bone rather than flesh.

Sharon braced herself and raised the bullhorn again. Jake stumbled to a stop, breathing hard. Tearing the whistle-amulet from his neck, he thrust it up at the sky.

"Ithaqua! Hear me!"

For several heartbeats, nothing happened. Then a raw blast of snow and ice howled from that terrible gash in the clouds, knocking Sharon off her feet and slamming her into the building. The police surged forward, faces ghastly pale under the parking lot lights, but a second blast scattered them as well.

As buckshot and ice pellets spewed in all directions, Jake Fowler threw back his head and laughed in the raw ruined voice of a madman.

Then, like a sail in a hurricane, his whole body started to rip.

Cassie stepped back fast when the screaming stopped and the doors got spattered, but there wasn't all that much blood. Just bright frozen dust on a wind that shrieked and tore, shredding flannel and denim and flesh, whistling through bones and blasting the asphalt clear. There were no snow-twisters now. No spirals of flakes spewing down. Just one tightly focused, utterly unnatural exhalation of white, looping back on itself into the night sky.

Into that long slash through reality.

As the last of the gust died away, the police commander picked himself up and motioned to his men. Two limped over to where Sharon had landed, out of Cassie's sight. The rest grabbed a tarp and headed for where Jake had been standing moments before—then turned away, covering their noses and mouths with their sleeves. Cassie waited until they retreated to the cruisers, then pulled up the hood of her parka and slipped outside.

The truck plaza's parking lot was frantic with activity. Drivers warmed up their rigs as Flying K employees rushed around with plywood and wire and power tools, patching the worst of the storm's damage. The police commander's walkie-talkie chattered nonstop as he stood directing traffic, trying to keep bystanders from getting run over, and yelling for the county plows.

Jess stood a little apart from it all, still clutching her cell phone to her ear but no longer crying. Minutes later, an ambulance's siren split the night as the vehicle itself sped into view, slowing down barely long enough to let her climb in.

Cassie released a breath she hadn't realized she'd been holding. Then she glanced back toward the main building, where a mounded green tarp lay on the concrete. There were no police near it now. No more sirens on the way.

No glimpses of Sharon O'Reilly's face.

Reaching up to cinch her hood tighter, Cassie took another deep breath and headed for the only other deserted space in the lot. She owed Sharon that much, at least. Or perhaps her own fragile peace of mind drove her—her need to know that the Outside no longer intersected this piece of real estate.

By the time she reached the hastily flung tarp at the epicenter of Jake's remains, she had one mittened hand pressed hard against her nose. Long streaks she didn't care to identify marked the asphalt in every direction. Splinters of bone snapped underfoot despite her best efforts, and sodden plaid flannel rags were everywhere.

The tarp itself lay nearly flat. Cassie was willing herself closer when something hard and dark and cylindrical bounced off the toe of one boot.

She froze. So did the pit of her stomach.

How the thing had survived, she hadn't a clue . . . but there it was, shining greasily under the fluorescent lights and completely undamaged. Only its cord had snapped. The rest of it twisted and coiled and flared into a dozen nightmares, each eye-symbol and aquatic horror staring up at her in challenge—

Or welcome.

In the next frozen moment, Cassie raised her head to see the police commander and several other locals watching her. They had moved much closer to the death site than she remembered, and their faces held neither fear nor disgust now. Only furtive hunger.

Somewhere beyond all clean, known stars, a new wind began to blow. Cassie wondered if she was the only one hearing it. The only one here who could truly understand it—could appreciate and respond to its call.

Then, twisting her boot heel down hard, she ground the whistle to black powder.

"Damn."

She didn't look around to find out who'd said it, or what he might have meant. She just made herself start walking: past the ruin that had been Jake Fowler, past the truckers and travelers and locals who were now very occupied with their own business. Past the long sad heap of green plastic she did not dare to acknowledge, or mourn.

The police never stopped her. No one did.

She had parked her Jeep behind the Flying K, at the end of a line of tractor-trailers. Nearly all of them were gone by the time she climbed in and began coaxing the geriatric engine to life. While she waited for it to warm up, Cassie took out her cell phone.

"Frank? . . . Yeah, I guess it is. For now."

The cold knot she'd banished from her stomach threatened to return. "Sure, I'll be fine," she lied. "I'll be home for breakfast. . . . You will? Great!"

Stowing her phone, she put the old Wagoneer into four wheel drive and headed out, eyes on the road and away from the clearing night sky, thoughts on Twenty Mile. For the next two hundred and sixty miles, Frank's buckwheat blueberry pancakes were the sanest things she could imagine.

ACKNOWLEDGMENTS

"Dark Equinox," first published in *Searchers After Horror*, edited by S. T. Joshi (Fedogan & Bremer, 2014).

"The Sweetness of Your Heart," first published in *Indigenous Fiction* No. 8 (June 2001).

"When the Stars Run Away," first published in *Dark Fusions*, edited by Lois H. Gresh (PS Publishing, 2013).

"Her Beloved Son," first published in *Fungi* No. 21 (Summer 2013).

"Desert Mystery! Gas & Go!" first published in *Lovecraft EZine* No. 8 (November 2011).

"Rehab," first published in *Everyday Weirdness* (18 November 2009).

"Scream Saver," first published in *Innsmouth Magazine* No. 2 (October 2009).

"The Water Lily Room," first published in *Noctober* (March 2009).

"Twenty Mile," first published in *The Darker Side*, edited by John Pelan (Penguin/Roc, 2002).

"Experiencing the Other," first published in *Strange Stars & Alien Shadows: The Dark Fiction of Ann K. Schwader*, edited by Kevin L. O'Brien (Lindisfarne Press, 2003).

"Paradigm Wash," first published in *Dark Wisdom* Nos. 10 & 11 (2006–07).

"Night of the Piper," first published in *Black Wings IV*, edited by S. T. Joshi (PS Publishing, 2015).

"Wings of Memory," "Custom Order," "The Death Verses of Yian-Ho," and "The Wind-Caller" are original to this collection.

CPSIA information can be obtained
at www.ICGtesting.com
Printed in the USA
LVOW01s1952060217
523343LV00002B/386/P